ABOUT THE AUTHOR

M. L. Tompsett is an emerging contemporary romance author — and this is her ninth published book.

She has been creating worlds to escape to since she was a little girl. Years later, she continues to enjoy her writing in imaginative make-believe worlds filled with exciting characters, diverse locations, and a variety of tropes. She is now moving into the big, wide, scary world of digital and print book publishing, including audio.

Married to her childhood sweetheart, they live in Victoria, Australia, and have two extremely talented adult sons. M. L. Tompsett is excited to see something she has been creating become a reality as a published book.

When not tapping away on her keyboard to draft the next page-turning book while drinking tea and eating licorice, she's busy working on her many talented clients' digital files for their next book release — or taking random scenic photos around Australia.

Check M. L. Tompsett out on her website, blog, or social media.

www.mltompsett.com

f facebook.com/M.L.TompsettAuthor

⊙ instagram.com/mltompsett.author

BB bookbub.com/profile/m-l-tompsett

ALSO BY M. L. TOMPSETT

CONTEMPORARY ROMANCE

SECOND CHANCE AT LOVE - series

Insta Bride

The Bodyguard's Convenient Marriage

Ghost of a Chance in Love

Secret Heiress

Paranormal Fantasy

SEX, LIES AND FAMILY SECRETS - series

The Guy Next Door - Book one

Dark Surprises - Book two

You Never Know - Book three

It's You - Book four

What You Know - Book five

OTHER VAMPIRE BOOKS

Her Vampire Fated Mate

Urban Fantasy

Shifter Romance

Kept in the Dark of Love and Lust

Kept in the Dark of Lies and Deceit - book two

Non- Fiction

My Travel Log

(Print Book Only)

SECOND CHANCE AT LOVE

Contemporary Romance

SECRET HEIRESS

M. L. Tompsett

Tompsett Publishing™

Tompsett
Publishing

For all your
digital
book
formatting
requirements

eBook
and
Print Books

www.mltompsett.com

NATIONAL
LIBRARY
OF AUSTRALIA

*A catalogued digital
record of this book is
available from the
National Library of
Australia.*

2ND Print Edition. 🤍 2026 M

For my Family.
Love you guys.

Also

To all my readers who have given me the chance to continue writing.

Thank you

♡
This is for you.
♡

BLURB

One last night of passion can purge the guy you've loved for the past twelve years from your mind and heart...right?

Izzy Delany, at thirteen, lost her parents in a tragic accident in Australia. New York became her new home with her aunt, and that is where she met her best friend, Mel Astor. The day Izzy met Mel's eldest brother, Tristian, her teenage heart and mind fell in love.

At twenty-five, Izzy is successful with three companies. Under the guise of using her grandmother's maiden name, the Astor family has no idea that their biggest competitor is little Izzy.

Tristian Astor is a master at being in charge of everything in his life, and his sister's best friend is not part of the equation. Pity his heart does not agree to keep the woman of his dreams at arm's length.

When Izzy discovers her life is in danger, can she survive long enough to inform Tristian that he is the father of her baby and that she loves him? Or will she lose everything, including her life, in this friends-to-lovers, best friend-brother romance?

In this plot-twisting, romancing, action-packed, who-can-you-trust, page-turning book.

*To trust in your ideas and your abilities to think, create,
and complete what your heart is destined to achieve.
Your future is what you make it.
Start your new chapter today because tomorrow may
never arrive.*

— *M. L. Tompsett*

SECRET HEIRESS

Chapter One

IZZY

*S*eriously.

After twenty-five years, my life boils down to six large packing crates. Six. And they aren't even that big. Thankfully, my housemate and best friend of twelve years, Melika Astor, hired this moving company to handle all the work, sparing us from any lifting — and rightly so.

Memorized, I continue to watch the sexy specimens before me. Envisioning their muscular arms, legs, and backs supporting a woman just right against a vertical surface.

My tongue slips along my parted lips — hoping to catch any drool — at the hunky fantasies, flaunting their flexing muscles under their wife-beater tops. Oh yes, indeed, my thoughts align with Mel's. It has been far too long between lovers and hard surfaces — well, any surface, for that matter. And my battery-operated friend can only do so much.

The sight of the USA Movers Today employees —

powerful physiques, confident, flirty smiles — holds my attention hostage. Their friendly banter and the sounds of furniture being expertly moved and loaded into trucks fill the air. The whole scene in my front yard is mesmerizing, a choreography of strong bodies and coordinated effort that has left Mel captivated and unsure if she should flirt or simply stare.

Have I mentioned that all those delicious, muscle-bound movers, with their chiseled features and captivating flirting smiles, could grace the cover of GQ magazine?

Even though I love the view, I'm still annoyed because Mel is being manipulated. Thanks to her brothers — especially her eldest brother — my top lip curls into a snarl, and I bare my teeth. Don't even get me started on that man. My feelings about him are far too intense to share.

As for Mel and me, we are like two peas in a pod, sharing a deep bond and similar tastes and ideas. If she goes somewhere, I'm right behind her, and the same is true for her. To me, she is like family. My family. And why we are packing up my house and heading back to the East Coast.

How did this all come about?

Mel's youngest brother, Nicholas — the little snitch. He arrived for a surprise visit while I was at a conference two weeks ago, leading to her two older brothers discovering she was pregnant. Now her siblings want to control their only sister, pressuring her to go back to New York and under their roof.

"Bloody annoying," I mutter under my breath.

Visualising Tristian — that sparkling dark-blue-eyed man — is getting on my nerves again and refusing to get out of my head.

Anyhoo... Mel's brothers have always underestimated her, never realizing how smart and creative she is. Our start-up, MeBe Tech, has been successful in just three years, thanks to her creativity and my business vision.

Lost in thought, I barely feel Mel coming up behind me. "Hey, girl. You okay?" she whispers. I look over my shoulder and see her smiling aqua eyes before she frowns. "What has your mind busy this time?"

That's Mel. She knows me so well. At times, she knows me better than I know myself.

The corners of my mouth droop into a frown. With disappointment, I shake my head. Before I can speak, Mel mumbles, "You're thinking about my stupid moron eldest brother Tristian."

With a small nod, I silently acknowledge her words. My best friend is a smart woman. In the past, she confided in me about her desire for me to be her sister despite my romantic feelings for her older brother. She advised me that even though I have rocks in my head, I still must be careful and protect my heart.

Mel's advice is a bit late now as I affectionately stroke my growing belly, feeling my baby move about.

Chapter Two

IZZY

"*T*he day you reveal your true identity to the world, my brothers will beg for your forgiveness — especially Tristian," Mel declares, wiggling her eyebrows like she's auditioning for a cartoon villain.

If only she knew.

Upon my arrival in New York at thirteen, after losing my parents, my aunt made one thing clear: stay hidden, stay safe. With her meticulous planning — and the help of her very resourceful friend — I received a new identity.

Using my great-grandmother's maiden name, Delany, I slipped into a new life. A scholarship to a prestigious school. A clean slate. A chance to breathe without looking over my shoulder.

On my first day, I saw three blonde, busty teenagers bullying a small, light-haired girl at lunchtime. I didn't hesitate. I stepped in, protected the slender girl with the stunning aqua eyes... and the rest is history. Mel was so impressed she declared me her best friend forever and dragged me home after school to meet her family — a "home" that turned out to be an enormous mansion.

And that's where I met Mel's oldest brother, Tristian Astor. My teenage heart didn't stand a chance. His sparkling dark-blue eyes were the first thing I saw.

I froze, speechless, pulse racing, butterflies rioting in my stomach.

He smiled — that devastating, heart-stopping smile — and I was done for. The moment he looked away, I could breathe again... and admire the rest of his well-built body.

Unfortunately, my heart didn't receive the memo to stay away from him.

With a nod, I reply to Mel, "Yes. One day soon, your obnoxious brothers will learn who my loving father was..." I rub my belly as my baby kicks. "They'll be more than amazed — and shocked — to learn who I really am."

When they discover I'm one of their biggest business rivals, it will not be pretty.

Even Mel doesn't know the full extent of my past or finances.

Her brothers have always assumed I'm some poor girl from the wrong side of the tracks. As the saying goes: If you don't ask, you won't know.

Not known to the Astors — and thanks to my handsome, talented father — I became an heiress to a multi-billion-dollar empire the day he passed away.

My parents were both successful entrepreneurs. My mother placed over ten million dollars in my offshore account before her death — giving me a tremendous head start. According to experts, my father's empire is worth over ten billion dollars as of the last financial year. And that doesn't include my mother's company, her assets, or my own secret investments.

The thought of scavengers discovering my father's assets still concerns me. I fully expect mysterious "relatives" to crawl out of the woodwork demanding their share.

With all this money, I live a double life.

My secret life.

I have to — for my own safety.

Chapter Three

IZZY

My breath catches as I feel my baby change positions with a full somersault. "Whoa, little one, take it easy on me."

Moves like that will leave me bruised on the inside. I swear this child is training for the Olympics.

The thought of being pregnant at twenty-five never crossed my mind twelve months ago, but now that I have this little guy growing inside me, I can't imagine my life without him.

Unless he continues to use me as a bouncy pillow while practicing his martial arts moves.

Mel's not wrong. There's truth in what she's saying. My secret relationship with her eldest brother — Tristian — who also happens to be the father of my baby, must remain hidden from prying eyes.

From the moment we met when I was thirteen, I've been drawn to him in a way I couldn't explain. He avoided me socially until my twenty-first birthday. What started romantically ended in casual hookups. Despite wanting more — wanting him — he valued his independence more than he valued a future with me.

If only things could have been different.

But the situation between us has completely changed, and we can't undo it.

Flashbacks of the masquerade ball Mel and I attended in March fill my thoughts. An exclusive annual fundraiser for New York's richest elite. Our final night in New York before leaving for California, and I was determined to end things — to free my mind and heart from Tristian and start fresh. No more late-night booty calls. No more last-minute hookups. No more rearranging my life to fit into his.

The night — marked by a final rendezvous in one of the hotel suites above the grand ballroom — was unforgettable. Precious.

Mel had planned a meeting with Corey Sheldon, her teenage crush and her brother's friend.

My breath races as I watch Tristian climb out of the bed and head to the bathroom. The intense sexual satisfaction lingers, the air thick with the musk of our passion and the unspoken words hanging between us.

My body still humming with pleasure, I'm eager for another round. But when he returns, something in him has shifted. A subtle change in his energy. He begins dressing.

That's when I know. We're not continuing. Something is wrong.

Even though his hungry gaze memorizes every inch of

my nakedness, I can tell he's fighting an internal battle. He wants to come back to me — I see it — but then his smile vanishes. Replaced by a cold, hard stare.

His words hit like a splash of icy water.

"We can't do this again. I'm sorry, Izzy. We don't have a future together..."

The euphoric high evaporates. My brain freezes.

What the hell?

And a few other not-so-nice things.

"Listen... We never did, and you need to move on with someone else."

As the last of his words sink in — insinuating I don't belong in his world — the orgasmic buzz I had going disappears entirely.

His actions leave me speechless and numb. My mind fails to process what just happened as my gaze fixates on his well-toned butt walking out the door.

Why couldn't he just say, I had a fantastic time — have a safe flight, goodbye?

Nope.

He had to act like a selfish bastard.

Several hours later, with his words still ringing in my ears, Mel and I left for the airport. We were eager to move to another state and start anew without interference from her brothers. It was time to let go of what we had in the past and prioritize our future.

Wonderful weather, kind locals, and the blissful absence of the Astor family's prying eyes marked the start of our new life. Anticipation coursed through our veins as we set off on this new adventure.

Our company, MeBe Tech, thrived. We even won an achievement award for new upcoming business. Life was fantastic — filled with laughter and adventure. Our lives flourished in so many ways...

Until we both fell ill. And everything came to a halt as the doctor confirmed our suspicions.

Pregnant.

Tristian is in for a surprise when he sees me. I don't care about his opinion. When he consistently ignores my calls — don't get me started on his abrupt return email — my decision becomes final: I will raise my baby on my own.

In his opinion, a relationship between us is impossible.

If he wants a relationship with my child, I won't stop him.

But he will soon realize I won't be standing beside him when the time comes.

Karma has a funny way of interrupting our lives.

Back then, at twenty-four, single and pregnant was the last thing either of us wanted or needed.

My cell phone's camera app continues to make shutter sounds with each sneaky photo I capture from my large bay window of the furniture removalists. These men are responsible for our possessions arriving at my multi-story beachfront home in the outer suburbs of Long Island, New York, at the end of Connecticut Ave. A girl can never be too careful.

Plus, the visual of all those manly muscles is rather satisfying.

My cell chimes several bars of an old eighties tune, informing me of an incoming call from my beautiful aunt. Perfect timing. I glance at Hazel's picture on my screen and smile. My aunt always makes me feel better.

Since I was a little girl, I've told her she's a magical fairy, which always makes her laugh. I swipe the screen. "Hello, my favorite aunt."

Before she says a word, I know exactly what she'll reply with and mouth it silently.

"Z... I'm your only aunt," she mumbles through a laugh. "How are you and your precious baby going?"

My eyes roll. Predictable woman. It's been just my aunt and me since we moved to the States when I was thirteen, after my parents died.

The attractive mover catches my eye settling into my car. My heart races. I shake my head and turn away from the window. That's it. No more watching. I don't need to see him loading my car.

Okay — now I understand how Mel felt. Watching others handle your car and belongings is stressful.

I force myself to focus on the call. "We are good, Hazel." My babe kicks near my ribs, and I rub the area soothingly. Since my parents' deaths, my aunt drops the "aunt" moniker and demands I call her Hazel in public. Despite her business alias as Hannah Ewington, few realize she's a multimillionaire — rapidly approaching billionaire status.

Aunt Hazel had a dual role as a high-powered attorney and a silent partner in my mother's company. After my mother's passing, Hazel took on multiple roles, apart from my loving aunt, she also stepped up, being a mother figure when I required one, otherwise, Hazel was just there. My family. We have been together for one another ever since that dark day. Back then, she became my legal representative, guardian, and CEO of LaniD. She successfully added cosmetics, perfume, and clothing to the company sales line. Every clothing piece, every design, every concept comes directly from my mother's sketchbooks — Hazel uses only my mother's original drawings and creations, preserving her memory exactly as she envisioned it. Hazel expanded to Australia, the UK, and the US, all with my full support.

"Z, I called because I want to plan something special for your parents' and baby brother's anniversary soon."

Bugger. With everything going on, I forgot all about the anniversary of their deaths next month. Now I feel like I've let my parents down.

Few people knew my parents were married for over fourteen years when they died. My father kept their relationship out of the public eye. He wanted his family life private and safe.

"Hazel, I don't think I can join you this year. Before you say anything... my doctor advised me this will be my last flight until after the baby is born."

"Shoot. I forgot how far along you are. Look, I'll join you, and we'll go out for dinner or something, okay?"

This is why I adore her. She always goes the extra mile for me.

"Only if you're sure. Thank you. That would be great."

"Have your people discovered anything regarding that friend of yours? Something seems off about that man."

I initially agreed, but Gavin — Gavin Davis — convinced me otherwise. We kept meeting at different charity events. His passion and innovation inspired me to give more. He seemed to be everywhere I went.

"My private investigator's still searching, Hazel. I'll hear from him when they learn more."

"Okay... Have you spoken to my precious nephew's daddy yet?"

I roll my eyes. Yeah, right. I still haven't confirmed who my son's father is. But I think she suspects.

"H, if he had bothered to return my calls, I would. For now, I will continue living my life."

"Oh, Z. I am sorry. Men can be such beasts."

A laugh escapes me. My aunt always knows how to make me smile.

"There is one thing, though. Can you prepare a prenup for me? I never want to be caught unawares."

"Are you trying to tell me something?"

"No. When the opportunity comes, I want a prenup ready."

"That's a rational request. Above all else, I want to protect you from exploitation."

"Yes. I thought you'd agree. Oh — and have my real name on the document. I'd prefer it to be all legal."

"Got it," she says. I hear her tapping away on her keyboard. "The other thing I need to discuss is that

Astor International is attempting another takeover with the New York branch of Heartson Industries."

What? Not again. Tristian will give me a headache before the end of the day.

"H, do what you must to stop it and prevent it from happening."

"My darling niece, it is time you spoke to Tristian and his brothers and inform them to back the hell off your company."

I shake my head. "Aunt Hazel, I know. I have to speak with Mel's brothers. They won't believe me when I say I'm the missing heiress."

Her brothers need to grow up. I'm not taken seriously in their male-dominated world. I could go on about Mel's treatment — her ideas ignored, dismissed. Little do they know, Mel has requested help from H. She's ready to prove herself.

"Z, that will be their problem, not yours."

"Aunt Hazel, I don't think they appreciated my company outbidding them recently on several projects. And purchasing that hotel chain."

"As I said before, darling girl, that is their problem. It's business. If they can't handle it, then they're in the wrong business."

I completely agree.

Time to change the subject. "Aunt Hazel, are you attending the Calloway New York annual gala?"

Which means she'll be in New York early.

"Yes. That is another reason I'm calling. Oh — and don't think I didn't notice you changed the subject, young lady. Remember, you must appear at your father's company table as my guest. Maybe even surprise the old kooks by announcing you're the heiress of Heartson Industries."

"Nooo. H."

"Izzibella, stop right there. You're a strong, independent woman. After the baby is born, it will be time for you to step up and fill your father's position. Before you say boo — your father's Will stipulates you will be situated in his office as the CEO on your twenty-fifth birthday. Your multi-billion-dollar company is your birthright."

I know she's right. Despite my birthday passing, I won't assume the role while pregnant. Thank goodness my father stipulated that my aunt would act as my legal representative until I step in full-time.

The old kooks have attempted to adjust my father's last wishes to favor themselves for years.

"Aunt Hazel, during my time undercover at the company, I worked my way up but faced obstacles because of my youth and being a woman."

"Z, you worked from the bottom, learning the skills, learning the staff. No one knew who you were. You know who you can trust and who to watch out for."

"But—"

"No buts, Z. It's a pity you left mid-March."

I roll my eyes. Moving across the country prevented me from continuing my employment.

"We have much to discuss regarding the latest minutes from the quarterly general meeting I somehow missed!"

Huh? Since when?

"Why would you miss a quarterly meeting?"

"That's just it. I attend every one. Someone changed the meeting to an earlier time and didn't notify me."

Sounds exactly like something those old kooks would do.

"Whose head is going to roll?"

"The usual suspects. Brown and Davis."

Typical. "Why does that not surprise me?"

Her sarcastic laugh makes me laugh. "Look, I've emailed you a copy of the minutes. Read through them and highlight anything you think requires attention. And add your recommendations."

"Just my luck. I'll discover more corruption disguised as fake business trips and expenditures that have nothing to do with my company. Don't get me started on the other fabricated expenses."

Her laughter fills my ear. "You realize you're the only one to dispute their claims. Hypocrites fear your rightful ascension day."

Damn the woman. She's just as pushy and stern as ever.

With a humph, my eyes narrow. How dare those men abuse my father's trust and memory.

"Why do the old kooks make my life so hard?"

"Izzibella, lift your game. You are more than the CEO. I raised you better than to act this way." She hits me straight in the chest. "...Shoot," she adds quickly. "I have an incoming call. I have to take it. Phone you back."

Before I can say anything, she ends the call.

"We love you too, Aunt Hazel," I mumble, rubbing my belly.

A sigh escapes me. The woman can make you feel like you've worked a twelve-hour shift with one phone call.

I require tea or scotch and a seat.

Chapter Four

IZZY

*T*he gorgeous movers carry the last box out the front door and load it onto the truck, leaving an echoing silence behind them. I'm going to miss this house, I think as I look around the empty room.

"Izzy?" Mel catches my eye as she steps inside. She gives a mischievous smile to the attractive removalists, openly admiring their muscular physiques. "The guys," she mumbles, wiggling her sharp brows, "are wondering if there are any other items we need to load."

Typical Mel — always flustered by gorgeous men.

I shake my head despite her antics. My smile widens. I love her dearly. We've been inseparable since our teenage years. She's my best friend, like a sister. And despite her long-standing crush on her brother's best friend, she's not oblivious to eye candy. We both appreciate handsome, sexy men — just look outside my door.

My eyes roll at her joyful behavior. "No," I say,

shaking my head as I glance around one last time. "That's everything."

Mel nods and steps back out the front door.

Several seconds later, I hear her flirting with the moving guys.

Unbelievable. The gorgeous woman deserves credit. Even seven months pregnant, she still flirts with the best of them.

If it weren't for Mel's younger brother Nicholas — and the other two Astor brothers — our lives would have been content here instead of stressed and forced into moving back across the country.

When I think about Mel's brothers, their attitude and behavior fill me with anger. Since their parents' deaths, they've considered themselves superior solely because they hail from a six-generation, all-American, old-money family. Furious as it makes me, I can't even begin to express my frustration over how they exploit, control, and emotionally manipulate my best friend.

Mel's brothers insist she return to the Astor family residence until the baby is born, determined to identify and find the father.

Little do they know, the father is closer to them than they think.

When I see Mel's obnoxious brothers, all I know is that I'll give them a piece of my mind.

Chapter Five

IZZY

*W*alking through each room, making sure nothing has been left behind, a 1980s tune sounds on my cell, reminding me of my aunt's promise to call me back.

With a quick swipe, I tap the answer icon. "Hello, Aunt Hazel," I say politely.

"Z, I'm sorry about what happened before. The call was important."

I roll my eyes — yeah, right.

"Now, I can complete our conversation from this morning."

What is she going on about?

"I had been waiting on AngelStar to return my call."

My foot pauses mid-step. AngelStar? Why would my charity organization call Hazel today? Everything better be okay.

I don't have time for an emergency. "H, what is going on?"

"Izzibella, before you blow a fuse. Allow me to finish."

Why hasn't my assistant contacted me if something was wrong?

"Make it quick, Hazel. My patience is wearing thin."

Her laughter reaches my ear. "Oh, my darling girl. You sound just like your mother. God, I miss her."

My annoyance softens instantly. The last time I saw my mother was the day my baby brother was born.

A sigh escapes as my eyes mist. "I know, Aunt Hazel. I miss her too."

How I've missed my loving mother and father. I wish they were here.

"My dear girl, the bushfire-devastated zones have received the latest donations of portable small housing modules and water tanks. The follow-up water tankers and trucks of food staples were a godsend. You have saved hundreds of people, if not more. The media are requesting a meet and greet with the CEO of AngelStar!"

Without thought, I'm already shaking my head. No one from the media will have my picture. They will not use my name or face against me.

"No, Aunt Hazel. I will not meet the press. Eric Bronson, my assistant manager, can speak with them. That is what I pay him for."

"That is what I thought," she replies. "I explained to Eric that I'm the charity organization's legal representative, and that he's required to speak with the media on behalf of AngelStar. And that the CEO has a brief press release."

I nod. "Thank you. If Eric cannot handle the press, he is unsuitable for the position."

"Yes, I agree," she says. "I thought it best to bring you up to speed. I've organized for twenty more housing modules to be sent before the end of the month."

Only twenty? No. That won't do.

"Double it, Aunt Hazel. All those devastated people... I imagine they're feeling very lost. And to lose everything... I can only hope my little contribution will help."

"My girl, for those who have received a portable home, they think you're an angel sent from heaven."

"You know, Hazel, triple the order — but send it as flat packs. That way, the modules will arrive sooner. It will give the people something to build with their own hands. Something else to focus on — something good. Add tools, generators, and fuel."

"Are you sure, Z?"

"Yes. I'm sure."

I can only think about the displaced children, with nothing left.

"Okay," she says. "I'll have the order placed with the building company by the end of the day."

"You know, H... include those twenty built modules as well."

"All right, my dear. Leave it with me."

"Thank you for all your assistance."

"It was nothing. From what little you've said today, I'll add those words to your press release."

I laugh. "Only you can turn a few simple words into a full, brilliant article for the press. Thank you."

Then it occurs to me. "Aunt Hazel, can you add another fifty housing modules separately? Have my family company foot the bill. There is more than enough funding for donations to cover the cost."

Her laughter fills my ear. "Oh, sweetheart, those old farts will protest."

What the Board of Directors thinks does not bear thinking about.

"Regarding the fundraising gala, it is crucial that Eric Bronson attends and presents a generous check on behalf of AngelStar to Mrs. Calloway. You know the amount. Also, please create another one of those oversized checks for fifty thousand dollars. This donation will be presented on behalf of Heartson Industries. It will be worth seeing the old kooks' expressions."

"I love it. Leave it with me."

"Mrs. Calloway is successful each year in organizing these fundraising events. She deserves a medal. The hundreds of millions she's raised for good causes is mind-blowing."

"Yes, the woman is a working machine. Righto... I'm messaging my assistant as we speak to start the ball rolling while I'm in court today."

Hang on... Hazel has retired from court. "I thought you were placing your court days behind you."

"So did I. But a dear friend found themselves in a spot of trouble. I'm helping."

Only my aunt would bend over backward for others. "Thank you, Aunt Hazel. I'll see you at the gala," I sigh. "Please remember, I will sit with Mel for a while."

"Okay. Bring Mel. She can be your plus one at the company table. Love you, sweet girl."

Hearing those words, a lump forms in my throat. Stupid hormones.

My aunt is all I have left. I don't know what I would have done without her after my parents died. "Love you too, H," I manage as my eyes mist.

*R*elief fills me as I watch the back of the contractor's vehicle drive away, finally taking everything with them — unlike earlier today when I discovered they'd left my house keys with the chosen sample tiles and paint-color palette on the back patio.

Tomorrow marks the beginning of extensive renovations on my beach house, and although it may be expensive, it will prove to be a valuable investment. They plan to replace the old, small swimming pool with a larger solar-heated one that includes a spa, surrounded by a big entertainment area. The place will look incredible once it's completed. By the time I come back in late spring, my three-bedroom vintage beach house will have transformed into a sleek, modern design with walls of bulletproof glass, five extra bedrooms and bathrooms upstairs, and a new spacious modern chef's kitchen.

In this house, I experienced a strong sense of home

and a deep connection with my parents. The beach was our sanctuary — our escape. I can still picture my father lifting me onto his shoulders as the waves rolled in, my mother laughing as she tried to keep her hat from blowing away. The smell of sunscreen, the warmth of their hands, the sound of their voices carried on the wind...

God, I miss them.

Sometimes the memories feel so vivid I swear I could turn around and see them standing behind me. Other times, the ache is so sharp it steals my breath. Thirteen years might have passed, but grief has no concept of time. Some days it feels like yesterday.

And then there's the darker thought — the one that creeps in when I'm alone. My uncle, my cousin, my parents, my baby brother... all gone in similar accidents. Too similar. My father, being a wealthy businessman, would have had enemies. The pattern is too neat, too convenient.

But I push the thought away before it swallows me whole.

My eyes mist, and I blink hard to keep the tears at bay. I miss my parents so much. I miss their warmth, their laughter, their unconditional love. I miss having a mother to call when I'm scared or overwhelmed. I miss my father's steady voice telling me everything will be okay. I miss the family we were supposed to be.

As I reflect on them, my baby shifts, rolling and stretching, reminding me of his presence. A tiny life anchoring me to the present.

"Easy, little one," I whisper, rubbing the spot where he presses against my ribs.

While I didn't expect to be pregnant at my age, my love for this little guy knows no bounds. If only my parents were here to witness the wonder of their grandchild's first steps, to hear his sweet babble, to share in the joy of his laughter, his growth, his milestones.

They would have adored him.

And he would have adored them.

The thought squeezes my heart until it aches.

Chapter Seven

IZZY

*M*el walks toward me from the open doorway with a radiant smile, holding a handful of business cards from the movers. "Izzy, everything is gone," she says, her gaze meeting mine. "Including all the attractive men," she adds mischievously, her eyes lighting up.

I know that look — she has something planned.

"Mind if we grab doughnuts and sandwiches?"

Ha. See? I knew it. Mel and her sweet tooth.

She affectionately places her hand on her pregnant belly. "Bubs is hungry!"

Unbelievable. She'd devour a full box of doughnuts daily if I let her.

Our doctor warned us about consuming too much sugar. After a chaotic morning assisting the moving company and coordinating with my contractor, I might relent and grant her request. Who knows when we'll have the chance to eat something delicious again? The contractor's delay left a sour taste in my mouth.

I nod. "You're paying. Make sure there are several jelly ones."

Mel beams, displaying all her straight white teeth. "Yes, Margy's Bakery, here we come."

I shake my head, already imagining the bakery sold out. Mel pauses, eyes sparkling with mischief. "I knew you would agree, so I already ordered everything."

Cheeky, bloody woman.

Now I can imagine myself with red jelly stains down my front when we reach the airport.

As we fill our faces with yummy goodness, on route to the airport, I tap out a text to Benny, my main driver, who will collect us from the airport, saving us a taxi fare and a long queue.

> **Me:**
> Benny, we will be arriving at LGA by 4:40 p.m. Mel sends her love.

Three dots appear, followed by his reply.

> **Benny:**
> See you there. And give my love back to Ms. Mel.

Thankfully, we land at LGA — LaGuardia Airport — with no red stains.

To remain anonymous, I've limited my use of two drivers over the years.

After collecting our bags, I tap another message to Benny.

> **Me:**
> We are here. Heading for the front entrance now.

Just as we walk through the doors, I glance to my right and see Benny. He zeros in and pulls up in front of us along the curb.

I've known Benny for eleven years. He's one of the few drivers I trust. The auto-release on the trunk opens, and Benny is quickly by our sides. His shocked look shifts into a huge smile. He reaches for the door handle and opens the rear car door.

"Wow. Good afternoon, Ms. Izzy. Is there something I should know?" His gaze drops straight to my expanding belly. No one knows about my pregnancy — which is exactly how I want it.

He reaches for my hand to help me into the vehicle.

"Whatever do you mean, Benny?" I reply cheekily. "We need to drop Ms. Mel off at her family estate. You remember the way..." I slide onto the rear seat.

Before I can say anything else, he nods. "I sure do, Ms. Izzy."

As I slide over to make room for Mel, I hear her speaking with him. "How are you going, Benny? It has been a while."

"It sure has, Ms. Mel. Is everything okay? Do I need to stop somewhere?"

Benny has always had a fondness for Mel despite their eighteen-year age gap. His actions are reminiscent of a caring older sibling — not like her own brothers.

"Sorry, Benny, not today. Thank you," she says.

Mel settles beside me, and Benny shuts the door. After packing our cases in the trunk, he drives away.

"Ms. Izzy?"

I glance up. "Yes, Benny. What is it?"

"I wish you had let me know. I could have collected your bags and brought them to the car."

You have to love the man. At least he shows he cares.

"Benny, we can manage tasks independently. But thank you. Though you better expect changes in the upcoming weeks."

"Yeah, Benny. Be prepared to drive at all hours," Mel laughs.

I notice Benny glance into the rearview mirror. Our eyes meet, and he smiles.

"Call me anytime. I mean it."

I nod in appreciation before glancing at Mel. We both smile and turn back to Benny.

"I'll take that into consideration. Thank you, Benny."

He focuses on the road, giving us privacy.

"Izzy, it's important to be careful until the trucks arrive with our belongings and vehicles. I will be concerned about you."

I'm still purchasing replacement furniture for my beach house. While we had been away on the other side of the country, I had this beach house updated with new extensions. A lot of work went into it, making it modern and extra safe. Thankfully, the contractors completed the work last week. It doesn't matter if it's the East or

West Coast — I'll always have a beach house somewhere.

I reach over and hug her. "Mel, I will take extra care. After all those strange problems I had with my old car."

"Izzy, your car was not old. It shouldn't have had the mechanical problems to begin with. Or your previous cars, for that fact."

True. It's peculiar that my last three vehicles all had varying mechanical problems.

"Mel, look. I'll speak with Gavin again."

Despite initially being a stranger, Gavin became a trusted friend in my life. After discussing that I'd be installing car surveillance, he convinced me to trade my old car for a new one, especially since the mechanics couldn't find the cause of the numerous mechanical issues. "He appears knowledgeable regarding cars. I'll have him look over my new one... That reminds me, I haven't contacted him to let him know I was moving back to New York."

I watch Mel shake her head. She has never liked him. He showed up six months ago out of nowhere. He won me over with his smile, innocence, sincere honesty, and, most of all, his charity work.

"Izzy, wait until you're settled. Remember, he is not your keeper. You had a life before he showed up. Gavin doesn't need to know every little detail of your life."

Okay... Mel has a point. Approximately three months back, she asked me why I was depending on Gavin. Somehow, he wormed his way into my daily life and became excessively clingy. Despite his plans, Mel objected to him moving in.

And she wasn't wrong.

Sometimes I wonder if I let him in too easily. If I mistook his constant presence for comfort instead of control. If I leaned on him simply because he made himself available — always there, always helpful, always ready with a solution before I even asked for one.

Maybe I shouldn't trust him as much as I do.

But then... he's never actually done anything wrong. He's helped me. Supported me. Checked on me. Listened. He's been there in ways no one else has — especially when Mel was busy or when I felt alone.

Is that dependence? Or is it just... nice to have someone care?

I'm not sure anymore. My feelings are tangled — part gratitude, part habit, part something else I can't quite name. And maybe that's the problem.

Mel is right. I'll contact him after I am settled.

Chapter Eight

IZZY

*M*el's words register when I hear my name. "Izzy, are you even listening to me?"

"What... I mean, yes, Mel."

I try to keep the sarcasm out of my tone. *Try* being the key word.

"Don't be coy with me, missy. What are you doing? Because you are not giving me your full attention!"

I roll my eyes — a clear sign of my annoyance.

"I'm packing the last items for a meeting that I cannot be late to."

My business partner in my security company, Simon Townsend — usually a godsend — has suddenly and unexpectedly come down sick. He was fine last night. The last thing I expected was to attend an in-person meeting at this stage of my pregnancy.

"What meeting, Izzy? I thought you were on maternity leave for in-person meetings!"

My shoulders slump. Yes, before arriving back in

New York, I decided I wouldn't risk my baby or my health by working and traveling long hours. But what else am I supposed to do?

"Mel, Simon has fallen ill."

When he phoned me this morning, it was a shock. He's one of the healthiest people I know. "I'm the other person who knows the security system for these tricky clients. Look — before you start — it's an hour from you."

Great.

I just reminded myself of the fundraiser tomorrow night in New York City. I still haven't organized a gown. Something keeps niggling at me to avoid the gala altogether.

"Look, Izzy. I am not happy that you're driving about. But I know I'm not able to stop you. Now, regarding tomorrow night…"

She's good at changing the subject and turning the attention back to herself.

"I have a spare dress that should fit you. I have everything here."

Of course she does. Mel would dress me every day if given the opportunity. Between Mel and my aunt demanding my attendance at this gala — and sitting at two different tables — good grief, I can only do so much as one person.

"Come directly here after your meeting," she demands. "Tomorrow, we can relax before getting glamorous for the gala. And show off our pregnant bellies," she laughs.

It seems Mel has everything planned.

What about her brothers? They still don't know I'm pregnant.

What will I do when I see Tristian after everything that happened in March?

As if she read my thoughts, she adds, "I know what you're thinking. My brother can take a flying leap. Anyway, we can call Benny, and he can drive us. I am not relying on my brothers for transport."

From her tone, her brothers have pissed her off.

"Mel, what have they said or done this time?"

Mel puts up with a lot from her brothers, but being pregnant, she now has a short fuse. All I can say is — don't piss Mel off.

I've been in my ocean-view home for a week and a half. The movers placed our vehicles inside the four-car garage. The men shifted heavy boxes inside. They put our beds and furniture in place, making sure everything was functional before leaving. I'm grateful they finished before my groceries arrived.

Mel will move in with me after her baby is born. My plan is to avoid her brothers once she informs them of her living arrangements.

Mel's voice interrupts my thoughts. As much as I love the woman, I don't have time to stand here. I focus back on her words, waiting for the opportunity to cut in, say goodbye, and leave.

"Izz. Don't get me started. They threatened to cut my money off if I did not tell them who the baby's father was. Can you believe that?"

Uh-oh.

I know for a fact Mel is wealthy in her own right — I

should know. Her business bank account is exceptionally healthy thanks to our IT company. I cannot remember the last time she spent any of her family money — her "allowance" her older brothers gave her after their parents' deaths. She decided long ago to place her allowance into an account for her future child's education. All her brothers would see is that the money was withdrawn from the trust account — not how it was spent.

Stupid idiots.

Her brothers are unaware that Mel and I are partners in a business venture. Her expertise lies in app creation. The woman is brilliant. Our company has succeeded through her creativity, my business insight, and my initial financial support. We created the company with the intention of hiding the identities of the owners.

We now have a team of ten creators and designers. Mel still oversees everyone's work. She implemented back doors in her system to shut down hackers, stopping them in their tracks with surprise tactics. Her computer and coding knowledge are impressive.

My house has a high-tech office with computers for Mel and me. She set up my website and app for my security business. She even created the website for AngelStar. She doesn't know the full extent of my dealings with my father's company. She knows the truth about where I came from and who my father was — but not everything.

Despite being one of her family's top business rivals, I wouldn't admit it. Especially after hearing Alex and

Tristian complain about my father's company causing one of their business ventures to fail.

"Mel. Look, I'll arrive this evening sometime. My business meeting should only last around two hours, max. Then I'll head over to you."

"Izzy, why is Simon not handling the meeting online? How sick is he?"

I huff and turn toward my room. This is not like Simon. I'm worried about him.

Come to think of it, I better throw some things into an overnight bag. I'm not big on clothes. A pair of leggings and a long men's shirt is my go-to wardrobe at home. If Mel's brothers don't like what I wear — stiff.

At least for meetings, I have a suit. My maternity black suit pants, a blouse that covers my belly, and a black blazer, matched with ankle-length black boots with a small wedge heel to give me a little height. Easy to slip on and off — my forty-five-dollar bargain boots from Australia. I had several pairs shipped back to the States last year in different colors, making sure there were at least three pairs in black. My kind of trip — business mixed with pleasure.

Oh, what was I saying... oh yes, meeting and Simon.

"I really do not know. Something must be wrong if Simon cannot attend a meeting physically or online. I'll call him from my car and make sure he has booked in to see a doctor. The last thing I require is for Simon to be out of action for longer than a day or so."

"Izzy, please drive safe. I need you by my side when my brothers show up for a family dinner this evening."

Oh, shitters.

"Meelll," I groan. "No. Not a family dinner."

Her family dinners have been like a World War III exercise.

"Sorry, Izzy," she states firmly. "You have to be here. I need you for moral support."

I restrain myself from refusing by biting my tongue.

So much for taking it easy tonight — it's going to be a shit show for dinner, and Mel's brothers are on the menu.

Chapter Nine

IZZY

*T*he temptation to tell this client to shove it where the sun doesn't shine plays havoc with my business persona.

It's one of those bloody days when my blood pressure is increasing.

This client... seriously. I'm still fuming, counting to fifty to calm down as I walk out their door. Now I remember why I pushed Simon to handle these clients. Frustrating is an understatement.

The close-minded individuals refused to believe I was associated with Security Consults Today.

The moment I inquired about the computer issue, their expressions confirmed my day was about to take a turn for the worse. Once I resolved their computer problem and finished up in their restroom, the old kook startled me by accusing me of neglecting and failing my responsibilities.

As soon as I glanced at the computer monitor, I had an ominous feeling something terrible had happened.

Someone had mysteriously erased all the data. Under my breath, I expressed frustration as I embarked on the tedious task of reinstalling everything — this time implementing multiple layers of encryption and making additional adjustments to prevent a recurrence. This would allow Simon or me to monitor it remotely.

The afternoon has been and gone as the sun slowly makes its descent.

Great.

I hate driving back to New York in the dark.

Once I pack my laptop and other equipment into the car, I slide into the driver's seat and send a text to Mel.

Me:
Finally finished!!

Me:
SOS. If I could, I would down four doubles right now!

Three little dots appear, showing she's reading my message.

A ding follows.

Mel:
I was about to send out a search party.
Where are you?

Me:
About to leave clients' premises at the corner of Chalmers Blvd and Amawalk Avenue, Amawalk. See you in an hour or so, depending on the traffic.

> **Mel:**
> OK. I'll be waiting with a strong, non-alcoholic drink just for you!

I smile. You have to love Mel. She knows I'm stressed, and thankfully she decided not to mention Benny. Just imagine the looks on the client's faces if I'd shown up with a driver. No. It wouldn't have been appropriate. After the afternoon I've had, I should have had Benny come and pick me up — stuff the clients' opinions. Too late now.

> **Me:**
> Thank you. How are you feeling?

> **Mel:**
> Don't ask.

Reading her text... uh-oh. That is not good.

> **Me:**
> Mel big hugs. I'm starting my car now.

It's time I get out of here. Mel's family home sounds preferable to being here.

> **Mel:**
> OK. Drive extra safe.

With a cheeky laugh, I send back a smiley face, knowing Mel hates them.

Me:

Three dots appear, disappear, appear, and then disappear.

Mel:
...

My lifelong friend decides not to reply. I couldn't help it. I have to laugh.

With that, I place my phone in its holder and push the starter button near the steering wheel. Then I remember I better enter Mel's address into my GPS so I don't get lost. I enter 95 E 7th Street, New York, save it under Mel Family Home, and tap go.

Not even fifteen minutes up the road, my knuckles have turned white on the steering wheel as I navigate the rough road. I'm sure the stupid GPS has sent me the wrong way. I'm positive this is not the way I was supposed to travel. Twice now, I've come close to biting my tongue as the tires hit yet another pothole — these potholes are more like tiny sinkholes. Poor Bubs is getting shaken up more than I am, and he kicks my ribs in protest.

"Sorry, little one. Momma is trying to concentrate here," I grit through clenched teeth.

My eyes become dazed from another oncoming car with extremely bright headlights. As the vehicle approaches, it becomes apparent their headlamps are on full brightness, the glare blinding me. After several blinks, hoping my vision clears enough to see, my breath catches and my eyes widen when my brain registers that the oncoming vehicle has veered into my lane.

"Oh, shit, no," leaves my lips as I pull hard on the steering wheel, narrowly avoiding the dark car with its bright headlights flashing.

My SUV leaves the pavement, past a large bush on my right, and somehow straight onto a side dirt road. My four tires remain on the ground until a loud noise fills the SUV, followed by an awful shudder before it forcefully shakes, leaving me without steering. I grip the wheel and stomp on the brakes — nothing.

What the hell?

"Come on. Work!" I shout, slamming my foot on the brake, desperately praying to whatever god may be listening to keep us safe and for the brakes to function.

Panic sets in as my car refuses to slow down, and all I repeat is, "Oh shit. Oh, shit."

Before I overthink it, I slam my foot on the clutch, push down on the shift knob, and force the car into a lower gear.

"Come on. Slow down," I scream as a group of trees grows larger in front of me. "Come on. Damn it."

Again, with my foot pressed down on the clutch, I push through to the next lower gear, then repeat the process until I'm in first gear.

"Slow the duck down, now," I growl through clenched teeth.

As if my car heard me, my SUV decreases in speed. Thank ducky. It worked. Relief fills me, and I try pulling back on the handbrake. I don't know if it functioned, but the car swerves a little and comes to a rolling stop.

My heart pounds, a frantic drumbeat in my chest, as I reach for my cell phone with one hand and fumble to turn the engine off with the other. My finger trembles as I squint at the screen, but somehow, I tap on my friend's number.

The distinct sound of the phone dialing — a series of short tones — fills the silence.

Come on, pick up... pick up.

Finally, after what feels like an eternity, Mel answers. "What has happened?"

Gotta love her. She must have sensed something was wrong.

My lips quiver as I form the words. "I need to know where I am. Can you pinpoint my location?"

"Huh? What's going on, Izzy?" Her voice fills with concern.

I take a slow, shaky breath. "Some asshole just ran me off the road. I need help."

"Shit, Izzy. Hang on."

I hear her walking, then tapping away on a keyboard. "Right-o. Give me a second... ta-da, I now have your location." Her voice fades, then returns sharp. "Are you okay? Are you hurt?"

The first thought that comes to mind — I'm paralyzed with shock. I haven't been able to move my feet or legs. My mind races as I try to make sense of what just happened. My hands shake, making it impossible to grasp the steering wheel.

The deafening pounding of my heart reverberates in

my ears, drowning out all other sounds. I strain my eyes, scanning the surroundings for any sign of the ominous dark car that caused this turmoil. When I don't see that blasted car, the tension in my chest eases, and a breath I hadn't noticed I'd been holding finally escapes.

"Izzy, are you still there? Speak to me," my friend demands.

I give my head a small shake and blink a few times to focus. "Yeah, I'm here."

What did I need? Help. Truck. "Mel, request a tow truck. Maybe the police."

"Did you crash into anything?"

My focus moves to the trees ahead of me. If I didn't stop, my car would have hit them. "No. I didn't crash, but my car is not drivable either."

"Shit, Izzy. Okay, I need you to remove the memory card from the onboard dash cam. Maybe the camera captured the other vehicle."

I didn't even think of that. "Thanks, Mel. That thought had not crossed my mind."

"Why would it? You're in shock."

"Yeah," I mumble as a notification appears on the screen. A text from Gavin.

Why would he be texting at this time of day? I am not in any frame to look at his message, let alone answer him.

"Iz, you still there?"

Huh... Lost in thought, I reply, "Yeah. I just received a message from Gavin."

"What does that wanker want now?"

My bestie does not hesitate to let me know her

feelings toward Gavin. The tone in her voice could freeze ice.

"I don't know, but I'm not opening the message. I'm not in the mood for him right now."

"Iz, should I call the EMS and request an ambulance as well?"

I try my toes and feet — they move and wiggle. "No, Mel. I'm not hurt, just badly shaken up. I can call the local sheriff."

"Izzy, don't forget to place the memory card in your purse or cell if you have one of those extra slots."

Wow. I forgot all about that feature. "Thanks, Mel. I'll look while I wait."

"We can discuss this further tomorrow. Thanks for the heads up," I say to my assistant and slip my cell back into my pocket.

Bloody hell, not again. Heartson Industries has interfered with another contract.

Of all the things to happen, that annoying company has destroyed another project we spent months on — all those dedicated months — gone, wasted. Securing that contract would have been a turning point for Astor International. Nicholas and Alex are not going to handle the news.

My sister's voice catches my attention as I walk by her room a few minutes later. I pause near her ajar door, listening to Melika hurrying about. Given her condition, she shouldn't be rushing. Her voice drifts out, low and urgent, and I watch her through the small gap. With her cell wedged between her ear and shoulder, typing on her laptop, something must be up.

I wonder who she's talking to. And what is that — *being run off the road?* Who?

"Izzy, don't forget to place the memory card in your purse or cell if you have one of those extra slots."

My ears perk up. Mel's speaking with her off-sider, Izzy.

A woman I haven't laid eyes on since March. A gorgeous woman I haven't been able to remove from my mind. If only things were different, I would ask the woman to marry me. But she is not from my world. She wouldn't handle our way of life. Plus, she's my baby sister's best friend.

What? Her words register. *Did someone run Izzy off the road?* Has she been in an accident?

"Why would it? You're in shock," Mel replies.

My first instinct is to protect Izzy. Who would do something like that? I push the door open just enough to hear Mel say, "I've organized Smith and Sons Tow Trucking to assist you, and they're on their way to your location. I think it might be best to phone the police from your end. I am sending through the coordinates to where you are."

I watch my sister tap away on her keyboard like a professional. Since when has she had all this computer equipment in her room? I didn't even know she knew how to operate a computer.

"No. Izzy, I'm coming to get you. Wait with your car. The tow truck should be twenty minutes away."

Tow truck. Driving.

Uh-oh.

My sister is not going anywhere in her condition.

She notices me in her doorway, turns her back, walks into her walk-in closet, and comes out with her long coat.

"Yes... Do you have anything to drink?" She awkwardly slides her arms into her coat and reaches for her purse. "Good. Lock yourself into your car... Keep safe, Izzy. I'll be there as soon as I can."

She ends the call and stares at me with a raised brow.

"How much of that call did you listen to?" she demands.

I feel uncomfortable — I invaded her privacy. Even though she's my younger sister, she definitely has a feisty attitude. The girl should have been a boy.

"Did something happen to Izzy?" I ask, avoiding her question. "Is she okay? Where is she?"

Mel arches her eyebrow sharply and shakes her head. "Tristian, why does it matter to you?" Why would she say that? What have I done? "When you bid farewell to her in March, you ended your relationship with her. And yes, I know that you two spent the night together before Izzy and I departed for California, so there's no need to deny it."

Oh, fuck. No one knows I spent the night with Izzy. How am I going to get out of this one?

"Look, Mel. It was a mistake. I know she's your best friend. It will never happen again."

She scoffs and shakes her head. "Tristian, I do not have time to listen to your bullshit. Grow some balls, would you, and return her calls. I have to leave. My best friend might be in danger, and she needs my help. So, get your ass out of my way."

Like hell I'll get my ass out of her way. I block hlf her doorway with my body.

Mel barges by me anyway and walks out of her bedroom.

Shit.

My baby sister is very pregnant. I will not allow her to drive — god knows where — by herself.

Heart pounding, I scramble back into my room, snatch my wallet, house keys, and jacket, shove everything into my pockets, and run after her. We reach the eight-car garage at the same time.

"I'm driving, Mel. No arguments."

She shakes her head and sighs. "We have to head towards Amawalk. That is where she had her meeting today."

Great — out in the sticks. I reach for my LandCruiser keys from the lock box.

She exhales sharply and shakes her head when I press the key fob. The lights flash as the doors unlock.

"Tristian, I'm serious. No yelling. No telling me what to do. Izzy needs us."

She opens the front passenger door and climbs in.

Shit — I should have assisted her. I forgot about the extra front weight of the baby. True to Mel-style, she proves her independence again. Once I'm in and start the car, Mel reaches for my GPS and types in the address. She settles into her seat and fastens her belt.

"Hurry up, Tristian."

*A*s Mel said, *"Wait with my car."*

Yeah... no argument from me. I'm not in the mood to be murdered in the woods tonight. Who knows what is out there? Bears? Serial killers? My ex? Hard to say which is worse.

The sun disappears as evening temperatures drop and darkness wraps around me like a cold, damp blanket. I settle into my car, shifting around until I find the least uncomfortable position — which, let's be honest, doesn't exist at seven months pregnant — and secure my doors.

I check online for the local sheriff's number and tap the screen to make the call.

The first time, it just rings.

The second time, it goes to voicemail... and then cuts out.

Okay... fabulous. I'll try again later. Maybe the sheriff's department closes at 5 p.m. out here. Wouldn't surprise me.

In the fifteen or twenty minutes since speaking with Mel, I extract the memory card from its slot in the GPS and slide it into my cell. Thank god for multiple SIM and memory card slots — one of the few smart decisions I've made today.

As the minutes tick by, I answer two business emails and send a confidential one to my employee, Tereasa, explaining she's now in charge of running the security business until Simon drags himself back into the office. From tomorrow onwards, I'm working from home. No more office. No more clients. No more idiots.

A couple of years ago, Essy Raiker recommended some of her staff for my company. Tereasa Maclyn — former Navy SEAL, brilliant, terrifying, and rocking an artificial leg — has been a godsend. It's time to upgrade her position. She's earned it.

Depending on how long Simon is out sick, I'll need to contact Essy again. Simon and I need people we can rely on — not flaky sheriffs who don't answer their phones.

Keeping my mind busy, it only occurs to me now that I haven't turned on my hazard lights. Pregnancy brain strikes again.

With the glowing orange lights flashing around me like a sad disco, I finish another email and hit send. I take a sip of water — because apparently hydration is important — when bright lights flood the area around my car.

Oh good. Either the tow truck or the beginning of a horror movie.

I tap my door lock again, just in case, and recap my

water bottle. My mind races. This better be the tow truck. I close down my email account and pack up my papers before my imagination creates a full-blown crime documentary starring me as the victim.

The bright headlights stop several meters behind my SUV. I focus on the mirrors, watching the truck door creak open. A dark silhouette steps out and walks toward my car. My hand hovers over my cell, ready to dial for help — or Mel — whichever one answers first.

The man stops beside my window. A hand lifts, then taps on the glass.

To be safe, I tap the record-video icon on my cell. If I die tonight, at least there will be evidence. Hi, Netflix. Here's your next true-crime special.

"Ms. Delany?" the dark figure asks in a friendly, muffled voice. "Are you okay? I'm here to load your vehicle."

A sigh escapes me. Thank god.

I nod. Good. I can finally get out of here and press the button to lower the window a couple of inches. "Hello."

His truck lights illuminate his profile, and I smile when our eyes meet.

Not bad looking. Powerfully built. Focus, Izzy. Not the time. "Can you show me some identification?"

He smiles — white teeth, nice — and nods. He pulls out a card from his chest pocket and slips it through the gap.

I grip the card and read: Keith Smith. Smith & Son's Tow Trucking Company. He flashes his driver's license too. Relief washes over me. At least this handsome man is who he says he is.

I lower my window some more. "Thank you, Keith."

"Ms. Delany, what happened for you to be here?" he asks, glancing over my car.

The memory of that dark car coming straight at me makes my stomach twist. My heart pounds. Fear and worry spike again — for me and my baby.

I take a deep breath. "Keith, I was driving on the main road, carefully avoiding most of the deep potholes. A dark car veered into my lane, coming straight at me. I swerved onto this dirt road, narrowly missing it, but then something was seriously wrong with my car. A hard jolt, shaking, loud noise... and suddenly no brakes or steering."

Keith shakes his head, glances around, then back at me. "How did you stop?"

Ah. There it is.

"I used my gears." His eyebrow rises. "Forcing the car into each lower gear, hoping it'd slow down."

"Wow. That probably saved you." He glances toward the trees. "If you kept going, you would have hit those trees up there."

A shiver runs through me. Yes, Keith. I noticed the trees. I'm pregnant, not blind. As much as I'm enjoying the view, I want to get out of here.

"What do you need me to do now?" I ask.

His face turns stern. "Have you been in contact with the local police?"

I shake my head. "The phone number online took me to an answering machine, then cut out."

He mutters something under his breath and pulls out his cell. Within seconds, he's speaking to someone.

"Hank. Can you come out to a car I'm about to load? ...A woman ran off Pines Bridge Road. ...Yeah. I think you need to have a look."

He nods. "Thanks, Hank. Ten minutes."

He pockets his phone. "The local sheriff will drop by shortly. While we wait, remove what you want from your vehicle. You can place it in my truck."

He steps back so I can open my door. I stand — slowly — and within seconds he blurts, "Holy cow, how pregnant are you?" My head snaps toward him. Brow raised. "Sorry," he blurts. "No filter." At least he's honest.

I open the back door, grab my oversized puffer jacket, and shrug it on. "Seven months. And the kid has been bouncing on my bladder."

Hopefully, he gets the hint — because this cold air is not helping.

"Look, I'll be quick. Want me to grab anything? My truck cab is warm. You can sit out of the cold."

Oh wow. A man who understands pregnant women. A rare species.

"Thank you, Keith."

I stop the recording and slip my phone into my coat pocket.

Keith helps me load my equipment and bags into his truck. Somehow, I climb into the passenger seat and sit quietly, watching him. Minutes pass as he circles my car, inspecting the tires, then crouching to look underneath with a bright torch.

Mel crosses my mind. I better text her.

> **Me:**
> The sexy tow truck driver is inspecting my car now. I'm sitting in his truck keeping warm. 🚗

I hit send and glance up. Keith is still taking his time, looking under the front and back of the car.

My phone dings.

> **Mel:**
> I'm more than halfway there. Is he built?? 😳 🤭

I laugh at her built reference as relief fills me. Mel will be here soon.

Several seconds later — or maybe minutes, time has lost all meaning — a bright glow grabs my attention from the side. The glow grows stronger until it clicks that I'm watching a set of headlights approach.

Great. Round two of Let's Terrify the Pregnant Woman in the Woods.

Keith angles his head, observing as the car draws near. Once he identifies the person, he walks toward the driver's side. A man exits the vehicle and greets Keith with a handshake. They talk quietly as they make their way toward my SUV in the dim lighting.

They crouch, scanning the underside and surroundings of my car with a flashlight. I hope this is Hank — the sheriff — and not some random man Keith found in the bushes.

The unknown man jots down a few notes before

approaching me alongside Keith. When he steps closer, the uniform finally comes into focus. Sheriff. Thank god.

I open the truck door, carefully slide down, and stand facing the two men.

Keith speaks first. "Ms. Delany, this here is Sheriff Stone."

I nod and smile. "Nice to meet you, Sheriff."

Sheriff Stone looks me over from head to toe and back up again, lingering on my belly like he's trying to calculate my due date. "Ms. Delany. Can you explain to me what happened?"

Straight to the point. No warm-up. No *"Are you okay?"* Just business. Lovely.

I repeat everything — again — while he takes notes and copies my license and registration. He pauses to watch the dashcam footage. Thank god Mel reminded me about the memory-card slot in my phone. Pregnancy brain would've had me eating the card instead.

"Can you send me a copy of that video, Ms. Delany?"

He gives me his details, and with a few taps, I forward the file. His phone dings.

"Thank you, Ms. Delany. I'll watch the file back at my office on a bigger screen and look for more details about the other car. Apart from that, I think I have all your details and will contact you when I have more information."

"Thank you, Sheriff."

I climb back into the truck cab — which feels like scaling a mountain in my current state — and settle in.

After twenty minutes or so, the Sheriff leaves. Keith finishes securing my car on the flatbed, then climbs into the driver's seat.

"Ms. Delany, was someone coming out here to pick you up? I should have asked you earlier."

Why ask that now? Is he planning to abandon me in the woods? Because honestly, that would be the cherry on top of today's shit sundae.

I glance out the window, nodding, hoping nothing has happened to Mel. Driving this far alone, pregnant, and avoiding her brothers... yeah, I'm worried. "Yes," I say. "My friend will be here any minute."

Keith nods and looks through the windshield. "I hope you understand. I can wait another ten minutes or so, but I need to return to my family's garage."

Bugger. Of course. Why wouldn't the universe add a countdown timer to my misery?

"I understand. Thank you for waiting thus far," I say, reaching for my cell. "I'll call my friend and see where she is."

Chapter Twelve

TRISTIAN

*A*nticipating the encounter with Izzy has my mind in a full-blown cyclone, making driving a challenge — especially with my heart racing and a very inconvenient situation happening behind my zipper.

The annoying woman's GPS voice fills the car. "In six hundred and fifty meters, turn left."

Fantastic. Even the GPS is nagging me. I really need to change the voice and volume on this stupid device.

Headlights blast toward us, nearly blinding me. A police patrol car. Interesting. Were they with Izzy? Wouldn't surprise me — trouble seems magnetically drawn to her.

Mel's voice slices through my thoughts. "Tristian, as your annoying GPS said, we're nearly there." She glances at her phone. "Slow down. The road is just up here."

Right. Time to focus. Time to be the responsible eldest brother — the role I inherited the moment our parents died. Lucky me.

"Remind me. What brought Izzy here initially?" I ask casually, easing off the accelerator.

I've been chewing on that question for a while. What the hell is she doing out here? This desolate, wooded stretch is no place for Izzy. She deserves luxury, comfort — not... this.

Mel sighs. "Tristian, Izzy does work, you know. What is her life to you, anyway?"

If only I could confess the truth — that I'm in love with my sister's best friend. That I think about her naked in my bed every damn night. That she's lodged herself so deep in my head I can't shake her loose.

But sure, Mel, let's pretend I'm just being nosy.

Ignoring her, I take the dirt road she points out. Up ahead, headlights face us.

"Ahh, good. The tow truck is still here," Mel murmurs.

Her phone rings. "Izzy, we're here. ...Tristian pushed the issue and demanded he drive. ...No, I have said nothing."

Said what? What conspiracy are they cooking up now?

My headlights sweep across the scene — a tow truck, Izzy's car on the tray.

I pull up beside it. The insect chorus grows louder as I step out. Izzy stands by the truck, concern etched across her face. Mel jumps out and slams the door.

"Oh my god, girl. Are you okay?" she screeches, throwing her arms around Izzy.

"Mel, settle. I'm okay. Let's grab my stuff."

They separate. Izzy's eyes meet mine in the dim light.

She nods. "Hello, Tristian. Thank you for driving Mel and coming out here to pick me up."

My fingers twitch. I want to pull her into my arms and keep her there. Instead, I lift my chin. "I couldn't let Mel drive so far in the dark."

She nods. "I've been concerned for her. I'm relieved someone drove her."

The truck driver walks up beside her. "Ms. Delany, you have my card. Give me a ring in the morning, and we'll decide what to do."

She smiles at him. He smiles back.

Great. Now I'm jealous of a tow truck driver. Perfect.

"Thank you for waiting, Keith. And all your assistance."

He nods, smiling again. My jealousy spikes. "Make sure you take care. Until tomorrow."

Then he turns to me, tilting his head toward the back of the truck. What? He wants to talk. Why? What now? My mind races with different scenario's.. Does he want to know if she's single? Is it about her car?

While Mel and Izzy pull belongings from the cab, I follow him around to the tray.

"How do you do? Are you close to Ms. Delany?" he asks.

I nod, cautious. "As you can see, she's like family."

He glances at the girls, then back at me. "Technically, I should say nothing, but... I'm a little concerned."

My breath freezes. Concerned about what?

"I would like you to know Ms. Delany has serious vehicle issues. How she did not crash her car... well, she is extremely lucky."

A cold weight settles in my gut.

He flashes a light under the front of the SUV. I crouch, trying to make sense of the damage.

"Look under the front. Start with the axle. Notice the damage? More than expected. Tomorrow morning, the sheriff plans to re-inspect the SUV on the hoist."

"What are you saying? Do you think someone tampered with her car?"

If someone tried to hurt Izzy, they're going to regret it. Deeply.

He nods and hands me a card. "Yes. Here are my contact details." He glances toward Izzy again.

I slide the card into my jacket and hand him one of mine. "Thanks."

"Does Izzy know about this?" I ask.

He shakes his head. "No. I have said nothing. When we're sure... and from what we've seen so far, we both agree — her vehicle appears to be tampered with."

My jaw tightens. Who the hell would want to hurt my Izzy?

"Thanks for letting me know," I say, shaking his hand.

When I return to my car, the girls are already inside. I slide into the driver's seat and start the engine.

"Where are we dropping Izzy off?" If it's her home, maybe I'll finally see where she lives.

Mel shoots me an annoyed look. "Brother, my friend is staying the night. If you do not like it — STIFF!"

Fantastic. Izzy under my roof. This will be hard in more ways than one.

Her favorite fragrance fills the car, and my zipper situation gets worse. By the time we pull into the multi-car garage at the mansion, I'm barely holding it together.

Before I can even turn off the engine, the girls bolt out of the car and rush toward the house, abandoning all of Izzy's belongings.

"Hey, where are the two of you going?" I call, hitting the start/off button.

Without stopping, Mel yells over her shoulder, "Bathroom!" as they disappear inside.

Chapter Thirteen

TRISTIAN

I'm starving. We delayed our family dinner to collect Izzy from the middle of nowhere — the sticks, the bush, the land of zero cell reception and questionable life choices. Thankfully, our cook left everything in the fridge, including those thick slices of roast beef that practically melt on the tongue.

It doesn't take me long to stack two roast beef sandwiches with gravy. I devour them like a man who hasn't eaten in days.

For once, I'm away from my noisy siblings. Sitting by the large kitchen window overlooking the pool garden, the silence settles into my bones. My body finally relaxes as I finish the last bite. I drain my drink, clean up, wash and dry everything, and put it all back exactly where it belongs. Order restored.

I flick the light switch. The kitchen drops into darkness except for the faint blue LED strips along the floor. They guide me toward the pantry. The scent of herbs and spices hits me as I reach for a bottle of cold water.

I turn the bottle in my hand, but all I can think about is scotch. A stiff drink would hit the spot. Instead, I'm grabbing water like a responsible adult. With Mel pregnant, I want to keep my wits about me in case something happens.

Not that I have any wits left where Izzy is concerned. She has me tied in knots. My dick hardens just thinking about her sleeping down the hall from my room. Tonight, sleep is a fantasy. She's too close. Far too close.

I turn to leave the pantry — and a sudden light blinds me. Someone switches on the overhead light for the island bench.

I pause.

Izzy walks in, absorbed in her phone, wearing a long white man's shirt and black leggings.

My brain short-circuits.

She's pregnant.

Her belly is round, swollen, unmistakable. A lump forms in my throat.

What the—

How—

Since when—

I freeze. Feet glued to the floor. Jaw unhinged. I hold my breath so I don't startle her, watching her move around the kitchen completely oblivious to me.

She loads two plates into the dishwasher. I can't look away from her baby bump. She pours juice, drinks it, sets the glass down, then turns on the kettle.

Why didn't she tell me?

My patience snaps. I can't wait another second. "Izzy, is there something you want to tell me?"

She startles, spinning toward me. "Oh, Tristian. It's you." One hand flies to her heart, the other to her belly. "You scared me."

Despite the irritation boiling in my chest, she's gorgeous. Pregnancy suits her in ways I'm not prepared for.

My eyebrow lifts. "Come on, Izzy. When were you going to tell me?"

She rolls her eyes, leans forward — and her enlarged breasts practically punch the air out of my lungs. "Are you serious?"

Uh... yes?

Valid question, I thought.

She gives me a sharp, dark look. "For all intents and purposes — let me just say — I contacted you, Tristian." Another eye roll. "You didn't want to speak to me."

What?

Whoa...What the hell is she talking about?

I open my mouth to ask — and of course, that's when my youngest brother strolls in.

Nicholas stops dead. "Holy shit, Izzy. Is there something in the water?"

Brilliant. The king of oblivious commentary has arrived. "Anyway," he continues, "Mel said she'll be waiting upstairs in her room for you to bring the hot chocolate, cookies, and a couple of doughnuts."

Izzy smiles, rubbing her belly.

She moves around the kitchen like she owns it,

preparing hot chocolate and snacks while I stand there, useless, watching her. She arranges everything on a tray, then glances over her shoulder.

"See you later, gentlemen."

And just like that, she's gone.

Looks like I'm not getting my answers anytime soon.

he moment I sink onto the end of Mel's bed, my cell phone vibrates, signaling a notification. The screen lights up, displaying the sender's name, which makes me frown in confusion as I look at the excerpt of the text. I can't understand why Gavin would reach out to me again today and at this hour.

We met at the Book Bar Club, a haven for bookworms at 197 E 3rd St., a few days ago. Over lattes, he voiced his disapproval of my decision to move to New York. What could he be after now? That's two texts within hours. Seriously...why is he sending these useless text messages?

Mel reads the preview of the message on the screen, and her head shakes in disapproval. "You're not considering replying to that, are you? There's something off about Gavin. I can feel it."

I do not intend to reply to Gavin's text or mention that to Mel. Her ego is already big enough. I meet her gaze and with a firm voice, I reply, "Mel, he's a friend. I can't just cut him off like that."

Her eyes fill with a mix of annoyance and concern. "Yes, you can, Izzy. He's always given me the creeps, and I can't shake that feeling."

I dryly reply, "Yes. You have made that very clear." The two have never gotten along.

"Did you see him the other morning?" If Mel had her way, she would have stopped me from going.

"Yes, I did. Gavin was visiting relatives. We met for coffee at a bookstore that doubles as a coffee shop. He asked me to fix a computer problem he couldn't sort out. It had taken me longer than I expected."

"Why?" she says, frowning.

Huh? Mel is aware of my skillfulness when it comes to computers. My brow rises as I meet her eyes. "What do you mean, why? He asked. I was there, so I helped."

"Izzy, I don't mean your skills on a computer!" Glad to see she remembered. "When I met the guy, he made out he was some wiz computer guru," she says with a frown.

What? "No. That can't be right." Gavin said once he avoids working on computers. Maybe I had taken his words the wrong way.

"Izzy. Why would he say one thing to me and something different to you? I don't trust the guy. Be careful around him. I would avoid him."

"Mel, he's been a good friend." Well, he had been until his behavior became a little erratic, and he told me off for moving to New York without him. Is that a bit stalker-ish?

"Izzy, sorry, but I don't care. I wouldn't be surprised if Gavin's responsible for your car issues, just to make himself look good each time he rode in on his white horse to rescue you."

That thought had crossed my mind, especially since he knew how to fix my car, even though I had not told him what was wrong with it.

"Look, Mel. I have other things to contemplate," I mumble around a mouthful of doughnut, followed by the delicious hot chocolate.

Just then, Mel's cell chimes.

We both look at her screen. I huff at seeing the name. Monica Snells. Miss rich bitch. She has had the hots for Tristian since we were in school.

"Why would Monica be texting you at this time of night?"

Mel shakes her head, then taps the screen and reads the message.

"Do you believe my so-called friend wants to catch up tomorrow?"

"I'll bite. The bitch hasn't contacted you since before we left over seven months ago. Why the sudden need to meet with you?"

My best friend laughs. "Probably because I'm back in New York, and she wants to worm her way closer to my brothers."

Just what I thought. "Seriously!"

"Yep. I would never have believed it if I hadn't overheard Monica in March."

"Why? What happened in March, and why didn't you say anything?"

Using her fingers, she counts out her reasons. "One: Monica has the hots for my brothers. It makes me sick the way she flaunts herself at them. Two: She has sexually propositioned both Alex and Tristian in front of me. Three: Instead of putting me on hold, she added our call with her friends. I had heard every sick word she spewed."

"Oh, Mel." If the skank were here, I would punch the bitch in the face for the way she had treated Mel over the years.

"Yeah, well, let me just say she revealed her sick plan for my brothers and me. She was only using me and was planning on setting one of my brothers up, forcing a marriage."

I lean towards Mel and wrap my arms around her.

"*That* should complete the schedule," Mel says, her words slightly muffled by a mouthful of delicious crumbling cookie. "The apps for the two clients are now completed." She wipes her mouth with the back of her hand and continues, "My in-house team will be meeting with them tomorrow, and I'll follow up the day after to address any last-minute changes the clients might have."

As she wipes her hands together and brushes off the crumbs from her front, she gives me a smile. I shake my head at her lack of decorum, noticing the crumbs on her laptop, bed, and floor. Just as I go to open my mouth to comment on her lack of manners, my cell phone vibrates with an incoming call. Glancing at the screen, I see that it's Simon's neighbor's number.

Suddenly, it hits me — I forgot to call Simon. With everything that has happened, I wonder what Vicki wants and answer the call, saying, "Hello, Vicki."

Before I can say anything else, she interjects with her uppity posh voice, "Izzy, don't panic." I hate it when someone says that — it only makes me panic more.

Concern fills me, and my voice reflects the alarm as I respond, "Vicki..."

However, before I can say anything else to her, she interrupts me with urgent news. "Izzy, Marty received a strange message from Simon earlier today. Long story short, we found Simon on the floor in his apartment and rushed him to the hospital."

My back straightens as I try to edge myself to the edge of Mel's seat, ready to stand up. "Oh, my god, Vicki. Is he okay?" I realize now that I should have insisted on him going to the hospital instead of making a doctor's appointment. He assured me he would be fine, but next time I'll trust my instincts.

"Izzy, listen," Vicki's voice captures my attention. "We'll know more in a few hours." Huh? Confusion fills me with her vague statement. What few hours? "I'll let you know when we know more." I pause, taken aback by her words.

"Huh?" I glance toward Mel, hoping for some clarity. "Vicki, what happened? What's going on?" I ask, hoping she will cut to the chase.

"We're not sure. Simon thought he was coming down with a bug." She pauses, then murmurs, "Izzy, we suspect he's been poisoned."

My mind races at the word '*poisoned.*' When did this happen? Then a hundred questions fill my mind at once.

"Oh, my god. No. Who would...?" I trail off, my thoughts consumed by the need to see him. "Which hospital is he at? I'll come straight over."

Her sigh reaches my ear. "No, Izzy. Stay where you are." What the hell? "The hospital wouldn't allow you to see him, anyway."

What is going on? Why do I feel Vicki is not telling me everything?

"When can I speak with him?" I hedge.

Did she just sigh again? "Izzy. The doctors sedated Simon twenty minutes ago."

Huh? "What do you mean sedated, Vicki?" Now, I'm annoyed. What else is she keeping from me?

She mumbles something, then says, "I'll be straight with you, Izzy. An hour ago, Simon deteriorated. They've placed him on a ventilator until the specialist can discover what is causing Simon's symptoms and his lungs to fail."

My misting, concerned eyes meet Mel's. I think my heart is ready to stop. Lungs? Poisoned? What in the world is going on?

"I don't understand. Will Simon improve, or am I losing my close friend and business partner?"

Another sigh reaches my ear and Vicki replies, "For now, the machine is taking the stress away from

Simon's lungs. The next twenty-four to thirty-six hours will determine what will happen. His specialist has him in the ICU. Marty and I will remain with him. Simon is lucky he lives next door to two doctors who were home. Or things could have been different." Oh, my god. No.

I should be at the hospital. Maybe I'll discover more... "Do you need anything? I can bring in food or something."

"For now, no, she says. "Thank you for offering."

Well, that was a bust. "Okay. Remember, I'm only a phone call away."

"Thanks, Izzy. Before his sedation, Simon left a message for you to pass on to others. 'He cannot be reached, as he has been called away to a family emergency.' And to have Franky reschedule his meetings, pushing them back a week or more."

I nod. "Yes. Sure, I can do that." I glance back at Mel. She can hear Vicki speaking. I wonder if my face resembles hers. Her smiley face has vanished and turned pale, and she looks concerned and scared.

I'm lost in thought and nearly miss her next words, "Keep what has happened confidential." Huh? Okay, it makes sense. Our business does not need the bad press. But still...

"Vicki, give Marty a hug for me. Hold Simon's hand and tell him I said he has to fight and survive."

"Izzy, I will. Look. I really have to go. I'll phone you tomorrow. Take care."

Before I can say anything else, she ends the call, leaving me staring at my cell. When I glance at Mel, I watch tears roll down her cheeks. Then I realize my cheeks are wet as I wipe my face with my other hand.

"Oh, my god, Mel. Simon is sick. Did you hear Vicki? They believe he's been poisoned."

She nods, reaches for the box of Kleenex, and passes me a tissue.

"Izzy, you spoke to him this morning..." she said as a statement, not a question.

I nod. "Yes. Simon mentioned he thought he had a bug of some kind. His head hurt, his chest was heavy, and he's been throwing up. At first, I had thought he wanted a day off." I should have done something...but what? Maybe I should have contacted Vicki and Marty to check on him.

Doubt sets in deep in my soul. What kind of friend am I? I should have tried more. Done more.

"Izzy, I know that look. There was nothing you could have done."

I nod and reply, "I phoned his number before the meeting. But he didn't answer his cell." I shake my head. Why didn't I do more? "Now I know why. I have failed Simon."

"Izzy, stop right there. You were busy contending with his business meeting, which was on short notice. And don't forget what happened after that meeting. Someone tried to run you off the road. We watched the footage." Another chill sweeps over me. I still cannot believe I didn't crash. My baby could have died. "You survived. You didn't crash. Now you're here under my family roof. We will get through this."

All I can do is nod. I feel so lost. Mel wraps me in her arms, and I hold on tight.

*S*omething wakes me from a sound sleep, taking a few seconds to realize I am at Mel's family home. Then I glance at the digital clock on the nightstand. 12.39 a.m. Seriously!

My brain begins to race, and Simon fills my thoughts. Oh, no. My friend... How can I sleep knowing Simon is sick in the hospital? With a bit of a roll, I reach for my cell to check for a message from Vicki. Nope. Instead, I notice a message from Franky, Simon's PA, who wants more information regarding Simon.

Before I went to bed, I informed Franky via a verbal message on his message bank.

Franky needs to follow my direction, or he will look for a new job. Franky's condescending attitude has always grated on me.

Before I phone and yell at the man, I quickly tap out a text.

> **Me:**
> Franky, Simon, had to leave right away, making him unreachable. That is all I know. You'll be assisting Tereasa while Simon is away.

That should do it. Short and sweet, and hit send before focusing on sleep.

*N*o matter how hard I try, sleep eludes me. My boy moves and presses against my full bladder. I know going back to sleep is useless, so I roll out of bed, turn on the bedside lamp, and head to the bathroom. Relief fills me when the kid stops bouncing on my now-empty bladder.

As I walk back through to my dimly lit bedroom, a scream leaves my mouth as I notice someone sitting at the end of my bed.

"It's me, Izzy. You don't need to scream."

My brain catches up when I realize it's Tristian who scared me. My conflicted heart yearns for him, unsure whether to hold or harm him. Strangling does sound good right about now. But then I have to get close to him.

What is he doing here at this time of night?

"Tristian, stop scaring the crap out of me. My heart cannot take it."

"Izzy, I said we need to talk. I'm serious."

I glance at the clock. 1.06 a.m. "Can't it wait until daylight hours?"

He shakes his head. "No, Izzy. I want to know, is this baby mine?" His focus remains on my belly.

Is he serious right now? I reached out and left messages for him, but he did not return my calls once. He had his chance, and he blew it.

"Tristian, seriously? When we verbally spoke back

in March, you informed me we have no future and I should move on with my life. I did." It is slight, but I notice him flinch at my words. Yeah, buddy... you should have chosen your words more carefully.

With a shake of his head, he straightens his back and focuses on my face.

"Iz, why are you hesitant to answer my question? Is the baby mine?" Talk about avoidance. He's the one who refuses to acknowledge my calls and says we have no future...

"Tristian, I had taken your words seriously. I made a choice to keep my baby. My baby!"

"Izzy."

I shake my head and say with narrowing eyes, "I have contacted you several times, Tristian. I even sent you an email when I had my first scan. You replied with, and I quote. *'Do not send me any more emails.'*"

Chapter Fifteen
TRISTIAN

onfusion. That is what I'm feeling. What is she talking about? What correspondence and when?

My mind races with memories of the two of us together before she moved away, a whirlwind of images, passion, and never repeated sensations. Since that night, I have received no messages or emails from her.

On the other hand — her admission that the baby is mine echoes in my mind, each syllable a stark, undeniable truth. A wave of happiness, joy, and a thrilling anticipation crashes over me, leaving me breathless. I'm going to be a dad. All I want is to hold Izzy close and never let her go. And, most importantly, to experience every moment of our pregnancy together.

As my brain processes the rest of her words, I pause, feeling ashamed. Why did I break things off with her in March? We could have been together all this time. As my eyes wander over her body and then return to her belly, I take in the miracle of our child growing within her body. No one else will raise my child, or me being left out of its life. My internal self flinches at my thoughts. I have to stop thinking of my kid as an 'it.'

With another shake of my head, I'm certain I've had no communication from her, and reply, "Izzy, you haven't sent me any messages or emails." Her tired yet stunning eyes narrow and blaze at me. Whoa. When she's passionate, she's breathtaking. My excitement stirs within me, thankfully concealed by my denim jeans, unlike my sweatpants, which would have revealed my true feelings for the alluring woman in front of me.

As I take in her clothing, my thoughts turn to money. "Izzy, you'll need financial help at least." Her angry eyes make it clear that she's furious. What is she angry about? I thought she would appreciate my money.

"Listen carefully, Tristian, to what I'm about to say. Your money is not necessary. I have my own, and I always have," she states. Huh? What does she mean by '*always*'?

I focus back on her and notice she's basically vibrating with anger. "Open your eyes and get your head out of your butt. If you had asked the right questions from the start, you would have known who my parents are," she declares, heading towards her bedroom door. She pauses and looks back at me over her shoulder. "Tristian, I'd appreciate it if you weren't here when I come back. I can't sleep with you in my room."

She turns and walks away.

Okay. Who on earth are her parents? Countless questions swirl in my mind, and this is just one of them.

Since when has she had money? Does Mel know? In mid-step, I pause and wonder why I'd question that thought. Of course, she would know as I storm out of Izzy's room, heading straight for my sisters. My little sister and I need a serious talk about her questionable friend, and Mel will provide the answers!

"*T*ristian, get the hell out of my room," my sister orders, throwing a pillow at me. "How dare you wake me to ask questions you should have looked into years ago? It goes to show how narrow-minded and selfish you are. Now, get out." If she's not careful, she'll go into labor, then I will be in the doghouse.

"Listen, Mel. I know that I have acted like a jerk. But, come on. Izzy has never let on that she has money." Holy crap, my sister's eyes are like laser beams, ready to cut me down. She's pissed. What is her problem? Why can't she answer my questions?

"Tristian, why would she do that? Why bring unwanted attention to herself? At least she learns about people. She learned about you." Mel lifts her hands and, with her fingers, forms air quotes. "Says the guy who stated — '*We have no future. But we can still fuck.*'"

My shoulders flinch at her comments. "Hey. Watch your mouth." Rolling her eyes, was her response to my words, as she lowers her hands to her sides.

"In my room," she says, her voice tight and strained, "you have no authority over what I say, Tristian." Huh? But I'm the head of the family. Of course, I have... "If you have a problem with my language, I will move out," she announces.

What? No. Mel won't leave until I find out who got her pregnant and take responsibility. On second thoughts, I haven't done the right thing by Izzy. She's having my baby without me. I have a ring, and Izzy will find it on her finger soon. She'll be my wife before our child's birth. I just need to arrange a prenup for us.

"Mel, you will remain here. And give me a hint... Who's your baby's father?"

"What? No to both."

I hold my hands up in surrender when Mel reaches and prepares another pillow to throw at me.

"Okay. I'll go for now. But we will talk in the morning."

She shakes her head. "No, Tristian. Question or pressure me once more, and I will leave and never come back."

I pause mid-step.

Anger fills me. I flex my fingers. I know it's her hormones speaking, but still... Mel's an ungrateful girl.

Agitation claws at me, a sharp, irritating feeling amplified by her irritating words. That is how I feel. Best to play it cool for now and bide my time. I'll get my answers. Maybe not tonight, but I will get them.

I nod. Turn and walk out of my sister's door.

The time has come to phone my attorney. I have some major decisions to make.

*T*he steam from my tea, a comforting cloud, warms my face as my fingers encircle the tall mug, feeling the intense heat pulse through the porcelain to my fingertips. My gaze drifts over the crisp, white rectangular card, its smooth gloss surface catching the light. Thoughts of Keith, the tall, dark, rugged, and handsome truck driver from last night. Despite his handsome features, it's time to discuss my car and any repair estimate. Today.

As I take a sip of my hot, fragrant tea, the shrill ringing of my cell phone pierces the quiet, announcing an incoming call.

The screen lights up with a soft glow as I swipe with one hand and blurt, "Vicki, how is everything going?"

"Good morning to you, Izzy," Marty, Vicki's husband, states with his British business tone.

Marty?

Why's Marty using Vicki's phone?

One way to know. "Marty," I ask, "How's Simon?"

SECRET HEIRESS

His smug British tone fills my ear. "I called because of that."

Why is he being irritating instead of answering? "Marty," I interrupt. "What's going on?" I can't process any more bad news right now.

He doesn't make me wait. "Let me start with, Simon will continue to be sedated twenty-four to forty-eight hours to ensure his healing. A meeting is scheduled to evaluate his progress and determine the next course of action."

Huh? What's happening? Vicki stated the timeframe was twenty-four to thirty-six hours. "I don't understand what..."

Marty interrupts. "Basically, Simon's lungs are taking longer to respond to treatment."

Why? I anxiously ask, "Marty, what did the doctors discover?" Poor Simon.

"Izzy, Simon's in the best place. He's on a ventilator to help his lungs and body heal."

"But?"

"Keep positive thoughts for him, and focus on visiting him in a couple of days or so."

I can see him... Can it be true? "I'm sorry, Marty. It's just I'm scared for my friend. I don't want him to be alone."

"Simon is not alone. Vicki is with him. Then there is the nursing staff. He's in safe hands."

Vicki implied my friend had food poisoning. Should I mention the takeaway meal? Will it help to mention it? "Marty, Simon ordered Chinese food the night before. The food came after I left. Could it mean anything?"

"Thanks, I'll investigate that poisoning angle."

Hope this helps. "Appreciate it, Marty. Thank you for updating me."

"Simon is where he should be. Vicki will update you later."

Marty then ends the call before I can speak.

Despite my fear and confusion, I'm glad Simon lives.

I contemplate my next steps as I rub my thumb on the stiff corner of the business card that the truck driver gave me last night. Watching Keith and the sheriff inspect the front of my car, something felt off. My focus moves back to the card, and I dial the number printed on it. The digital sound of the numbers dialing and then ringing before someone answers on the third ring.

"Good morning. Smith & Son's Tow Trucking Company. How may I direct your call?"

"Hello. My name is Izzy Delany. Keith gave me his card when he picked up my car last night after I was ran off the road."

"Ah, yes. Hello, Ms. Delany. Can you come to the garage? Other than the usual paperwork, there's something about your car you should see."

So, I was right. Only one way to uncover what has happened and reply, "I'll be there in an hour."

"Thank you, Ms. Delany. See you then." The woman ends the call.

It only takes me a few seconds to tap out a message to my driver, Benny, informing him I require his services ASAP.

He doesn't make me wait, his reply is instant.

Benny:
I'll be there in ten minutes.

At least I can rely on Benny. I drink my tempered tea and head for the kitchen to make a sandwich. If I don't eat now, I'll be starving by the time this afternoon arrives.

"*I*zzy, you look beautiful." Huh? Lost in thought, I'm wondering why I'm dressing up instead of being with Simon at the hospital. Then there are the issues with my car and what happened. Who would want to hurt me? As I turn and face Mel, my eyes meet her smiling ones as she says, "That dress is perfect."

What is Mel going on about? I give in and glance at my reflection for the first time in the large mirror on her walk-in robe wall.

Wow!

I'm surprised. I actually look good.

The stylist styles my hair in a French twist, with a few long strands curled, framing my face. My eyes pop with expert-applied makeup in natural shades. As for the dress, I'm at a loss for words.

Wow. Is all I can come up with.

The black dress of Mel's showcases my pregnant, enlarged breasts, and my baby belly sits proudly in front of me without looking gaudy. It feels tailor made for me. The dress falls to my ankles in a moveable lightweight fabric, exposing my toned thighs through slits when walking and dancing.

The shoes are one of my pairs, which I keep in Mel's walk-in wardrobe. I have several other pairs of shoes and a couple of non-pregnancy outfits in there for special occasions. I wiggle my exposed toes in my clear wedge high heels, which have a black lining and ankle strap with a silver heart charm full of genuine diamonds attached.

My feet look as if they are floating.

I love it.

My eighty-nine dollar Australian purchase will remain a secret, but as for the diamond heart charms, they were a special treat for me. They only cost me five hundred for the two, and a special clip holds them in place. Okay, now I have to give it to Mel.

She has a good eye and fantastic taste in clothing. With a cheeky smile on my face, I mumble, "It will do for tonight."

As my gaze roves over my best friend, I can't help but think, Wow, Mel is a knockout in red. She looks stunning.

Her sharp brows move up her forehead. "What? Are you kidding me? The dress is perfect. You look amazing. My brother will regret what he said to you all those months ago."

However, my smile soon vanishes as Mel mentions Tristian. In my heart, I love him, but in reality, he's shown me his true colors. He is a bigot who only cares to be seen with someone from a wealthy family. Well, my son and I will be happy without him. My baby will learn the value of money and people. I firmly believe in the saying, "Never judge someone until you know them." Respect is a two-way street, and he will learn manners.

Mel's voice cuts through my thoughts, saying, "Izzy... are you listening to me?" Huh? What? My attention snaps back to reality with her words. "I'm sorry, I should never have mentioned Tristian." I nod as Mel embraces me. "Come on, we have a party to attend. Buzz Benny. We will blow his mind when he lays eyes on us." I smile at that. She's right: Benny's mind will be blown.

*W*e successfully evade Mel's brothers back at her family's mansion. Benny, my loveable driver, of course, fusses over us by the car and demands he'll escort us into the venue on the second floor.

With our heads held high, the air around us buzzes with excitement as we walk through the large doors into the radiant event. Hundreds of elegantly dressed people are standing or sitting at large round tables. I feel eyes upon me, accompanied by hushed whispers with each step. Several couples nod and smile, a few women turn their heads with raised brows. Does the excitement of two pregnant women warrant this level of attention? Mel's radiant and glamorous presence enhances our appearance. That must be it.

The sounds of serious business negotiations mingled with bursts of joyful laughter as we walked by, a vibrant mix of tones filling the air. A visual sweep quickly draws my attention to my aunt, holding court. With a captivating smile on her face, several wealthy New York patrons surround her in their finest attire.

With a quick nod in my direction, she smiles and gracefully excuses herself from her entourage, the murmur of their conversation fading as she approaches us. As soon as we step through the doorway away from the main crowd, Aunt H engulfs me in her loving arms.

"My darling girl. You're glowing. My... you remind me of your mother. You look gorgeous," my aunt says, before stepping back and then giving Mel a hug. "Hello, dear. How you both look beautiful. Pregnancy agrees with you both."

Mel smiles, then says, "Thank you, Hazel."

"Thank you, Aunt H. Come on, we best keep moving," I say.

Hazel glances at her watch and nods. "Yes. Our presentation checks are due to take place in a few minutes. We better meet our host."

The fancy decorated room vibrates with the sound of cameras and the hushed murmur of reporters' voices as the presentations of large company donations are given to tonight's hostess. The hundreds of suspended crystals and the polished surfaces reflect the flash of cameras, creating a dazzling spectacle.

Aunt H, tall and elegant, beams, awaiting her turn to present the hostess with a large check for fifty thousand dollars from Heartson Industries. I'm so proud of what my aunt has achieved. She is a natural in the spotlight. Her presence demands attention and respect. Photos and small speeches with each handover warrant extra questions from the media.

A few minutes later, my representative from AngelStar, Eric Bronson, handles himself professionally as he hands over a large cardboard check as the press clicks away, taking several photos and the reporters asking questions about AngelStar — Eric announces the fantastic achievements AngelStar has made towards fundraising and donations to the fire victims' charity and the additional housing being supplied that I — I mean AngelStar started several months ago.

The large portfolio I had Eric bring tonight, showcasing photos of the portable homes and including donation information — website and phone number — helped tremendously at tonight's event. With this incredible advertising opportunity, our message will reach a massive audience of diverse organizations and wealthy individuals, providing unmatched brand exposure and the potential for significant impact — imagine the possibilities! Proud of the successful interviews, I couldn't have planned it better myself. The destitute families will benefit from tonight's exposure.

*M*el and I entered the grand room via the decorated entrance on the second floor for the main event and quickly found our table and seats, including eight more table settings. At these types of events, guests sometimes can not choose who they prefer to sit with, which leaves them stuck with people they do not know.

Something catches my attention, as I look towards the main doors of the gala. On no. There she stands — Monica Snells, Mel's ex-close friend, wearing a red dress that clings to her like it was painted on. I tap Mel's leg under the table and mumble, "Seven o'clock. Your buddy is here."

"Who?" Mel asks and turns her head to look. "Ah, shit. What is she doing here?"

"Probably to cause a scene."

"Sadly, that is probably true," Mel murmurs. "If she approaches me, I won't take responsibility for my actions," Mel declares.

I agree with a nod and take another sip of my glass of water when I hear my name behind me.

"Izzy, is that you?" I glance up and notice three beautiful women approach us with smiles. "Oh, my. Look at you. You're gorgeous and glowing."

A beautiful woman, Essy Raiker-Bianchi, one of the best bodyguards I know, leans down and hugs me.

"Thanks, Essy. You're looking fantastic. How are you doing?" I ask before glancing at her sister, Laini Raiker-Travelli, and their close friend, Missy Jamés-Steele, with a huge smile. I met these girls a couple of years ago, and we turned it into a girl's weekend. Plus, I have hired Missy's advertising business and Essy's bodyguard business several times. "Missy, Laini, it's great to see you."

"I see you've been busy. I didn't know you were seeing someone." The floor becomes interesting, avoiding her questions. Her friendly gaze notices my discomfort, a slight frown touching her lips. "Oh, I'm sorry, Izzy. I should know better than to ask that question," Laini states. Laini had a daughter, which she had kept secret. Her now-husband had married someone else at that time. He never knew that he would be a father back then, leaving Laini to raise her child alone.

Essy had twin boys and two daughters. She had a complicated relationship with her *secret* husband. Then there is Missy. She met her husband in Vegas. They thought they had a fake marriage, only to discover later that they were legally married and Missy was pregnant in another country. These three have had entertaining lives and more unexpected pregnancies.

I shrug my shoulders. "The guy in question is not in my life regarding the baby. All I'll say is it's complicated." The three beautiful women all nod. Complicated is one thing they know well.

"Regarding your request, I have organized Raymond Streets to join Tereasa. He can start tomorrow morning. Also three more security patrol staff."

What a relief. Now that Simon is in the hospital, we require more staff. "Thank you, Essy. You're a lifesaver. Can you thank Raymond for me? Tereasa can show him the ropes and what needs to be done."

"I'll let him know," Essy says, glancing at my best friend.

I feel a tap on my leg. Shit, I'm a horrible friend. I forgot I had not introduced them.

"Where are my manners? Essy, Missy, Laini. I

would like to introduce Mel Astor." I turn and face my best friend. "Mel, these beautiful women are Essy Raiker-Bianchi. Missy Jamés-Steele and Laini Raiker-Travelli. Essy has that bodyguard business I told you about."

Before I can say another word, Mel cuts in, "Essy, Missy, and Laini, it's a pleasure to meet you all. Essy, I think Izzy here might need to hire your services."

I shake my head. What is Mel doing? Essy frowns and glances from Mel to me, then back to Mel.

"I take it has nothing to do with Tereasa or Raymond? Explain what has happened?" You have to love Essy. She is straight to the point.

Mel doesn't wait for me to respond. "A lunatic ran Izzy off the road last night. The car cam footage looks bad. Today, we discovered someone tampered with her car prior to the incident."

Upon visiting the garage earlier today, the situation proves far worse than expected.

Who would want to hurt me?

Essy frowns, then reaches for her cell phone in her glittery clutch. "Who was the towing company?" she asked.

Mel lists the details and goes on, as Essy asks about any recent oddities or new acquaintances in my life. Before I can reply, Mel mentions my friend Gavin and the trouble I have had with my two previous cars.

"Leave it with me, Izzy. Having one of my bodyguards following you might be in your best interest. Just to be safe. My danger radar is going off."

Essy cannot be serious. I don't require a bodyguard.

Surely it is overkill? "No, Essy. I don't want to waste your time."

"Don't underestimate Essy's gut feeling, Izzy. Let her check everything. Better safe than sorry. Consider your baby," Missy advises.

My shoulders flinch as I glance down and place my hand on my belly. They're right, and I should take it more seriously. I have to protect my unborn son.

I meet Essy's eyes. "Okay, Essy. I'll take you up on your offer for a few days."

She nods, speaks into her cell again, and places it back in her clutch bag. "Izzy, I'll have my staff look into your car situation. From tonight forward, one of my guards will be your new shadow, keeping a discreet distance. I'll send a text with their details when they are in place. We had better keep mingling with the other guests and speak with our host before sitting at our table. Have a good evening, and we'll speak soon."

We say our goodbyes, and I signal to one of the waiters. I require a drink with some bubbles.

"Izzy, I'll return shortly. I just saw someone I better say hello to."

Huh? Who did my friend see? And glance over my shoulder, looking for whoever has caught her attention. "Okay, Mel. I'll order our non-alcoholic bubbles while I wait."

"Sounds great," she says as she turns and disappears into the crowd.

Where is she going? A male server interrupts me before I can figure out which way she went, asking what I want to drink. Ordering our sparkling cider and a few nibbles for the table, the waiter moves on, allowing me to look for Mel. But she wasn't anywhere to be seen.

Who did she see? Where did she go?

A few minutes later, the server places our drinks and table nibbles on the table. I reach for my glass and take a sip as I continue to watch the dancers and scan the room for Mel.

Just as I place the tall slender glass to my lips for another sip, my friend appears, settles beside me on her seat with a smile, and lifts her glass. "Cheers, Izzy. May our night be one of fun and entertainment."

Despite Mel's smile, I question the toast's meaning. We tap our glasses together and say, "Cheers."

An elegant couple interrupts our toast. Across the big round table, they settle in with smiles and nods. I instantly recognize the captivating pair. Mr. and Mrs. James and Mary Lowdon, who reside in the Hamptons, own a penthouse in New York. They have careers in real estate.

Mel and I return a nod. "Good evening," Mel says just as another couple arrives, sitting in their allocated seats. They pause long enough to nod and smile.

We nod back, and Mel says, "Hello, everyone. I'm Mel Astor, and this is my friend Izzy Delany."

"Hello, ladies. I'm Doctor Howard, and this beautiful woman beside me is my wife, Sara."

Apart from being at least ten years younger than the Lowdons, it soon became apparent that Doctor Howard enjoys hearing his own voice as he explains his occupation as a neurosurgeon at the children's hospital in New York. His wife, Sara, works at one of the many art galleries in upper New York.

You don't have to be blind to notice Sara doesn't like her husband ogling me. But, then, neither do I. She frowns as she asks, "Izzy, what do you do?"

I turn to Mel, shrug my shoulders, then face Sara with a smile. "I work in security."

Mike smirks and then buts in. "You don't look like a security guard. What is it you do in security?"

I prevent myself from rolling my eyes at the couple. "I run the company with my business partner. We work all over the States. Presently, we are not accepting new clients."

Sara gives me a strange look and asks, "Why?"

I attentively smile and reply, "We cap our client list at two hundred per year. We provide constant security for clients' work and home properties."

"Since when do you work in security?" A voice startles me from behind. Tristian. Great! What is he doing here? He sits beside me just as I'm about to speak. "This is the first I have heard about it."

I give him the stink eye. "There's much you don't know about me." And turn back to Mel.

Warmth engulfs my side, and his voice brushes my ear, sending chills down my body. "Maybe you should speak with me, Ms. Delany. For we have much to discuss."

"Tristian, back off," Mel hisses. "What are you doing here and at our table?"

"Someone needs to keep an eye on the two of you. Why did you leave the house without us?"

I glance over my shoulder. My lips close to his. "We were safe in one of my cars. I have a driver when the situation calls for one."

He glances at my lips, then at Mel.

She nods in affirmation. "Oh, brother. If only you use your brain cells for good!" Mel says with a straight face.

I smirk and shake my head. "Tristian, you can see we are okay. Now go wander off. I'm sure your date is wondering where you are."

He frowns at my words. "Izzy, you are and will be my only date." He zeros back on my lips. My breath catches as my traitorous heart increases. A slight lean forward, and we would be kissing. Instead, I lick my lips.

Mel makes a gagging noise and attempts to stand. "Tristian, notify us once you gain manners." She turns and squeezes my shoulder. "Come on, Izzy. My kid is bouncing on my bladder."

I glance at our other table guests, noticing their faces. Not liking Sara's smiling eyes at Tristian causes my shackles to rise. Great, why do I feel protective of Tristian? He's not mine. "Excuse us, it's time for the little girls' room," I murmur and push against my chair to slide back. Tristian stands and moves, giving me more room.

As soon as I stand, I hear the muffled voices of our table guests. "Look, they're both pregnant."

My eyes meet Tristian's. He smiles, flashing his straight white teeth. "You look beautiful, Izzy."

Because I have manners, I nod, "Thank you."

Before I can say anything else, Mel demands, "Come on, Izzy. We gotta go."

Tristian takes another step back from me. "You better go before she pees on the floor." I smile, nod, and turn.

We don't take long in line once we enter the ladies' bathroom. "Why did you rush off earlier? Who did you speak with?" Knowing my friend is up to something, I watch Mel in the mirror. Her eyes avoid mine. Guilty!

She turns her head away and sighs. "Look, Izzy," she mumbles. "I spoke with Essy." What's going on? Mel going behind my back is not like her.

"Why?"

"Iz, you require protection. I need to ensure she is ready for the task." I narrow my eyes at her. She's lying to me, and she knows I know she's lying. I shake my head and drop the subject. Mel sighs, then whispers as we dry our hands, "He's here, Izzy. I saw him?"

I frown, wondering who she saw. "Mel, who?"

She steps closer and says beside my ear, "Corey is here." The long-lost lover has returned. Why hasn't he contacted Mel since his return? I turn my head and look her in the eye.

"Corey Sheldon, the one who somehow vanished off the planet, has reappeared..." She nods.

Concern flashes across her face. "Iz, he only left that one message. *'We'll speak when I return.'* I did not expect him to be gone all this time."

Corey must do right by Mel. For years, she has loved him. Corey has kept his relationship with Mel secret long enough from Tristian and the rest of the family. "Come on, Mel. Let's go find him."

*S*he's gorgeous!

I can't help but notice how beautiful and glowing Izzy looks with my child. However, I find it difficult to keep my hands off her.

Just then, I catch a glimpse of my sister between guests, leading Izzy towards the restrooms with a knowing smile. Brat. My sister will pay for her behavior.

Meanwhile, the annoying wives at our table continue to flirt and hit on me. Why would they do such a thing with their husbands nearby? I can't comprehend it. Finally, at least one husband notices or has had enough. I watch the pair over the rim of my glass. He growls at his wife and then forcefully pulls her away from the table. Well, that's one way to deal with the woman.

My brother's voice startles me. "Hey, bro," he whispers yells in my ear. "Where's our sister?" I turn in my chair to face my obnoxious youngest brother

Nicholas. As I glance past him, I realize our other brother, Alexander, is nowhere to be found.

I meet Nick's gaze and demand, "Where's Alex?" deliberately avoiding his question. Nick simply shrugs his shoulders, takes a seat beside me, and quickly finishes his drink before signaling a waiter for another. The kid is going to be a problem if he doesn't cut his alcohol intake down.

"He wandered off five minutes ago. I haven't seen him since," Nick informs me, glancing over his shoulder.

Concern for our sister, I urge him, "Nick, go find Alex and bring him back here. Our main responsibility is to watch over our sister."

However, my youngest brother narrows his eyes and shakes his head in disagreement. "Tristian, how much trouble can Mel get into? Maybe we should give her some space. She's even threatened to leave if we don't back off," he suggests.

Mel already gave me that lecture. Nick doesn't need to stick up for our sister. I know how ungrateful she can be. Frustrated by Nick's suggestion, I respond firmly, "Nick, Mel is not going anywhere. If she decides to leave, I'll cut off her allowance."

Nicholas shakes his head in disapproval at my words and replies, "That's low, bro."

Now I'm feeling conflicted. I'm damned if I do, and damn if I don't, and ask, "What do you suggest I do, then?"

"Tristian, how about being there for our sister? I do

not want to lose her. She's stronger than you think, and she will leave if you continue to push her."

"Nick, go look for our brother and bring him here."

Nicholas finishes his drink, turns, and gives me a strange look. "Hey, what's with the gossip tonight? Word has it you'll be popping the question to Simone this evening."

Huh? I shake my head. Never. I can't stand that antagonizing woman.

Before I can answer, I smell Izzy's perfume — a familiar, comforting scent — lingering in the air behind me. Shit... No. Of all the times for her to return, she chose this moment.

"Yes, I would like to know the answer to that question myself," she says in an annoyed tone.

Great, without trying, Izzy is angry with me. One: I am not marrying Simone. And Two: It is the last thing I want Izzy to hear, especially when I have to convince her to marry me.

"Hey, Izzy. Wow, you look fantastic. Pregnancy really agrees with you," my stupid brother announces.

I turn my head enough to look at her. "Thanks, I think," Izzy says with a raised brow.

I turn my head back to Nick and give my brother the *you'll pay for that* look. Nick shrugs his shoulders and stands. I swivel in my chair, glance back over my shoulder, and see Izzy standing there with her brow raised high and shaking her head at me.

Shit. How am I going to get out of this? Just then, the sound of music signals the start of the dancing.

That's it! I stand and reach for her hand. "Izzy, come on, let's dance."

Not giving her the chance to refuse me, I led her towards the dance floor with my other hand on her lower back. Just one touch and the emotional pull and need to protect her increases.

Taking Izzy in my arms has never felt so good. The sensation of never letting her go fills my soul. Her pregnancy belly pushes into me, reminding me I have questions.

Many questions.

Several couples dance around us in time to the music. At least we are not the only ones on the dance floor.

"Tristian, what do you think you're doing?" I watch her eyes dart around. Izzy has always been the type to avoid confrontation and attention to herself. That was always Mel's department.

"I believe dancing, Izzy," I whisper beside her ear, feeling her shiver, knowing it drives her crazy. "What do you call it?"

She gasps, and I feel her shiver again. "You're a dick," she pants. "And you know it."

My lips twitch. "I can be all dick. I seem to recall how much you enjoyed it."

We dance to the rhythm of the music, and I see Mel walking away from our table. Where is she going? "Don't be obnoxious. There are rumors circulating that you're proposing to Horsey-Girl tonight. I mean that bitch Simone." Wow. I know why I don't like Simone, but what has she done to Izzy?

"Izzy, you called her Horsey-Girl — interesting. And let me say, I cannot stand Simone's childish behavior. She's not marriage material."

A noise fills my left ear. I turn my head enough and meet Izzy's eyes. Did she just snort?

"What?"

"Are you serious? She's not marriage material... Who would you say is?"

My fingers on her back spread out to bring her closer to me. I run the tip of my nose along hers before staring at her with a straight face, right into her eyes, and reply, "You. Your marriage material, Izzy."

Her eyes widen. She shakes her head and tries to pull away. "Don't, Tristian."

I hold her in place and move my face closer to hers. "Iz, I would marry you tonight if you allow it."

"Why? Because I'm carrying your baby?" Pride fills me as she acknowledges my baby, especially in public.

"No. Because I'm an idiot and should never have said what I did back in March. I love you, Izzy."

"Wow. Seriously?"

I nod. "Seriously, Iz. I want you in my life permanently. I have loved you for far too long and regretted my words and lack of actions from that night."

"Okay. What about your reply to my email?"

She keeps saying stuff about emails. I went through my inbox earlier, and there were no emails from her.

"Izzy, I checked my emails today while in my office. There was none from you."

She stops dancing, lifting her chin to look at me. "What did you just say?"

Huh? What is going on? "I pulled up my emails and never found one from you."

"That's it, time to show you," she announces.

The next thing, Izzy storms off the dance floor, and I follow her back to our table. She picks up her small, black, sparkly bag, retrieving her cell phone. With a few swipes and taps, I watch as she opens her emails. She taps on sent emails and scrolls through them. After several seconds, she stops and taps the screen.

"Here, Tristian, look at this and notice the date stamp."

She passes me her cell, and I immediately notice my name, email address, and date.

I take in the date May 31st. That can't be right. Izzy hasn't sent an email since March.

I glance up and meet her eyes, then back down at the screen and scroll. In front of me are several emails to my email address. I tap on one of them, which has an attachment dated July.

I scan the email and then the picture — a dark image with a white mass. Then it clicks. It's one of those sonogram images. Izzy's name is on the top right with her details. The white mass is my baby. I go back to the email and read it.

Sender: Izzy Delany [izzydelany@hotemail.com]
Subject: Answer me, Tristian.
To: Tristian Astor [tastor@hotemail.com]
Date: 23rd July

Hi Tristian,

I don't know what is going on with you, but due to what you said to me back in March about how we do not have a future, etc., you see, I still feel you should have the latest picture of our child.

After all the years I have known you, your lack of communication and the area regarding family seems strange.

Have you been so busy you couldn't return my calls? Look. You have made your choice. You do not want to be part of my son's life. That is your choice.

Yes, I'm disappointed. You have ghosted me where my calls and emails were concerned.

At least I know Mel has my back, and she is excited to become an aunt.

Kind Regards,

Izzy

What the hell? I would have thought this was fake without seeing the date stamp.

I glance from the screen and shake my head, meeting her eyes before re-reading the email.

"Izzy, I never received your messages or emails," I mumble, taking another look at my child.

"That's BS, Tristian. You sent me a reply."

I turn my head towards her so fast I nearly give myself whiplash.

Huh? When?

She taps the screen a few times. "Here, this is what you sent."

I glance down at her screen, and sure enough, I see an email addressed to Izzy. From my private email account address, dated 23rd July, the same day she sent her email with the picture.

What the hell? I never sent this. My head shakes in denial as I scroll down the screen.

Sender: Tristian Astor [tastor@hotmail.com]
Subject: Re: Answer me, Tristian.
To: Izzy Delany [izzydelany@hotmail.com]
Date: 23rd July

Izzy,
How do I know the picture is not fake?
I am not the father.
Please do not contact me again.
Tristian

With each word I scan, I re-read the contents several more times, completely taken aback by what I saw.

What the hell is going on? I never typed this. I would contact, no, I would fly out and see Izzy personally. This is a serious matter.

Someone has access to my email account. "Izzy, I never sent this. I would fly to see you if I received your email. Our baby is a serious matter. You're part of my family."

As she is about to say something, a beautiful brunette approaches us. "Izzy, is everything okay here?" I take a few seconds, but I'm sure I know this stranger. Izzy smiles at the newcomer.

"Essy," she says with a nod. "Tristian and I are just discussing emails and messages. He denies he received anything from me. When I showed him this reply from his email account, he completely denied he sent it."

She lifts her cell towards the woman named Essy. Why is Izzy discussing our personal matters with this stranger? "Can you briefly describe what the emails and messages are about?" The woman named Essy requests.

Huh? What business is it of hers? The urge to inform her it's none of her business, but I don't have the chance, as Izzy explains. What the hell? Once Izzy stops talking, Essy looks at me with narrowed eyes. Great. A pissed-off female is the last thing I require right now.

"Mr. Astor, you mention you receive no messages or emails. Is that correct?" I nod in agreement, then stop.

Wait a minute, I am not answering questions from this woman and reply, "I'm sorry, I am not about to discuss private matters with someone I do not know."

Izzy rolls her eyes. "Tristian, meet Essy Raiker. From Raiker Bodyguards. Essy, this here is Mel's eldest brother, Tristian Astor, from Astor International."

"Ahhh. I thought you look familiar. You worked with my husband on a business deal in January." The name Raiker does not ring a bell. "My husband's name is Declyn Bianchi." Ah. Now I know why she looks familiar. What did Declyn Bianchi mention about his wife? Oh, shit. Now I remember. His wife is ex-FBI who runs a successful bodyguard business. But why is she here with Izzy?

"Tristian, Mel requested Essy to investigate things after I was run off the road last night."

Chapter Nineteen

IZZY

I think I am in shock, or just confused.

If Tristian is telling the truth, then someone has access to his emails.

Who would do such a thing?

The only ones who cross my mind are his assistant or secretary. They both have access to Tristian's emails and phone calls. Then their dislike for me is evident.

"Izzy, are you listening to me?" Tristian's voice tickles the side of my ear. "You know. I'm feeling neglected."

Neglected? Is he serious right now?

"Huh? What?" I murmur, as my focus goes to the other dancers waltz by with each step we take. "What are you talking about?" I ask.

"Iz, I have been speaking to you. It seems you've been elsewhere," he murmurs. "Should I repeat myself?"

My lips twitch into a smile as I reply, "Maybe. Was it important?" We turn again and continue dancing with the other dancers. As teenagers, Tristian and their mother taught Mel and me to dance and waltz. It was one way to be in Tristian's arms.

I meet Tristian's smiling eyes. "Maybe..." His focus moves to my lips, then back to my eyes. "I was reminding you about our earlier conversation."

Surely he's not speaking about marriage again? I ask, "Really? And what was that again?"

"Ms. Delany, I was requesting your hand in marriage. I regretted saying foolish things to you in March," he confesses.

Not the marriage proposal again. If only he meant it. If only he loved me. Then I might take him up on his offer.

A frown forms on my face as I wonder out loud, "Why not act upon your regretted words earlier?"

"Good question." He sighs, and I wait for him to continue. "I am a fool. I have kept my feelings for you hidden."

"But I had taken your words to heart in March, especially when you ghosted me and sent that email a couple of months later."

"Izzy, I did not send that email. I would never ghost you."

With a raised brow, I reply, "So you say."

"Izzy, I want you and only you. How many times do I have to repeat myself?"

"When you mean it... Then I will listen."

We spin around the floor again until I notice two different women staring daggers at us.

"Um, Tristian, why would your secretary be here at the gala?"

"Huh?" He searches for her amongst the crowd. "Ms. Shirly should not be here."

"Well, look over my shoulder when we turn, and you will see her. Dark blue form-fitting long dress. She doesn't look thrilled to see us together."

While dancing, I couldn't help but notice the second woman grabbing my attention. A woman with a horse-drawn face. This woman I have never liked. Rumors suggest Tristian plans to marry her. Mel and I had nicknamed her Horsey-Girl.

"Oh, for god's sake." Tristian spins us and leads us in the opposite direction. "Izzy, follow my lead and play along for our son's sake," he pleads.

We turn in time with the music when a bitchy tone reaches my ears. "Tristian, why are you spending so much time with that woman?" Horsey-Girl demands, I mean Simone Holts, as she stops behind Tristian.

"Shit," Tristian hisses. We turn enough for Tristian to face Simone. "What is it you want, Simone?"

"What do you mean by that, Tristian? Tonight, I heard you plan to propose to me. How can you manage that while dancing with her?"

Tristian winks at me. His expression grows serious as he faces the girl with the horsey face. "Simone, I would recommend not listening to rumors. I would never marry you. Remove that ridiculous idea from your mind. I'm not the type to propose when already engaged."

I pause. No. Tristian does not mean…?

Horsey-Girl's attention snaps to me, and she looks me up and down as her eyes are ready to spit fire.

As I lift my chin, my eyebrows rise at her reaction. I kick Tristian in the shin. His grip tightens around my fingers.

"Tristian, why are you paying attention to someone who is clearly beneath you?" Irritated, my eyes narrow, and my molars grind with annoyance.

This bitch dares to insult me. Just as I move forward, Tristian squeezes my hand in warning. Even though my eyes scream attack, somehow, I keep my mouth closed.

"Simone, never degrade the woman I love like that. You're the only one who would do anything for success. I learned that the hard way. Now, walk away before I have security escort you."

Her eyes snap to his. "You wouldn't dare," she hisses.

"Try me, Simone." He glances to his right and nods his head to someone. "Why don't you run along and help your daddy with his friends? I believe there is a millionaire or two waiting to be admired." Simone glances in the same direction, then glances back at him.

"The conversation is not over. I don't know how she brainwashed you..."

Three suited men appear to Tristian's right. "Is there an issue, Mr. Astor?"

"Yes. Ms. Holts here was leaving and required assistance to leave the building."

She shakes her head. "Don't do this in front of these people, Tristian."

"Simone, run along to your daddy and get out of my

sight, or these gentlemen will escort you out. Your choice."

"You are a bastard, Tristian."

He smiles. "And never forget it either, Ms. Holt." We watch her stride away with her head held high.

That woman is going to be trouble, and mumble, "She'll make my life a living hell, you know."

His concerned eyes meet mine. "If she threatens you. Let me know."

"Tristian, I have my own people."

"That might be the case. But I would prefer to handle it. I want you and our child protected at all costs."

I shake my head and notice Mel from the corner of my eye. What is she doing?

The song ends, and we walk back towards our table.

Mel smiles and nods her head to the right. I glance that way and notice my aunt. She indicates with her hand for me to join her. I give a slight nod and turn to Tristian.

"You and I will have words later. Someone has just requested my presence, and I'm needed elsewhere for a meeting upstairs. Now. You behave. I will be back."

Seizing my clutch, I pivot on my heels and proceed in the direction where my aunt had vanished from sight.

Chapter Twenty

IZZY

*M*y aunt waits for me just outside the gala entry with her foot tapping, waiting for me to join her. "Come on, Izzy," her tone is terse. "Let's get this show on the road. The Board of Directors called a meeting on the eighteenth floor, so that's where we're headed. I'm unsure of the attendance count," she states with a frown.

"Seriously," I growl, "why the rush today?"

She shakes her head and huffs. "The old kooks are adamant to meet with you and question your ethics regarding the funding for the charities. The greedy stuffed shirts do not like you spending profits. According to them, their profits should line their pockets. After seeing the books, we're aware that certain Board of Directors members are taking bonuses they do not deserve or have a right to."

Our eyes meet, my brow rises at her words. "That's an understatement, Hazel. My father would strongly disapprove of the board's actions."

"I wouldn't disagree with that."

As soon as we turn the corner for the bank of elevators, I notice one of the stuffed shirts from the Board of Directors stepping into an open, waiting elevator. He turns and sees Hazel. "Hannah, come on, I don't have all day," he announces, using my aunt's business persona name. What a hypocrite. He's one of the annoying men who has given me a hard time since the first day I started working at my father's company all those years ago. One thing I made sure of was to keep my identity secret.

The sound of Aunt Hazel's heels click-clacking on the marble floor announces her approach to the open elevator. The old kook steps to the side, revealing the polished silver walls.

As I go to follow her, I reconsider my options and slow down. I'd rather use the stairs than ride the elevator and risk encountering that unpleasant man.

Ahead, a foyer with double glass doors leads to the staircase. Behind the clear glass, a man wearing a dark suit appears. His dark eyes meet mine. He shakes his head, hand-signaling me to forgo the elevator and come towards him and the stairs. If I remember correctly, he fit Essy's description of her bodyguard employee.

With a nod to his suggestion, I turn towards my aunt and frown as I met her eyes. She smiles, then lifts her elegant brow in question regarding the elevator, and I shake my head slightly in reply. Hopefully, she realizes I refuse to share the elevator with that man and keep walking, heading for the double glass doors and the staircase, refusing to make eye contact with that obnoxious man.

As my aunt stands in the elevator's doorway, she announces, "Edward, you go ahead." The sound of her shoes echoes as she steps out on the marble flooring. "I need to visit the powder room first." Each one of her steps away from the elevator increase in sound as they echo along the floor.

His nasal tones fill the void behind me as he replies, "Seriously, Hannah, can't you hold it for two minutes?" A huff escapes my aunt, and then I hear footsteps trailing behind me. "You can take the stairs," he smugly states, his voice rising with the sound of the elevator doors closing.

Her favorite scent tickles my nostrils. As she comes up beside me, Aunt H remarks, "He's a pompous jackass." I fight to hold in my laughter as my lips twitch and fail. "The air in there was rank," she declares with a straight face. "Anyway. He must have been sucking on a garlic clove." Normally my loving aunt would never announce such a thing about people's breath. With one look from my aunt, we both burst out laughing. Between fits of laughter, Aunt H says, "How can he walk around smelling like that?" And she gives a little body shake.

Although it was an unpleasant topic, I still enjoy laughing with Aunt H about it and shaking my head, replying, "I don't know, H. Surely someone would inform him of his disgusting breath." And shudder at my words. Thank goodness we skipped the small enclosure with the smelly man.

Soon, my breathing evens out, and a sense of calm washes over me. A quick nod of my head in the direction we should go. "We'll need to use the stairs," I suggest. "The next set of elevators is up there." With each step, I monitor the man in the suit as he moves to the left of the clear glass doors and proceeds up the stairs, only to disappear behind a closing door on the upper landing as I murmur, "Besides, I need to talk to someone."

What is going on? Where is he going?

We reach the stairs and begin the tedious climb. My hand grips the handrail with my next step. "You didn't have to follow me," I say over my shoulder, but relieved that she did.

The sound of her sigh reaches my ears. "I know. If I had stayed in the elevator, I would have hit the man. The last thing I require is a lawsuit." My lips twitch with amusement, and I nod at her words.

"Fair enough. He's never liked me. Wait until he recognizes me, the woman he would demoralize in the corridors." The lengths I had taken in my father's company to gain experience and knowledge while I was incognito. "The look on his face will be priceless when it's revealed who I really am."

We continue to the next landing, containing a solid exit door in between floor levels.

"That is the reason for the meeting. The idiots are demanding they see the missing daughter in person. Plus, I can guarantee they'll try to intimidate you. They want the company for themselves and will try to kick you out." I half snort and chuckle at the same time. We continue the climb to the next flight of stairs to the next level. Glancing up to my side, I can now see the landing for the next-level elevators. Two sets of four elevators — good, we are nearly there and continue climbing up the steps.

"As if I would allow that. I've foiled four of their attempts over the years."

From behind me, I hear my name. "Ms. Delany. Thank goodness you have taken the stairs. I'm Jackson." I glance over my shoulder to see who is speaking to me, and I recognize him as the man who signaled for me not to use the elevator. Just as we safely reach the next landing, I turn and face Essy's employee bodyguard.

He smiles his dimples on display. If it was any other time, I would be interested in this man. He urges us with his hands to move away from the edge of the steps and position ourselves against the wall.

"Why didn't you want me to go on the elevator, Jackson? What has happened?"

He extends his hand towards the handrail, gesturing for me to follow suit. "Suspicious activity detected with the elevators, ma'am. I've contacted Ms. Raiker and the others, and I was returning to inform you to stay away from them."

I raise an eyebrow in confusion. "Huh?"

Just then, there's a massive explosion from above. The staircase and walls shake, and I automatically duck. "What the hell?" I screech as I wrap my other arm around my belly.

My other hand grip intensifies on the handrail, and

Jackson yells, "Get down!" I'm trying to — my belly is in my way.

Then the lights go out.

My mind screams in panic, and somehow I hold the verbal scream, wanting to escape. Whatever is happening, this is bad. Extremely bad.

The entire staircase shakes again. Jackson covers us with his body. The overhead lights flicker back on, only to watch bits of plaster rain down on us.

"Was that a bomb?" My aunt shrieks as she wraps her arms around me tighter. The overhead lights flash on, then off, and then flicker several times before coming back on.

Just as I ask what is happening, screaming floats down from above. The sound of people in pain moaning as others are yelling for help. Whatever that explosion is, it is serious.

The bodyguard stands talking to someone. I glance up and see he has his cell to his ear. "Yes, she is safe. ... roger that. I'll escort her to the exit now."

Just as I go to pull myself up using the handrail, a strange thunderous whoosh noise fills the semi-silence, followed by a tremendous crash and boom — shaking the walls and stairs once more. "Stay down," Jackson demands as more dust and bits of plaster surround us.

What was that?

The overhead lights flash off.

"Was that the elevator?" my aunt's voice announces to no one in particular. The emergency lights flicker several times before coming on.

We look up as the sound of rushing footsteps echo

down the stairs towards us. Jackson stands, ensuring anyone rushing by does not step on or kick us.

The fire alarm activates, its wailing practically deafening me. Dust billows up from below us and fills the open area of the staircase. Several gala guests rush by us on the stairs, heading for the lower levels. One of the rushing people stops — a man — concern across his face.

"Are you ladies okay?"

We nod, and my aunt replies, "For now, yes."

The bodyguard focuses back on us and assists my aunt to her feet.

The stranger inquires, "What's happening?"

"Hurry, we must leave the stairwell and exit the building in case there's another explosion," Jackson says. "Can you assist Izzy while I help her aunt?"

The stranger nods, reaches for my arm, and carefully helps me stand. "Come on, Luv. Let's leave, as that gentleman suggested." It is then I notice he has his cell phone in one hand with the torch activated, sending a bright stream of light on the step.

"Thanks for your assistance. What is your name?" I ask as I cautiously take my next step on the dusty staircase.

"The name is Jones. Malcolm Jones. I was attending the gala with a mate. I wonder what happened to him?"

His accent indicates he's not American. Maybe British?

"What is his name? Maybe I might know your friend."

"I doubt it. But you never know. Sheldon. Corey Sheldon."

Huh? Out of all the names he could have brought up. He had to say the one person Mel had been searching for. The man she loves and the father of her baby.

"Are you serious? I know Corey. He's good friends with my best friend's brother."

"Brother, you say? His name would be?"

"Astor. Tristian Astor. My friend said she thought she had noticed Corey earlier. She wanted to speak with him."

Malcom turns enough and meets my eyes. Something in them hints he knows more than he's letting on.

Just how much he knows is the million-dollar question.

Hotel security appears before we can reach the next lower level for the gala.

"Ladies and gentlemen. You cannot go any further down. The building is unsafe. Please use the emergency door to your right to evacuate."

With relief, after several minutes, we exit the building alongside other guests.

My cell chimes, displaying an incoming call. With a quick swipe, I answer the incoming call from Mel, as she screams, "Where in the hell are you?"

"Glad to see you are okay," I say dryly. "Where are you?"

"Outside," she screams. "I'm with Corey. We're about to get into his car. Tristian is looking for you."

Relief washes over me when I realize Mel is safe. At least she can now speak with Corey.

"Let Corey know his friend Malcom is with Aunt H and me. We have just exited via the laneway. We'll head to the front of the building. Let your brother know."

"Okay."

A male voice reaches my ears through the speaker of my phone. "Come on, Mel, we gotta go. The police want the area clear."

"Corey, Izzy said your friend Malcolm is with her."

"Say, we'll meet up later," I hear Corey say.

"Look, Iz, did you hear that?"

"Yeah. Be safe, Mel. Talk soon," I announce.

"Talk soon. Bye." Our call ends, and my screen lights up with a text within seconds. I tap it. The message appears on the screen from Benny.

> **Benny:**
> Are you safe? I'm out the front, just from the main entrance.

I turn to Aunt H. "Come on. My driver is waiting out the front."

Then I glance over my shoulder at Malcom. "Hey, your friend is with my friend. They just left and said he'll meet up later. Do you need a lift?"

He shakes his head. "No. But thanks. I'll grab a cab and head back to the hotel."

I smile. "Keep safe. We might meet again."

He nods and says, "Maybe. Look me up if you're in London."

With that, he walks off and exits the alley before us.

I glance to my left and look at Jackson. Once again, he's busy speaking to someone on his cell. He ends the call and faces me.

"Ms. Delany, I have to go back into the building."

I'm not sure about Jackson leaving. He's my protection. What else can I say? Maybe he had other obligations before becoming my bodyguard for tonight. "Thank you..." I reply.

If it wasn't for him... Before I can say his name, he says, "All the best and keep safe, ma'am. Ms. Raiker will be in touch."

"Thank you, Jackson." Before I can complete his name, he nods and disappears into the alley's shadows. I shake my head at the man. My arm loops with Aunt Hazel's and head for the front street. Within moments, I spot Benny standing beside the car with a police officer in a deep conversation, waving his arms about.

We approach the two men with swift steps. "Is there a problem here?" I announce.

The young man spins and faces me. "I was explaining to this driver he needs to move his car."

"He can now," I reply. "He's been waiting for me. Do you know what has happened?" Benny opens the rear door as Aunt H climbs in. I step closer to the door, taking in the scene.

"Looks like a bomb went off," he states.

Jackson's words come to mind from the staircase, suggesting a bomb. Why would someone want to destroy a building? I ask myself. "Was anyone hurt?" I inquire anxiously.

The young man replies, "We're not sure. But if

anyone was in the elevator... They wouldn't have survived."

Feeling the need to move, I say to the officer, "Look, officer. We'll get out of your way."

With that, I slide into the car, and Benny shuts the door behind me. Inside the car, I reach for two chilled bottles of water and share the news with Aunt H.

"Did you hear that? The elevator was bombed," I say. "He confirmed what Jackson said. It might have been the elevator we intended to use." I glance at Aunt H over the bottle and notice her pale complexion.

Realizing she needs something stronger, I open the secret panel containing spirits and drinking glasses. I pour a couple of fingers into a glass and offer it to her. "Here. You look like you need this."

She nods, taking the glass with shaky fingers and throwing it back.

Just as Benny slides into the driver's seat, another explosion fills the night air rocking the car.

Chapter Twenty-One

TRISTIAN

lease be alive.

Panic fills me.

No.

Izzy has to be alive. I keep repeating in my mind.

My knuckles turn white and my muscles flex as I turn and dump more heavy rubble behind me.

She has to be here somewhere. The jagged metal, crumbling plaster, and dust-coated bricks create a terrifying, unstable landscape around us. My hands, filthy and aching, grasped another large piece of brick and plaster, remnants of the destruction before me, and I heave it onto my growing pile.

For all that is holy, I hope Izzy used the stairs instead of that elevator. "Where did she go?" I mutter to myself. I've been searching for her everywhere, but I can't find her. My hands are raw from shifting the sharp, jagged debris in the towering pile in front of me.

Another guest saw Izzy and another woman walking toward the elevator and assumed they'd gotten on. I hope she wasn't in the elevator that plummeted to the bottom of the shaft.

I'm startled by the sound of someone speaking right next to my ear; only then do I feel a heavy hand on my shoulder. "Sir, I appreciate your help. However, we can handle it from this point. You should get yourself examined." The man in uniform glances over my body, from my head to my hands. "You're bleeding," the emergency man says, looking at my hand. "Your hands need medical treatment."

Huh? Sure enough, I look at my hands and notice droplets of blood splatter to the dusty, dirty floor from my hand. Shit. I'm bleeding more than I realize and pull the handkerchief from my pocket, wrap it around my injured hand, and step away from the emergency people.

I nod at the worried man and turn. With a swift glance around me, I continue to search for her among the throng of people. I have to find her. I need to see Izzy with my own eyes.

The sounds of people screaming for help, moaning in pain, and calling out names overwhelm me. The urgency to head toward the main entrance increases with each step. My cell vibrates before its chime tickles my ears, and I reach for the device with my bloodied hand from my pocket. My sister's picture fills my screen. With a tap, I answer, "Mel, have you seen her?" Are the first words out of my mouth, not bothering with hello.

"Chill, Tristian," Mel says. "Izzy escaped with her aunt. They were heading towards the front street from a side alley when I recently spoke to her."

"A side alley?" I ask. "How did she end up there?"

"I don't know, ask her. Look, I gotta go. Someone is giving me a lift home. Bye." Before I can question her further, the call ends. Bloody sister …just wait until I see her next. At least I know she is alive. Now, as for Izzy, I have to see for myself that she is safe and rush towards the main foyer, dodging gala attendees, police, medics, and firefighters.

With each step, away from all the dust and debris fragment-filled air, the urge to cough increases. In moments, I'm outside on the sidewalk, glancing left and right as the emergency vehicles and city sounds fill my ears, as I attempt to fill my lungs with clean air — instead, my throat and lungs protest and I cough hard. Each cough tears through me, expelling the contaminated explosive dusty air from my lungs until my breathing eases.

With tear-filled eyes, I blink several times to clear them and use the back of my hand to wipe my wet face. With my vision clear and search again, looking at everyone nearby, hoping to catch a glimpse of my girl until I glance to my left again, a vehicle moves away from the curb, people walk by, and there, as if it was the red sea being parted is Izzy in the distance.

My knees nearly buckle as a wave of relief washes over me. There she is, in all her glorious pregnant beauty, speaking with a police officer beside a dark vehicle I don't recognize. On the other side of the vehicle, I watch her aunt slide into the back seat.

Before I realize what I'm doing, I'm scrolling for Izzy's name on my cell to phone her. Only to discover I no longer have her in my contacts. Where is she...? Damn it. I bet whoever tampered with my emails was also responsible for removing Izzy's details from my contacts. Why didn't I grab her cell number when we were inside?

My brother's voice reaches my ear as a hand grabs my shoulder. "Tristian, thank god, man. I've been looking for you everywhere," Nicholas pants from beside me.

"As you can see, I'm alive. Did you find Alex? I haven't seen him?" I fix my gaze on my brother. With not a hair out of place, Nick appears flawlessly clean.

"Yeah, Alex mentioned he was leaving right before the explosion occurred. He had a meeting or something. More like a booty call. He's not responding to his cell phone."

It's time to contact my driver, and I tap on his name on my screen.

"Mr. Astor, thank goodness. I have been concerned," my driver Wayne states. That makes two of us.

"Wayne, can you make it to the building's front to pick up Nicholas and me? We'll wait for you."

"Mr. Astor, the emergency services are not allowing non-emergency vehicles through."

I glance to my right. Another medic pulls up near the curb. He's right. It's better to meet the car. "Wayne, let's meet near the intersection."

"Yes, Sir."

I end the call and face my brother. "Come on, Nick. We have to walk to meet our car."

"Seriously...With our name..."

My stupid little brother can be selfish. "Nick, stop being a spoiled brat. It will not hurt you to walk up to the intersection."

With one last glance over my shoulder, I watch Izzy sliding into the dark car. At least she's safe.

Nick persists in complaining with every step we take. While we are waiting for our driver, I try to contact our brother only for the call to go to voice mail. "Alex, call me. I want to make sure you're safe and avoided the explosion." What is it with siblings? They are nothing but stressful.

"Nick, do you have Izzy's cell number?"

"Yeah, why?" he says, his attention captured by a couple of women walking past.

"Why...the girl is pregnant, and I haven't seen her. I want to make sure she is safe." Not wanting to inform him she's only thirty meters away.

"Oh. Okay. I'll text it to you." He grumbles something else and then slides his cell back into his pocket. "There, that's it. Why don't you have it?"

My cell dings, and his message appears. I save it to my contacts list under Izzy's surname only.

"Huh? Um. I did. Somehow, it disappeared."

"How can a name and number disappear from a cell phone?"

"That's what I'd like to know," I murmur.

Just then, a loud explosion fills the air, and the ground shakes. We stumble as I turn to see more smoke billow out of the gala building.

Shit. Who in the hell is blowing up the building? Time to get out of here.

As I turn, relief hits as our driver appears several vehicles away. We flag him down and slide into the back of the car.

"Thank you, Wayne. Take us home, please."

Nicholas turns to look at me. "Dude. Why ...home?" His smile disappears, his eyes widen as he looks at my face. "You have blood running down your face." He glances at my hands. "Your hands are covered with blood." Nick has a way of exaggerating. Usually, he freaks out at the sight of blood. "Shit, bro, since when have you been bleeding?"

My eyes roll to his stupidity. "Since before I walked out of the building."

It is time for me to consult with my lawyer, the one I pay a hefty yearly retainer. He should have connections to help screen my office staff. Better yet, I'll get in touch with Essy and request a thorough investigation by her staff.

With Mel departing with Corey, I consider avoiding a return visit to her family home, my gaze drifting to Hazel. "Aunt H, would you mind if we went back to your apartment?"

She smiles and nods. "Yes, dear." She reaches for me and squeezes my hand. "I would feel better if you were safe under my roof."

I nod and smile back. "Me too. And, thank you."

"That is what family is for."

I call out to my driver. "Excuse me, Benny."

"Yes, Ms. Izzy."

"Benny, can you take us to my aunts, please?"

"Sure thing."

"Thank you, Benny."

A strange look crosses her face. I know that look. She has thought of something. Something bad.

"What is it, H?"

My aunt looks towards the window. "Izzy, I have a

bad feeling that the explosion," she turns and looks straight at me, "might have been for us."

No. That can't be right. All the people hurt... "Why would you say that?"

As if she's in deep thought, her facial features change to a frown. "Too many little things, my dear."

Suppose, given the strange happenings with my car — the poisoning of Simon and now the elevator explosion... I'm agreeing with her.

"H, once we are back at your apartment, I'll shower, get cleaned up, and call my friend, who has a bodyguard business." I take another sip of water. If only I could drink something stronger. "It was one of her bodyguards that indicated I should not go on that elevator." My cell chimes, showing a notification. I glance at the screen. Speak of the devil. Essy.

I tap and open her text.

> **Essy:**
> Are you safe?

Aunt Hazel takes another drink. "Thank goodness you listened. But then. The look on your face was priceless." A giggle passes her lips. "I think you would have skipped the elevator, anyway."

I tap back.

> **Me:**
> Yes. I'll phone you once I'm settled at my aunt's apartment.

My lips twitch at my aunt's words. "In no way, shape, or form, would I be willing to share an elevator with him, not even in a million years. I would have preferred the stairs than be anywhere near that annoying, obnoxious man."

"Thank goodness we took the stairs."

Yes. Thank goodness.

*M*y lovely aunt loans me a soft, fluffy robe and oversized pajamas, perfect for wearing after my long, relaxing shower. Despite everything, a bone-deep coldness overcomes me. I wonder if the shock is setting in. After all, coming face to face with death is not normally an everyday occurrence, and this was already my second time in less than twenty-eight hours.

With a hot cup of chocolate in hand, I stretch out on the spare bed I use when I visit. My feet are tired and I need a moment to relax. As I lay here, my mental list of tasks for the day came to the forefront of my mind. The first thing I need to do is to call Essy.

Thankfully, Essy picks up on the third ring. "Essy Raiker, speaking," she greets me.

"Hello, Essy. It's Izzy Delany," I reply.

"Thank you for the text. It was a relief to know you were safe. Both Mel and Jackson mentioned you made it out of the building," Essy says.

Speaking of Jackson, I want to express my gratitude to him. "Please, thank Jackson for me. If he hadn't warned me, I would have been on the elevator," I say.

Despite Essy's assurance, Jackson was responsible for reporting any suspicious behavior, which had ultimately saved lives.

Grateful for my safety tonight, I decide to make a request. "Essy, I agree with Mel. I would like to hire you on a full-time personal basis. It's time for a comprehensive security check of my life for the past few years," I tell her.

*a*fter making a fresh cup of chocolate, Essy and I cover a wide range of topics of my life over the phone, delving deeper into the issues I was having with my cars and the story of Gavin and how he cunningly became a part of my life.

"You're not wrong to let me know about your other vehicles and Gavin," Essy says.

At first, I'm a little taken aback by her words, but once my thoughts catch up with common sense, it becomes logical. "At first, I did not want to believe it — until Mel's words made sense. Then there is my other business partner, who is currently in the ICU."

"What? Why? When did Simon end up in the hospital?"

"Oh, Essy." How do I say... My friend might yet die.

"The doctors have said that he has been poisoned. It is not looking good for him. Now, the bombing. It feels like I am being specifically targeted."

Essy replies, "You could be right, Izzy." She pauses, before asking, "Just to make it clear, is Astor the father of your child?"

I confirm. "Yes, you already know that," I say. Wondering where she is heading with her questions.

"From what little I have gathered, Tristian Astor has his own issues. I heard rumors tonight that he would propose to Simone Halt," she states.

I couldn't help but remember the comical look on Horsey-Girl's face when Tristian told her he loved someone else. "Simone confronted Tristian and me while we were dancing," I reply. "He told her to get out of his life and that he would never marry her."

That reminds me. Tristian started his own rumor regarding the two of us. How soon will word spread and how far?

"Izzy, is it true that he's engaged to you?" Well, that explains that one.

Bugger. "Tristian told her we are engaged to get her to back off."

"Do you feel Simone might be a physical threat to you in any way?" I wouldn't put anything past that dreadful conniving woman.

"I do not know. But Simone will make my life hell. Plus, I do not trust her."

"Fair enough. I wouldn't trust her either. She seems to be a spoiled rich brat."

I laugh. "Yes, Simone is. She's accustomed to always having things go her way."

After speaking with Essy, I feel a lot better. Her expertise and experience from her FBI days have made her one of the best for hunting, discovering, protecting, and investigating. I better grab some sleep. I have a feeling that by morning, I will be busy.

*S*omehow, I manage an entire night's sleep, and to my surprise, even my baby behaved himself.

After a refreshing shower I put on the clothes my aunt left in my room and waddle my way to the kitchen, rubbing the annoying constant twinge in my lower back, where I find Aunt H already engrossed in her laptop and cell phone, completely unaware I arrived for breakfast. Typical Aunt. Always busy and working on something.

Remembering my manners, I smile at cook and signal for some toast and tea and nod in appreciation and thank you. The aroma of hot raisin toast fills the air, making my mouth water. My belly grumbles.

I spread soft butter over both toast slices and devour one, relishing the combination of spices and fruit, as well as the melted butter, of course.

This Australian favorite never fails to impress me, and Aunt H always made sure to supply it for my breakfast. "You'll choke on that one of these days," Aunt H remarks playfully, breaking her concentration on her devices, smiling at me.

Finishing my mouthful, I lean across the table, wrapping my arms around her shoulders and planting a grateful kiss on her cheek. "Thank you for this delicious breakfast. You're the best," I declare.

My Aunt H responds with another smile that reaches her eyes. In her usual style, she teases me about my predictable tastes. She sips her coffee as her attention shifts to the cook. "You can thank my talented cook for the spiced fruit bread," she explains. "Knowing you were here, she baked a loaf specifically for you."

Gratitude swells within me as I rise and embrace the petite tiny woman in a warm hug. "Thank you so much, Cook Sherry. If you ever decide to leave Aunt H's employ, you can work full time at my house."

"Thank you for the kind offer." Cook Sherry pats my back and I release her from my hug. "But I will be retiring soon," she says.

What? "No," I protest, realizing I would miss her incredible culinary skills. "What am I going to do without your fabulous food?" I exclaim.

"How about I give you a couple of numbers for you to call and interview for the job position?"

I sit down, stuff half the slice in my mouth, and enjoy the flavors. I nod, and once I swallow, I say, "If they can cook this scrumptious bread, they are hired."

With a genuine smile, she replies, "My granddaughter will be pleased to hear that. She is looking for a new job."

"Your granddaughter ...Josie? Is she old enough to be driving and cooking?"

Cook Sherry laughs and nods her head. "Si. My little Josie is only a few years younger than you, Izzy. I taught her everything she knows about cooking."

Josie's face comes to my mind. She was always polite, eager to help, and quick to please her grandmother.

I finish chewing, swallow the delicious toast, then sip my tea, and ask, "Does she also need a place to live?"

Cook Sherry nods her head. "Si. She's between places at the moment. If she can secure a live-in position, that would be fantastic."

Hmm. That would be fantastic. "Let her know I have a live-in position opening next week."

I write my details and pass them to Cook Sherry.

"I'll phone her after I cook you some more toast," she announces.

I smile and nod as I reach for another slice. The woman knows how to please my stomach.

"Izzy, dear. I have to head out. Last night's bomb blasts claimed the lives of two Board of Directors and left several others injured."

Oh, my. "Oh, Aunt Hazel. That is tragic. What do I need to do?"

She shakes her head. "For now, I want you to rest. I've ensured that I started all the emergency procedures at the company, and the families who lost a loved one will receive a personal note and flowers. There will be a lot of paperwork to follow up with, and their life insurance documents need to be submitted."

"Are you sure I can't help?"

"No, Izzy. I have it under control. Will you be okay here?" Silly woman. I can look after myself.

"I'll contact my driver when I'm ready to leave. I have several phone calls to make, and then I'll leave your fabulous cook alone."

Aunt H gives me an extra-long hug as she says goodbye before leaving.

Cook Sherry smiles and passes me several more slices of hot fruit toast. When it comes to this delicious breakfast, life is good.

"*T*hank you for the update, Vicki. I'm relieved Simon is alive. Goodbye," I say as I end the call.

My emotions scatter. Vicki says Simon will remain in a coma. I'm scared for my friend remaining on life support. At least his condition hasn't deteriorated.

My fingers tap against my cell when the thought of Mel fills my head.

Where did my friend go last night? Why hasn't she contacted me by now? But, then, I haven't contacted her either.

I tap her name on the screen, and her number rings in my ear, as it reaches the fifth ring, I wonder if she might be sleeping. It cuts out and goes to her message bank. I tap the end call and try her number again.

This time, after the fourth ring, she answers. "Oh, my gods, could you be any more annoying?" Ouch. I stare at the screen and wonder what has gotten into my best friend.

"Well. Hello to you too," I say dryly.

"Oh, shit. Sorry, Izzy. It's just that I'm in the middle of something and was talking to someone else."

"Yeah, right? Now start talking, chicka. You're up to something, and you've left me out. What gives?" I demand.

A male in the background says, "I'm heading out and will return after four." Was that Corey? A door shuts, and the sound of Mel making herself more comfortable fills my ear.

My friend mumbles something I miss then says, "Um...Izzy. You may remember way before we left for California — we were playing a drinking game with my brothers and Corey?"

Why is Mel mentioning that? A lot happened that night. Tristian and I had a quickie in his room, and we narrowly avoided getting caught. "What about it, Mel?"

She ums and ahs before speaking. "You see. That night, Corey showed me the paperwork his parents had forced on him. It was for a marriage license. The female's name was blank. I jokingly said he should write my name down. Then that way, no one else can fill the blank spaces in if the documents fell into the wrong hands."

"What do you mean, you said...?" Why do I have the feeling my friend has done something stupid? "Um, Mel. Where is this conversation leading to? You didn't marry Corey this morning without me being there?" I ask half-jokingly.

"Um... Maybe. Kind of. Shit. Izzy. It was... What am I going to tell my brothers?"

A sarcastic laugh escapes me. She didn't, did she? Not without me there. Different scenarios rush through my mind. Has Corey stepped up and done right by Mel? But then, what is Corey's agenda in all this? I don't trust the guy. Throughout my years of knowing Corey, he has never seemed committed to one woman. I hope he loves her and is faithful, for my best friend's sake.

"Mel. I need to ask. Does Corey love you?"

"What...? How dare... Yes, of course, he loves me." Wow! Someone hasn't had her nice pills this morning. Then, it occurs to me. She never said he had said it to her.

"Mel, I had to ask. The man disappears and does not keep in touch with you?"

"Look, Izzy. You're like a sister to me, but you're pushing our friendship to its limit right now."

What? Why is she being so testy?

"Mel. What is going on?"

"I don't appreciate your tone or accusations regarding Corey." Oh, man. Is it me being rude, or is there something else happening with Mel?

"Mel. I'm sorry if I'm coming across harsh. I love you as a sister and don't want to see you hurt. Last night, you left before I reached the front of the building, and I haven't heard from you since. I'm worried."

Mel sighs. "Izzy. I'm sorry. It's just that I've handled the last twelve hours wrong. I'm feeling judged. When I married Corey, I would have preferred you to be by my side. You have been a big part of my life. Seeing the man I've loved again and being wrapped in his arms has turned my mind to mush."

She doesn't have to tell me her mind has turned to mush. I noticed that for myself. I need to see her with my own eyes and make sure she is okay, but... I don't know; I feel something is not right with my best friend.

"What are you doing now? We should meet up and talk about last night and this morning. I would rather you hear a few things directly from me."

A strange noise reaches my ear, and I look at my phone. Is there a dog with Mel, or was she making that noise?

"Izzy, I need you. Can you get Benny to pick me up? I don't feel right?"

What just happened? "Mel, what doesn't feel right?"

As quickly as I can, I send Benny text.

> **Me:**
> Morning, Benny. I require ASAP pick up from Aunt H's apartment. Mel needs us.

With different thoughts flying through my head, I don't know what to think. When Mel requests to be picked-up, something is not right. She's usually independent and does stuff for herself. My main priority is Mel and her baby.

"Ow. Damn it. That was stronger."

Huh? What did she say? "What is going on, Mel?

What is stronger?" My first thoughts are …that she's in labor. I type another text to Benny.

> **Me:**
> I need to leave now.

After I hit send, I realize how rude I must sound.

I'll apologise later.

Thank goodness for the stretchy clothes Aunt H has found for me. Otherwise, I'd be wearing that ruined ball gown from last night. I slip into a spare pair of sandals. Thank goodness Aunt H and I wear the same size shoes, and then I reach for my clutch and head for the door.

Mel grunts and swears in my ear.

My cell dings. I look at the screen. A notification from Benny and tap the screen.

> **Benny:**
> I'm downstairs.

Now that is what I'm sayin'. My man is proficient. Benny is due for a pay rise.

The sound of Mel panting worries me before I hear her say, "Oh no. I've peed myself." That's it. The silly girl is in labor, and her waters have broken. What has she been doing this morning?

"Izzy, I think I just wet myself."

She thinks! And ask, "Mel, give me the address where you are. Grab your bag and unlock the door."

She rattles off the address of a hotel. Seriously… Why didn't Corey take her back to his place? At least

I'm less than ten minutes away. "Look, Mel. Do you remember the breathing exercises we have been learning? I want you to concentrate on those until I get there, okay?"

As I step out to the sidewalk, my hand rubs that annoying twinge in my back. I turn my head and spot Benny. He has the door open for me, and as I slide in, I give him the address and let him know Mel might be in labor.

Benny slams his foot on the gas pedal, the engine roars to life, tires screech against the blacktop, and I'm sent back hard against the backrest of my seat.

Mel has been silent. I check my screen to make sure we have not lost the connection.

"Mel, are you there?"

She must have moved her phone closer to her mouth. Her hectic breathing fills my ear. Relief fills me. She remains on the line.

"Izzy. Do you think I'm in labor?" Is she in denial, or does she hope I lie and say no?

"Mel, don't freak out on me, but yes, I think you are."

"Shit, Izzy. I was afraid of that." She makes more horrible noises. Then she makes noises that can only be described as dry retching.

Oh geez. That does not sound good.

I glance up and notice the hotel on my right.

"Mel, I'm almost there. ...Can you walk?"

She makes several nasty sounds and screeches. "Yes."

"Okay, I'll meet you at your door and we'll head straight to the hospital."

"Izzy ...what about Corey?"

Corey... Wait until I see him. I'll give him a piece of my mind before punching the asshole for leaving Mel by herself on their wedding day.

The car comes to a stop, and the concierge opens my door.

"Mel, let's concentrate on you and your precious baby."

I slide out and give the concierge my attention. "My friend is on the fifteenth floor and in labor. Can someone escort me up there? I'm here to take her to the hospital."

The man stares at me dumbfounded and then looks at my belly.

Seriously. I do not have time for this. Sick of waiting, I turn to Benny and say, "Stay here. I'll be back with Mel." And waddle through the revolving doors for the elevators.

A voice behind me demands my attention. "Excuse me, ma'am. You cannot use the elevator unless you're a guest."

I pause long enough, turn, and face the annoying man. "Do you have access to the elevators?" I demand.

"That is not the point, ma'am."

"Yes, it is. My friend is on the fifteenth floor in labor. And you are displaying how incompetent you are being."

"Ma'am. I will have to ask you to leave."

What the hell? I focus on his name tag, lift my cell,

and notice the call to Mel has ended. "Garard, I am phoning the owner of this hotel." I scroll through my contacts until I find Tristian's number. What were the odds Mel stayed here last night?

"Ma'am, call whoever you want. You are not going upstairs."

The idiot is pushing my patience. "Do you know one of the Astor owners is upstairs on the fifteenth floor and in labor at this very minute?" The annoying man's facade changes.

The call answers on the second ring. "Izzy, thank fuck," Tristian announces. "I've been so worried about you. Where are you?"

Speaking over him, I say, "Tristian, I am arguing with one of your incompetent staff members at your hotel. He's refusing me entry. Mel is in labor up stairs, and this idiot is not allowing me to get to her."

"She's what?" Thankfully, his focus moves from me to his sister. "Who are you speaking with? Put them on, now," he demands.

I indicate for Garard to come towards me. "Garard, your boss, Tristian Astor, would like to speak to you."

The idiot gulps. Lifts his chin and reaches for my cell.

"Who am I speaking with?" the man asks. Tristian's voice screams through the cell, and Garard's face pales. He looks at me before clicking his fingers for one of the staff to approach. "Yes, Sir. I will see to it personally." He passes me my cell. "I'm sorry, Ms. Delany. I will escort you to the fifteenth floor now."

Garard, with one of his staff members, and I step

into a waiting elevator. He hits the fifteenth-floor button number. When the doors slid open, I rush out. I don't require the room number. I can hear Mel screaming in pain. Shit. I rush faster, trying not to trip over my own feet. Mel emerges from behind an ajar door. I stop in front of her and wrap an arm around her.

Oh, my. My friend looks like shit.

"Come on, Mel. Time to leave."

"What about the mess?" I glance at the floor and see it's wet.

"Don't worry about it. Garard here will take care of it personally. Won't you Garard?"

His shocked face nods as he surveys the wet carpet. "Yes, Ma'am."

We hobble right past him and head for the elevator again. "What took so long, Izzy?"

"I'll explain later. We have to get you to the hospital."

"I can agree with that," she manages to say before groaning again.

As we approach the vehicle, Benny opens the car door. The first thing I notice is a towel and blanket lying on the seat. I turn to thank Benny for his thoughtfulness, only to see concern etched on his face.

Mel makes another of those strange, painful noises. Shit. "Come on, Mel, you gotta climb in."

She gives me the evil eye over her shoulder, and with a bit of effort, she's in. As I slide in behind her, I notice blood on the blanket. Oh, no. That is not a good sign, and yell the hospital address to Benny and demand to get us there now.

Mel leans to one side, grunts, and then screams.

"Mel, look at me," I demand. "Do not push. You have to wait until we arrive at the hospital." She gives me a look as if I'm crazy. "Mel, I mean it. Do not push. Do that panting breathing, and I better look to see how far you are."

She pants several times, then groans, "Izzy, the baby is too early to be coming?" We both know that. I hope we make it to the hospital in time.

"I know, Mel. Look, I'll phone our doctor as I check because she'll want to know what's going on down there."

She makes more scary noises. Benny says something I cannot understand and feel the car increase in speed.

Mel lifts her hips as I maneuver her gown out of the way — the one she was wearing from last night. Movement in my throat threatens to projectile at the sight of blood on her glistening thighs. The urge to run in the opposite direction increases. I take one of those useless breaths and demand myself to be brave for Mel.

I move her leg a little more and look and nearly throw up. Okay, a traumatic view of Mel with no underwear on. A sight I never want to witness again — blood oozing from her swollen vagina, sends a chill down my spine. Should there be this much blood?

I'm out of my depth here.

But then she grunts and begins panting. I can see she is having another contraction, and her vaginal lips, the outer labia majora, and the inner labia minora stretch wider and longer.

Oh, my god. The top of the baby's head is visible.

The contraction recedes, and the small part of the head I glimpse vanishes and more blood leaks out.

My finger taps the app on my phone, which is a direct number for our obstetrician.

On the third ring, she answers, "Hello, Izzy. How are you?"

My eyes meet Mel's as I say, "Hello, Doctor Hamlin. Can you meet Mel and me at the hospital right now? Mel is in labor. Her waters have broken, the baby's head is making an appearance, and there is blood." I hear Mel gasp as her eyes widen when she hears my mention of blood.

The sound of the doctor moving and picking something up before a door closes reaches my ear.

"How much blood is there, Izzy?"

I glance down and whisper, "A lot, Doctor Hamlin. We should be there shortly."

"Tell the driver to meet me at the emergency entrance."

"Thank you, I will."

I glance up and notice the hospital just up ahead. "Benny. Takes us straight to the emergency entrance. The doctor will wait there for us."

"Will do, Ms. Izzy."

Mel screams, and part of the baby's head makes another appearance.

Oh shit. I won't let this kid be born in a car.

"Mel, look at me," I demand. "Stop pushing. We've arrived at the hospital. Let the doctor deliver the kid."

She pauses, looks me in the eye, and screams, "Get me out!"

Benny comes to a screeching halt.

The door opens, revealing Doctor Hamlin. "Mel, you've been a bit busy. Let's get you out of the car."

Mel nods before grunting again. The medical staff reach for the blanket and slide Mel to the edge of the car seat before maneuvering her out of the car and straight onto a hospital trolley.

"Benny, I'm sorry, but the seat will require cleaning. Thank you for everything. I'll call later." Grabbing Mel's bag and my own, I follow the doctor with Mel, inside the building.

Chapter Twenty-Three

TRISTIAN

I couldn't help but wonder what had just happened.

Why is my sister staying at our family-owned hotel? She was supposed to have gone home last night.

If Izzy's words are true, does that mean my sister is in labor? Regardless of the situation, it was too early for that. Mel still has seven weeks to go in her pregnancy. She couldn't possibly be in labor.

Annoyance mixed with anger wells up inside me. What has Izzy done involving my sister? Just as I ponder this, my best friend, Corey, enters my office unannounced.

"Hey, man. Your secretary isn't at her desk," my long-time friend points out.

Yes, I know. I gave her the day off. I walk around my desk, and Corey and I exchange a man hug. "Man, it's great to see you. We didn't get a chance to catch up after everything that happened last night," I murmur by his head.

"That's why I'm here. I have something to tell you. Can we go..."

I interrupt him, realizing I don't have time for a chat. "Cores, I'd love to stop and chat, but I just received some news. My sister is on her way to the hospital."

Corey's face turns pale. "What? No, she can't be," he exclaims. Why would he say that?

"Look, Corey. I have to go. Mel's in labor."

"That can't be right," I hear him mumble as his face turns white from the corner of my eye. "Ah, Trist. I'll come with you," Corey offers.

Why would Corey want to join me? He was never close to my sister. I don't wait around. My sister must be scared. She needs me.

Thankfully, Izzy, sent the hospital information of the hospital. So I know where to go.

My driver meets us by the front doors of the building. We slide in; I give him the hospital address, and my driver takes off.

A few minutes later, my driver interrupts my racing thoughts. "Ah, Mr. Astor. We have a slight problem."

I glance out the window and notice traffic surrounds us. "What's the problem?"

"Mr. Astor, according to my screen, there is a traffic accident ahead of us. I'm sorry, sir. I'm not able to change lanes or change direction."

No. Now, what are we going to do?

"How far are we from the hospital?"

"Around eight miles, Sir."

This is unacceptable; we'll be late. I can't stop thinking about my sister. She's probably worried sick, and scared. We are going to miss the birth, thankfully; I contacted Alex and Nick, who assure me they're both on their way.

ear overwhelms me as we finally arrive at the hospital. Neither Izzy nor Mel are answering their phones. All I know is that I am a mess as I hurry towards the front desk.

"My sister is in labor. Where do we go?" I demand.

The older silver-haired woman behind the desk smiles politely and asks, "Her name?"

"Melinda Astor," I reply.

"Melinda Sheldon," Corey says.

The silvered-haired woman's smile falters, and she looks from me to Corey and back to me again.

"Which is it — Astor or Sheldon?"

Corey and I simultaneously utter our surnames. I look at Corey with a frown.

Annoyed, I demand, "Are you trying to say something, Corey?"

"Look, Tristian. We do not have time to waste. Mel needs us."

"Gentlemen," the woman behind the counter interrupts us. "Whichever surname, you need to go directly to the delivery suite on the fifth floor. Follow the signs for the labor ward and ask at the nurses' desk."

I say thank you and shake my head as I rush towards the elevator. I don't care if Corey keeps up.

Chapter Twenty-Four

IZZY

"You did it, Mel. You bloody did it. Look at your gorgeous little girl," I gush at the tiny, dark-haired baby. She looks like an angel. "She's beautiful."

The last thing I have ever imagined is cutting the thick umbilical cord. Yet... Here I am, unforgettable. What an honor!

Though unforgettable, I give the medical scissors to the nurse to my right.

Photos. I should be taking pictures.

Noticing my cell on the bench near the bed, I reach for it and promptly begin snapping photos.

The nurse on my left suctions the baby's nose and mouth again. Rechecks both clamp clips on the cord stump near the baby's belly, and then wrap the squirming baby in a towel before passing the screaming child to a shocked but smiling Mel. Her tearing eyes meet mine. "Izzy, I'm a mother. She's here. My Trinity is here!" I snap more pictures of my best friend holding her newborn baby and several close-ups of the baby herself.

Mel rolls her eyes at me, then glances at the doctor who had been busy between my friend's legs.

Mel's smile vanishes. "Doctor Hamlin. Is my baby going to be okay?" She demands before glancing down. Yeah. What Mel said. The baby is premature, after all.

Her baby calms in her arms before she looks back at the doctor.

Doctor Hamlin passes a covered bowl to another nurse, steps to the side of the bed, and reaches for Trinity.

"Mel, it's time for me to complete the thorough check of your baby. I'll also perform a few tests."

The doctor dodges Mel's question, and I trail her to the bench across the room. The doctor unwraps Trinity, who starts kicking and throwing her arms about — poor kid didn't like being unwrapped, and begins to cry.

With my camera poised, I switch it over to video and hit record as I watch the doctor listen to Trinity's little chest, stomach, and back. She measures her head with a paper measuring tape, places the baby on the weight scales, and goes back to the padded bench, where she then checks Trinity's hips, moving her little legs in different directions.

Doctor Hamlin pricks Trinity's heel with a needle. Wiping blood onto a small card, then tapes a cotton ball to the bleeding heel. The nurse hands the doctor a syringe, who then injects the baby before re-wrapping her in a towel. All while I continue filming everything.

Doctor Hamlin smiles and turns to face Mel with the baby in her arms.

"Mel, your daughter passed her examination, and she's healthy. As a precaution, it's best to keep you both in overnight."

Mel nods and reaches for Trinity, bringing her to her chest. "Would I be able to breastfeed her?"

"I shouldn't see why not. You can try to and see if your milk comes in. If it doesn't, we have formula ready just in case."

Mel nods. "Okay, I'll try breastfeeding Triny first." Mel moves her hospital gown, exposing her breast. The nurse explains what Mel needs to do. Both Mel and Trinity seem a natural at feeding. Swapping the video feature on my cell back to camera mode, I continue to snap more photos of the baby feeding.

My attention shifts to the doctor when I feel a hand on my shoulder.

"Izzy, how are you feeling? No pain, tightness, or contractions?" she asks.

I frown and shake my head. "No. I think I'm fine. Why?"

"I've noticed the way you've been holding your belly."

I didn't realize I had been. Then I feel it. My belly tightens, and the niggling pain strengthens. Oh, no. It has to be one of those Braxton contractions. "It's just one of those Braxton Hicks contracts."

The doctor smiles at me.

"Izzy, humor me. I'll set you up in the bed beside Mel, pull the curtain around, and check if it's a Braxton hick. If you're in labor, then I'll be admitting you. We might stop your little one from making an early appearance."

I glance at Mel and feel my belly tighten again. This time, the pain increases, and it goes straight to my back. Whatever is happening is not good.

Mel nods her head toward the second bed. Bugger. I better not be in labor.

"Okay, Doc. Just to make you happy," I smile, but it comes across as a funny face as a sharp pain hits me. Good grief. That was a strong one.

As Doctor Hamlin pulls the curtain around for privacy, she says, "Righto, Izzy. Remove everything from your waist down and hop onto the bed."

I do as she says, awkwardly leaning back on the bed and grabbing the sheet at my side to throw it over me.

The doctor pulls on her gloves. First, she feels around my belly. Her eyebrow rises as another one of those Braxton Hicks hits me, catching my breath. "Izzy, I need you to relax a bit." I nod as she proceeds to do an internal exam. Ha. That's easier said than done. I hate these things.

She frowns and shakes her head. "Izzy, you're over four centimeters dilated. No blood or fluid seen, which is a good sign. I'll order the medication to help slow and hopefully stop the contractions."

I just nod in disbelief. Oh, shit. I'm in labor. How?

"Izzy, you'll remain in that bed for the next twenty-four hours. Rest, and no walking about." The doctor gives me a stern look. What! Oh, no. I can't be on bed rest. I've got things to do... Places to be. "I'll be back after your admission paperwork is complete." Our doctor disappears out the door and I'm left overwhelmed.

The nurse comes in with one of those hospital gowns and encourages me to sit up. Before I know it, I'm wearing the dreaded cotton gown instead of my clothes, and the sheet pulled up over the baby bulge.

In a short amount of time, I have a hospital name band wrapped around my wrist. The nurse inserts a cannula in my hand with a bag of fluids hanging nearby. Before I can blink, another nurse wraps a blood pressure cuff around my arm and takes my blood pressure reading.

A different nurse appears with a cart and wraps a strange-looking wide band around my belly. Then, they attach wires and a machine with paper to this.

I reach for the nurse. "Can you open the curtain? I want to see Mel and speak to her. Please." She nods and slides the curtain back, opening the space again.

As soon as my eyes meet Mel's, mine fill with tears. "Mel. My boy cannot be born yet?"

She glances down at her daughter, then back at me. "At least you're in the hospital. The doctor seems adamant before about stopping your contractions."

I'm concerned about my baby and his safety. "I hope so, Mel."

Another nurse wearing red scrubs comes into the room. "Hello, ladies. I'm here to transfer Mel and baby Trinity to your new room."

Mel and I both shake our heads. "No. I am remaining here with Izzy," my best friend announces.

"It's hospital procedure," the nurse sternly says.

Mel sits up straighter. "I do not care. I am staying with Izzy. She supported me, and now I'll support her. So, make preparations for my baby and myself to remain here."

The doctor walks in and smiles. "Susan, keep these two together. Mel and her baby can stay in the same room as Izzy."

My eyes meet Mel's, and we both smile. "Thank you, Doctor Hamlin," I say.

"At least this way, I know you will remain in bed," our doctor says. My smile vanishes. Bugger. Now I'm stuck here.

Another nurse enters with towels and one of those shower wheelchairs and goes directly to Mel.

"Hello, Ms. Astor. I'm here to assist you with your shower."

Mel glances at me, then glances down at her baby, then back at me.

"Izzy, can you watch over my daughter while I shower?"

With a smile, I reply, "Yes, of course. My goddaughter will be in excellent hands, especially with the nurses coming and going."

The nurse places Trinity in her baby bed and wheels her to my side, then assists Mel to her feet before seating her in the chair and wheeling my friend into the adjoining bathroom.

Another nurse delivers two water jugs and places them on our individual bedside tables. Two other nurses then arrive, strip Mel's bed, and remake it with clean bedding.

Doctor Hamlin examines the printout and adds information to my digital file on the mobile medical computer. She then gives orders to the nurse, which I miss most of what she says, increasing my anxiety.

Now that I am stranded here in the hospital, I better start making plans and reach for my cell and tap on my aunt's contact name.

After four rings, my aunt answers, "Izzy, will I be expecting your return this evening?"

No hello. No greeting! It seems Aunt H is busy.

"Aunt Hazel, there's no need to be alarmed."

Her next words are immediate. "What does that mean, Izzy?"

It's best to be direct and say it as I take a useless breath. "I've been admitted to the hospital."

"What?" she demands. "Since when? Why?"

"Ah. Well...I arrived at the hospital with Mel. She was in labor and has since delivered her baby girl. The doctor says I'm in labor, too. Our doctor is hoping with bed rest and medication, she will stop the contractions to prevent my baby from arriving early."

"Oh, my darling girl. Which hospital are you in? I'll be there as soon as I can." That's my aunt. Drops everything to be there for me.

"Thank you, Aunt H. Would you be able to bring in my laptop and chargers? The only thing is, everything is at Mel's family home."

Just then, the bathroom door opens, and Mel slowly

shuffles back to her bed. The nurse assists her back into her bed, pulling the sheet and blanket up over her.

"Izzibella, why can't one of Mel's brothers retrieve your things?"

Ahh. I glance towards Mel to see if she has been listening, only to see her smiling at me. I pull a growling face at her, and she laughs at me.

"They've left and are on their way here to the hospital," I hedge. Apart from the quick conversation with Tristian, I haven't contacted them. Chances are Tristian would have contacted his brothers to meet him here.

The sound of fingers clicking has my attention. "Let your aunt know the staff will expect her," Mel states with a smile.

"Did you hear that? Mel will notify the staff and await your arrival."

"If I didn't love you so..." My shoulders sag in relief. "I'll see you later." Before I can say thank you and goodbye, the call ends.

"So, I take it your aunt is heading for my family home?"

I nod. "Yes."

"Speaking of home and my brother, when will you explain to Tristian who your father was?"

"Soon," I sigh. "Tristian has always underestimated me. He had with the both of us." I love the man, but he's looked at me as the kid from the other side of the tracks.

How can I live with someone who does not value love,

trust, and honesty? Okay, so I've kept my real identity secret, but that has been for my safety. My aunt has pushed that issue since I moved to the States all those years ago.

My eyes meet hers. "Mel, where will you live once you leave the hospital?"

Before Mel can answer, the doorway fills with a harried-looking Tristian. "Yes. I would like the answer to that question myself," he demands.

As he strolls into the room, Corey follows straight behind him and goes to Mel's side, smiling and reaching toward the baby.

He leans down, kisses Mel's lips, and then kisses the baby's head.

"What in the hell are you doing, Corey?" Tristian challenges, stepping closer to his sister, all tall and threatening.

Baby Triny stirs and cries.

Mel explodes at her brother, "Now look what you've done, Tristian, get away from me and grow up." My best friend lifts her daughter and places her against her chest, with Triny's head resting against her shoulder while she attempts to soothe the baby. "How dare you come in here and frighten my daughter!"

Tristian pauses mid-stride. "But, Corey…"

"So, what, Tristian? You do not get to order my husband around," Mel announces.

"Your what?" he chokes.

That is it. I've had enough of the big macho bully. The man I thought I loved.

"Tristian, leave and never return. In future, phone

Mel if you want to see her, and be polite." Then Tristian turns and focuses on me.

His face pales. "Izzy. Why are you in a hospital bed?"

"You're only noticing now?" I shake my head in disbelief. "Why? It's none of your concern. Now leave before we have hospital security escort you out."

He rushes to my side and reaches for my hand. "Baby, what is wrong? Are you okay?" All I can do is shake my head at his stupidity.

"Seriously, Tristian? If I were fine, would I be in a hospital bed, connected to a pole and machine?"

A nurse quickly enters, glancing at the two men. "I can hear you from out in the corridor. You can quiet down or get out."

"Nurse, please, you can escort Mr. Astor out. He is not required."

The nurse takes several steps closer to Tristian. "Izzy, you are carrying my child. Don't you think you should inform me if something is wrong?"

The nurse pauses and glances back and forth between Tristian and me.

"Why? Because you've been a big part of my life for the last seven months — not." I look back at the nurse. "Nurse…"

The nurse steps toward Tristian. "Sir, you've been told. You are not required here."

"Izzy, please. I want you and our child in my life. I love you."

Did I just hear him right? He loves me? Does he even mean it this time? It's a little too late.

"Tristian, if you meant it, you would never have treated me like you did back in March."

He flinches. "Iz. I was stupid and selfish. I thought I could keep you in my life, and we'd continue our secret relationship."

"Sir, are you completely stupid?" the nurse says. My lips twitch. See, even the nurse gets it.

"Please, nurse. I need to be here. I've only recently discovered I will be a father," Tristian pleads.

Corey's presence makes me anxious. The last thing I want is for him to discover what happened between Tristian, me, and my past. My focus shifts to the nurse, then to Mel, who then nods at me with a knowing look, glances at her brother, then back at me with her *tell him* look.

With a cheeky smile she says, "How about I go with Corey to the nursery and bathe Trinity?"

With a nod, I return a look of *thanks a lot*. "Thanks, Mel," I say through clenched teeth.

Tristian looks from me to his sister and back to me.

"What is going on?" Tristian queries. I lift my hand, indicating for him to wait.

The nurse steps in to assist Mel with the baby, placing Trinity in one of those baby cribs on wheels. Then the nurse informs Corey to grab the wheelchair for Mel.

He wheels the chair beside the bed as the nurse assists Mel with getting to her feet. Corey wheels Mel, and the nurse pushes the baby crib through the door.

Finally, we're alone. When I glance back at Tristian,

his face gives way to the many questions he's about to ask.

"Don't start, Tristian," I say before he can speak. "I had phoned, emailed, and tried to contact you. And you ghosted me."

He shakes his head. "But, Izzy. We've been through this. I never received your messages or seen your emails. If I had known you were carrying my child, I would have come to you. I would have made my feelings known."

"You don't get it, do you, Tristian? I'm not a poor kid from the other side of the tracks — I've never been." And glance at the monitor, watching the numbers change. I have to pull my big girl panties up and stop avoiding my past from Tristian. It's time I said who I am to him. "Why have you been attempting a takeover of Heartson Industries? The New York branch?"

I can tell by his reaction that I have caught him off guard with my unexpected question. "Huh? I only recently learned about the takeover. How do you know anything about that?"

"Now that is the million-dollar question. How would I? You will never get your foot in the door of my father's company."

He pauses, absorbing my words, and it's several seconds before Tristian's mind ticks over. "No." His eyes widen in disbelief. "You can't be... It was rumored his daughter was dead or missing."

"That's just it, Tristian. I've been under your very nose all along. If only you had asked the right questions, you would have discovered I am the missing heiress of Heartson Industries."

He shakes his head in denial. "No. How?"

"My aunt. She brought me back to New York. Changed my name because whoever murdered my parents and baby brother is still out there."

"Baby brother?" His face pales. "Murdered?"

"That's where you failed. You never asked the right questions. Your sister did. And I was truthful with her. Do you know she is independently wealthy?"

Oops. I didn't intend to mention Mel and her business wealth.

Sorry, Mel. I didn't mean to blurt that out. But I am sick and tired of your incompetent brother treating you as if you're a helpless woman. You are anything but. You are intelligent, talented, independently wealthy, and the best friend and sister anyone could ever ask for.

I focus back on Tristian. "Your threats of cutting off her allowance have been a joke. Do you even know how talented your sister is? What she has achieved in the last three years?"

His disbelieving look nearly has me laughing at him. "What are you talking about? How can Mel be independently wealthy? She's been spending the monthly allowance..."

I cut him off. This has gone on for long enough. "That's your stupidity and naïvety talking. Did you even check that she had spent the money? No. She's been banking the money for Trinity's college fund."

The sound of someone entering the room has me pausing. "If anyone is going to pay for my daughter's college education, it will be me," Corey announces as he walks back into the room and reaches for Mel's cell, sitting on her bedside table. Bugger. Corey had no business listening. Now Mel's going to be pissed.

I turn to him. "You see, Corey, you left my friend. '*We'll talk when I get back.*' Does not cut it. Plus, you were not the one comforting her at night when she was crying her eyes out because you didn't come back."

He flinches and lowers his head before looking back at me. "I'm back now. I married Mel. What else will you call me out on?" he growls.

"Do you love her? Have you ever loved Mel? Or did you think my friend was an easy target? Something to get back at Tristian for?"

I never told Mel how I discovered Tristian had slept with one of Corey's girlfriends. She dumped Corey so fast when she thought she had a future with Tristian, but she soon discovered her mistake.

"Izzy, shut the fuck up," Mel demands from the doorway. Oh, shit. I didn't see Mel arrive. It's not how I wanted Mel to discover the facts regarding Corey. "You have no right to say those things."

"I'm sorry, Mel. He never said he loved you or showed signs of being in love."

Mel pauses as we all glance at Corey.

"Well, Corey. Do you love my sister?" Tristian demands. "Was this a twisted game to seek revenge on me?"

Chapter Twenty-Five

TRISTIAN

*H*ow does my life spiral out of control so fast? As I question my own thoughts. How did I not know about my sister? When did she become wealthy without my knowledge?

What else have I missed? It seems like a lot. To make matters more complicated, she's married to someone I once considered a brother.

This revelation shakes me to the core, making me realize I don't know my own siblings. I thought I understood them. The more I think about it, the more I realize Alex's constant disappearances and Nick's mysterious actions provide no answers, only more questions. It's a stark reminder that I'm clueless about their lives. What kind of brother am I?

Can I ever forgive myself for failing Mel? Everything seemed under control until Nick called and informed us that Mel was pregnant. I was taken aback by the news, especially since she was heavily pregnant and refused to reveal the father's identity when she arrived back in the city.

And then there's Izzy, the woman I've loved for far too many years. She's currently in labor, adding yet another layer of complexity to my already chaotic life. To top it all off, she turns out to be my family's biggest competitor in business. How did I not know this?

I'm left feeling lost and unsure of what to do next.

As I touch my pants pocket, I'm reminded of a heart-shaped object that holds a one-of-a-kind ring. It's a compact velvet box containing a dazzling five-carat diamond ring I bought when I was eighteen.

This ring symbolizes my commitment to my little angel, a reminder of my past self and the importance of remembering my humanity. I keep it with me everywhere I go, as it serves as a constant reminder that family should always come first.

Unfortunately, my father failed to understand this. He was solely focused on work, neglecting sleep and family time. If only he had consulted his doctor, he might still be alive today.

"Tristian, I love your sister; I have for several years. It's up to you if you want to be part of our lives. If you cause trouble, we won't see you again."

What the hell? I shift my attention back to Corey. My fingers twitch, ready to grasp his neck or form a fist and smash his nose. He has transformed into someone unrecognizable, leaving me uncertain if I can ever trust him again.

"Corey, I cannot believe you went behind my back.

You've had sex with my sister." How could he betray me like that? Somehow, I force myself not to move as my fists ball up. "What happened to our friendship-the loyalty?" My eyes narrow at him. "You knocked Mel up. You left her for months, and then you secretly marry her." I turn enough to look at my sister. Once upon a time, I knew everything about her. What she was feeling and thinking. Now, all I see is her annoyance. "When did you get married and where?"

Mel shakes her head and sits up on her bed. "Tristian, the documents were completed in March before I left for California."

Huh? Documents? I look at each person, wanting answers. Izzy shrugs her shoulders.

Corey and Mel look away. Guilty...is what they are.

"What paperwork?" I demand, as I focus back on Corey.

Corey sighs. "The legal documents I had. We had spoken about the ones my parents forced on me. Mel jokingly wrote her name in the blank bride section. Somehow, my parents collected the documents after I left when I traveled overseas, and they submitted them."

"I don't get it. How could you allow the documentation to be submitted? You would still need to... see a judge or something. To speak the vows in front of witnesses and sign the documents." My thought process vanishes. I cannot think of what I need to say right now.

"We did that this morning."

What? "This morning?" They have to be kidding me.

My focus moves to Izzy.

Her eyes widened, and she shakes her head. "Hey. Don't look at me. I never knew. I found out when I was speaking with Mel before lunch."

So... I'm not alone in being excluded from the wedding.

"Corey, tell him," Mel says. I look back at them.

What are they going on about now? Tell me what? What else should I know?

He shakes his head and steps closer to my sister. "Ah, Tristian. Remember when we played a drinking board game with Mel, Izzy, and Alex back at the start of March? That was the day I showed Mel the paperwork. As a joke, Mel and I filled out one set of documents with your and Izzy's details."

"What?" Izzy and I scream.

Corey flinches. "Sorry. I didn't know they were submitted."

Submitted! Anger fills me. How could they? It's no joking matter.

Years of loving Izzy aside, I prefer to follow the legal steps along with my fiance.

A new arrival drew my attention to the door. Recognizing Izzy's aunt, burdened with bags, I rush to assist her.

"Hazel. Here, let me help you."

The woman narrows her eyes, then passes me a laptop bag and an overnight case. "Thank you, Tristian." She turns and walks up to Mel, hugs her, and passes her a gift bag. "Here, love, congratulations to you. Where is your gorgeous babe?"

SECRET HEIRESS

Mel smiles. "Thank you, Aunt Hazel. My baby is in the nursery. I was just on my way there to bathe my girl."

She stands and reaches for Corey. They say goodbye over their shoulder and leave. Hazel soon turns and looks at me.

I thought, 'What? I will not leave Izzy's side any time soon.'

The woman shakes her head and places another bag on Izzy's bed. "My dear. You have me worried." She leans in and hugs Izzy, then leans back and sits in the chair beside the bed. "What has the doctor said?"

Izzy looks at me, frowns, then smiles at her aunt.

"At the moment, I'm to have complete bed rest. Medication is being administered to stop contractions." Izzy points to the bag of liquid hanging from the pole beside the bed.

Their conversation highlights my failure with Izzy. I should have talked to the doctor. I should have pushed the issue to ensure Izzy and the baby are safe. What kind of man am I?

Hazel's voice brings my attention back to them. "The meeting I had this morning is completed, and that little matter we've had to deal with is no longer an issue."

Why do I feel this conversation is not for my ears?

"H, did you discover who was behind the attempted sale?"

"Yes. Yes, I did. Haslow, along with Browns, were behind it."

"Who was the other person?" Izzy asks.

Hazel narrows her eyes at me. I am definitely missing a whole other conversation here. "To my surprise, the person was none other than Alex, despite being from the same company," she states.

"What?" Izzy and I both say.

Chapter Twenty-Six

IZZY

*M*y eyes meet Tristian's as he shakes his head. "Sorry, I must be missing something here," he says, turning to my aunt. "Why would my brother be meeting with you, Hazel?"

I watch H, her eyes narrowing. "Seriously, Tristian, you're going to play the *'I don't know what you're talking about'* card!"

With a shake of his head and a shrug of his shoulders, Tristian pleads, "I'm serious. I do not know what meeting my brother attended today. He should be here…"

Aunt H interjects, "Okay, for all that is obvious, I attended a meeting with some of the Board of Directors of Heartson Industries this morning."

Confusion is obvious in his eyes. Unless Tristian is a good actor, he evidently doesn't comprehend the situation. "Why were you meeting with Heartson Industries? What am I missing?" he asks, his tone full of doubt.

My aunt responds, "You foolish boy. I've represented Izzy legally since before she had taken ownership of Heartson Industries. I am Izzy's legal counsel, attorney, and business partner." Tristian's eyes meet mine, and he looks dumbfounded. "Your brother attended the meeting intending to purchase Heartson Industries' New York branch. The sale failed despite the board's sneaky efforts. Sorry, Tristian, you will not purchase any part of my niece's company anytime soon," my aunt explains, turning her back to him.

Tristian pleads, "But... but... I don't understand why Alex was there this morning. I was not aware of any meeting." Desperate for answers, he continues, "Several months ago, Heartson Industries contacted me about the possibility of the New York branch coming up for sale."

My aunt's eyes narrow and faces him. "What?" her tone turns deadly, then she demands, "Who contacted you?"

Tristian replies, "Off the top of my head, I am not sure; I would have to look the information up in my notes, which are back in my office."

As the situation unfolds, I find myself unsure whether to believe Tristian. What happens in his company he should know about.

"Tristian, you better contact Alex. He should not have gone behind your back," I say.

"No. He should not have. I don't understand what I am missing. But, then, this day has been full of surprises."

As truths are being said, I should mention the

shares. "By the way, Tristian," I murmur. "Remember when you released 200 family company shares on the stock market... Well, I purchased forty-five percent of those shares."

"Huh?" He shakes his head. "How? That's impossible. The most shares anyone could purchase and trade were fifteen percent."

I shrug. "Nothing is foolproof. It was easy to get forty-five percent of the shares." I will not mention my aunt purchased fifteen percent.

"Thank you for informing me. Heads will roll when I discover who allowed a larger number of shares to be sold to any person or individual company."

"Yes. You will have your hands full."

"Where are they?" Mel says, annoyance filling her voice. "They were supposed to arrive over an hour ago." I don't blame her. She's clearly irritated because her two other brothers haven't bothered to make an appearance.

Tristian stands. "I don't know what is keeping them. They said they were on their way." He reaches for his cell. "I'll call them now. As well as a couple of other calls I need to follow up on. I'll be back soon." With that, he walks out of the room.

I wonder what could keep Alex and Nick away. It's not like them not to be here for their sister.

My aunt clears her voice. "It is time for me to leave. I'll be back either tonight or tomorrow. Keep me updated, and let me know if anything changes." She hugs me and presses a kiss on my head. "Remember, I love you. Look after yourself and rest."

"Yes, Hazel. The last thing I want is for my little guy to be born before he's ready."

My aunt walks to Mel and hugs her as well. "Congratulations, my dear. Take advantage of the nurses while you have them and rest. You are going to need it."

"Thank you for the lovely gift, Hazel. I love it."

"You're welcome. Now I better go. Bye, girls."

With a swish of her long coat, she's out the door. I still cannot believe when my aunt filled me in on the bogus meeting that went down at Heartson Industries. She had to stop herself from laughing when Alex saw her and realized that with her business and legal background, he knew the sale had failed.

Tristian could not believe his brother would do such a thing — he felt Alex's betrayal deeply.

Our doctor arrives to perform our check-ups. "Good afternoon, ladies. Let's get these examinations out of the way and you both can enjoy afternoon tea. You must be hungry by now."

Mel and I both nod. She checks Mel first, adding information to her notes, then changes her gloves and examines me.

"The good news is, you're still four centimeters, Izzy. But we still have a long way to go. Have you had any more contractions?"

I nod. "Yes, but they are not as painful."

"Okay. We'll keep you to the bed rest for tonight. Enjoy something to eat, and I'll check on you later."

We both say thanks and bye as two orderlies arrive with trays each full of delicious sandwiches, a slice of chocolate cake, a cup of tea, and a sealed cup of orange juice.

Food. The sandwiches look fantastic.

"Izzy?"

I turn to look over at Mel to see her take a bite from her sandwich.

"Are you okay, Mel?"

She nods and finishes her mouthful. "I just wanted to say thank you for being here. And I'm sorry. It's because of me you're now in the hospital."

I shake my head. "Mel, no one knows why I went into labor. It was probably caused by the explosion and all the excitement from last night." I take another sip of my tea. "Don't stress about it. I'm in the best place to be. Our doctor is looking after us. I don't know about you, but I'm starving."

"Me too. And thanks again, Izzy, for being here with me."

I nod and finish my food. With the room silent, I drift into a light sleep, only to be interrupted by the annoying ringing of my cell phone.

Glancing at the screen, I note Vicki's number.

Vicki?

Oh, god. How could I forget?

"Simon," I say out loud.

Chapter Twenty-Seven

IZZY

"Hello, Vicki. How is Simon?" I ask, wanting to know the condition of my friend and business partner.

"Hello, Izzy. Just a quick update, I'm afraid."

"Why? What has happened?"

"The specialist believes they'll test Simon's ability to breathe without the machine."

"Is that safe?"

"I'm not his doctor, Izzy. I cannot make that call."

"When are they going to try?" I ask, attempting to keep my voice calm.

"Later tonight. Are you able to be here?"

Damn it. I'm stuck in this bed. "Vicki. No. I am not. I'm on bed rest at the hospital."

"Bed rest! Are you and the baby okay?"

I sigh. "I think so. But as you know, anything can happen."

"I'm sorry, Izzy."

"Don't be. Lately, I've been in the wrong place at the wrong time. The trauma is catching up with me."

A nurse enters and gives me an annoyed look as she approaches my bed.

"Look, Vicki, I have to go. The nurse is here to continue monitoring my obs."

"Okay. Izzy. Text me the details of the hospital you're in, and I'll call in and see you."

"Thanks, Vicki. I would appreciate that and keep me updated. Bye."

"Bye." Our call ends, and I text Vicki the hospital's name.

The nurse gives me the stink eye, as she takes my temperature and then blood pressure. She adds the information on the electronic chart and then reads the graph paper on the machine, which is connected by wires to the big wide band wrapped around my belly.

Without saying a word, she then takes Mel's obs, being all friendly, enters the medical information on Mel's electronic chart, waves to her, and leaves the room without saying a word to me.

"What a bitch!" I say under my breath, and then I focus back on my cell, entering the information of the hospital address, floor and room details in another text to Vicki and hit send.

"I heard that, Izzy," Mel says with a laugh.

"Look, Mel. The nurse could have completed your monitoring before doing mine. The woman is a pain in the butt and rude."

My friend giggles. "I can agree with you there. She

was rude. But then, I noticed her eyeing off Tristian earlier. So that might be your problem."

I roll my eyes as I shake my head. That is all I need. Bloody Tristian continues to turn too many women's heads.

*M*y senses kick in as soon as I feel someone holding my hand. Opening my eyes, I realize that my room is darker and Tristian is fast asleep, with his head leaning against my leg. His hand grips mine while his other rests against my expanding belly. Annoyingly, my belly tightens, indicating that the contractions have not stopped. Bugger.

Glancing over at Mel, I see that she is also fast asleep. Suddenly, a thought strikes me — where is the baby? I can't see Trinity anywhere or Corey. Carefully, I place my other hand, which contains the cannula, on Tristian's head. He snuggles into my leg, making funny noises that make me laugh.

Soon enough, a different nurse enters the room. She notices that I'm awake and smiles. "Hello, Ms. Delany. How do you feel?" she whispers, wrapping the blood pressure cuff around my arm and beginning to take my blood pressure. After typing in my information, she takes my temperature and reads the readings from the tocodynamometer and Doppler sensor. "Do you have any pain or contractions?" she asks as she types more details.

I shake my head. "When I woke earlier, I felt another contraction. Luckily, it wasn't painful."

"That's good. I'll make a note."

Reading the name tag on the nurse's uniform, and with my bladder ready to burst, I ask, "Fiona, how do I go to the toilet while hooked up to everything?" She glances down at Tristian, then over her shoulder at Mel before meeting my eyes. "Hold on, I'll grab one of the commode shower wheelchairs, and we'll take your I.V. pole for a walk."

I smile and nod. I just want to go to the loo and empty my bladder without having to pee in a bedpan. Also, I didn't want to be in bed if my bowel functioned while sitting there.

Fiona is soon back beside the bed and parks the wheelchair containing a toilet seat opposite where Tristian sits and sleeps. She pulls the blanket and sheet to the side, allowing my feet and legs to be free, and assists me to sit up and slowly swiveling around so my feet and legs hang over the side of the bed. She unhooks me from the Doppler sensor and tocodynamometer. I then shuffle off the bed and sit in the commode wheelchair. My butt feels like it's on display for anyone passing by. Thank goodness this room comes with its own bathroom.

"Before I wheel you over the loo, I have to place a bedpan inside the bowl. We have to monitor your urine output." It does not take her long to place a pan inside the toilet bowl, then turn the wheelchair around and reverse me over it. "I'll leave you to it. Press the buzzer when you are done. Don't attempt to stand. I'll wheel you to the sink to wash your hands."

I nod, and Nurse Fiona shuts the door behind her, leaving me in peace to pee.

Thankfully, the time I spent going to the loo did not result in another contraction, and Fiona carefully assists me back into my bed and hooks me back up to all the machinery. I glance at Tristian — fast asleep and didn't even stir in this whole time — unbelievable. Then over to Mel. It is then I notice the baby is back.

"Where did the baby go?"

The nurse smiles and glances towards the baby. "She needed her diaper changed. We also have milk in the nursery to feed her, allowing Mel to sleep."

"Wow. Is everything okay with Trinity?"

"Oh, yes. She is a gorgeous little babe. Well behaved." She turns back to me and asks, "How do you feel?" As she places the sheet and blanket back over me.

"Tired, but good." She checks my lines.

"Okay. I'll bring you a cup of tea if you like."

My lips form a smile. "Yes, please. Thank you. White and no sugar."

Fiona soon returns with a cup of tea, placing it on the little side table.

"What time is it?" I ask, noticing the lights outside the room now dimmed.

"It's eleven twenty-seven."

"Really. Okay."

"I'll leave you to rest and go back to sleep," she says with a smile. "Good night." Fiona glances at Tristian and then over to Mel and the baby before walking out of the room.

Chapter Twenty-Eight

TRISTIAN

*W*ith the room shrouded in dim light, the lack of noise and the growing cold make me realize it must be very late. The absence of Izzy's hand in mine and the lack of her belly beneath my touch strike me immediately; something has changed. I look at her peaceful face, noticing her slow, even breathing, and realize that she is fast asleep.

At least she's resting, I think to myself, as a wave of exhaustion washes over me as I watch her sleep. I still cannot believe I rushed home and grabbed a shower and a change of clothes and a couple of other personal possessions, as well as Mel's baby and hospital bags, from her room. That was the best I could do, given the situation.

With a quick glance at my watch, I see that it's 1.30 a.m. My attention then turns to the tocodynamometer and Doppler sensor, and I'm relieved to see that the contractions have reduced and our son's heart rate is good. Relief washes over me. Thankfully, I had one nurse explain how the machines and monitors work and how to interpret the readings.

Strange little noises erupt from behind me, reminding me my sister and niece are there. I go to get up and notice a nurse appear in the doorway. "My niece is waking."

"I'll take her to the nursery. She's probably wet." The nurse begins to push the crib on wheels towards the door. "I'll bring her back when she's hungry." She continues out of the room, removing my niece and shutting the door behind them.

Not wanting to disturb Izzy, I quietly use the bathroom and return to the chair beside her. Suddenly, a sleepy voice breaks the silence, asking, "What's this?"

I turn to find Izzy holding and looking down at the heart-shaped ring box that I had forgotten to put back in my pocket. Oh no, this is not how I wanted her to see the ring for the first time. Trying to sound calm and not nervous, I reply, "It's a ring box."

Confused, she whispers, "Why is it here on my bed?"

My eyes meet her confused, sleepy ones. "Because it was uncomfortable sitting in my pocket."

"But why is it here?"

"It is something I had selected and purchased several years ago." I'm not prepared to say I purchased it for a little angel long ago.

"I'll ask again, Tristian. Why is it here?"

My mouth turns dry, and somehow, I swallow, delaying my answer for a few extra seconds. Who am I fooling? She's giving me her stop being annoying look.

"Why... You see, there are two reasons."

A crease appears between her eyebrows. "What do you mean... two?"

"Um, my answer to both reasons is linked."

"What are you talking about, Tristian? You are not making any sense."

"Wait and listen, and you will understand."

"Hurry up, Tristian. I want to go back to sleep this century."

My girl has far too much cheek for her own good. "Look, I have wanted to place that ring on your finger since I purchased it."

"What? When did you purchase it?"

"Izzy, I have loved you for a long time. Several years ago, I wanted to propose to you and make you mine forever."

"Huh?"

Now I have more details about that little girl — my angel — and I can finally fulfill my promise with love in my heart.

If only I could convince Izzy to marry me. I want her to be my wife before our son is born, and I prefer my boy and Izzy to have my name. While Izzy was asleep, I received an update from one of the private investigators I had hired, who finally discovered more information regarding Izzy's father, information I should have been made aware of.

The question is, why was I unaware of this? Why have my previous investigators failed to inform me of the facts?

Before Izzy can answer, one of the night nurses strolls in on her rounds, interrupting.

"Hello, Izzy. How are you feeling?" the nurse asks as she checks the machines and adds the information to the electronic chart.

"A lot better, Fiona. What do the tocodynamometer and Doppler sensor show?"

The nurse smiles and replies, "The readings are getting better. The doctor will inform you later in the morning."

"Does that mean the medication is working?"

My eyes meet Izzy's. Then I look at the nurse. She smiles. "It does. Anything can happen before the doctor arrives. One step at a time."

I nod. Hopefully, the doctor will deliver positive news in the morning.

Chapter Twenty-Nine
IZZY

iona, my nurse, quietly leaves my room as my best friend remains fast asleep. Suddenly, it dawns on me — her baby is not here with us. I turn to Tristian and inquire, "Do you know where the baby is?" Glancing back at Mel, I add, "Where's Trinity?" Next, I redirect my attention at Tristian, our eyes lock before he breaks into a smile.

"Trinity was wet. The nurse has taken her back to the nursery so Mel can rest. Whenever my niece needs to be fed, a nurse will bring her back to Mel."

Understanding the situation, I say, "Oh, that's good. I was just worried when I didn't see the baby."

Tristian nods, then holds my hand and gently strokes his thumb over my flesh. "Izzibella, I have a little story to tell."

"And what is this story about?"

"Well..it's about a princess."

"A fairytale?"

"No. Not a fairytale. It is a true story."

"Okay. So it's about a true story, princess. You have me intrigued now."

"Shhh. Now let be begin." I poke my tongue out at him and lean back into my pillows. "You see, once upon a time I met a gorgeous little girl when I was around eleven or twelve. She was one of my most treasured memories from that age. You see, she would follow me and cling to my hand. The precious little angel melted my heart. When I had gazed into her big, intelligent, gorgeous eyes surrounded by long dark eyelashes, the little angel informed me I would marry her when she grew up."

Aww. My heart melts. Tristian can be human when he wants to be. "See, you had admirers even when you were a young boy." He nods and smiles. "Do you possess a picture of this small angel? Otherwise, your story is not true!" I ask with my lips twitching.

His face transforms into his cheek big smile and mischievously pulls out a photograph from his pocket, surprising me. Oh, my. I was joking. I was not expecting him to produce a picture of his fairytale princess.

He passes me the photo as he says, "The beautiful angel kissed my cheek and told her parents that she would marry me when she grew up." My eyes meet his, and I smile. I can't help but be amazed. I didn't think he'd have a photograph.

"Oh, really? And who was this bold, brazen little angel?" I ask. Who would have thought someone so little would demand such a thing?

He smiles back as his gaze becomes serious. I glance at the photo and notice two children, then back at him as he speaks. "If you didn't already know, that photo was taken the day I met your parents." Huh? My parents. What? Is this picture real? How can that be? My attention returns to the photograph. "That's us," he remarks.

Surely he's mistaken and shake my head, unable to recall meeting Tristian all those years ago when my parents were still alive. "Izzy, you spoke to me in your sweet, angelic voice. Made me pinky promise that I'm only allowed to marry you when you grow up."

Huh? "Are you serious right now?"

With a straight face, he replies, "Extremely."

"Why are you only telling me now?"

"Why? Remember, I only recently learned of your real identity. And while I ran home and picked up Mel's things earlier, I also collected this old photograph from my safe, which triggered several flashbacks of my little angel."

I focus on the photograph again. No, it couldn't be. But how? An extremely young Tristian, around twelve years of age, smiling adoringly at a little girl. Me. Oh, wow! The more I examine the photo, the more memories of my old house flood back. I have not visited my father's mansion in a very long time.

My eyes meet his smiling ones. "Bella, it was you who demanded I marry as an adult."

A small laugh escapes as I can imagine Tristian, the little boy, listening to the bossy and determined five-year-old me.

"What else did I say?"

"That I was your prince. And do I have a horse?"

My lips twitch before I laugh. I recall a distant memory of repeatedly requesting a horse from my father. He said I had to wait until I was older before he would allow me to ride one. If I enjoy riding the horse, I can have one if I am extra good. Boy, did I think I had my daddy wrapped around my finger!

My eyes met with Tristian's.

"So, what was your answer? Did you have a horse?"

Tristian lips twitch as he shakes his head. "Sadly, I had to inform my young princess this prince did not own one, but one day, we can go horse riding in the park when she is older. You became excited when I said that. You wanted to know how to become older."

"Really. I think I was used to my father allowing me to think I could have anything I wanted when, in reality, I had to earn it. He had a knack for being crafty." I smile at my father's memory of how he would craft his wording in a way that made you think, but you knew you could achieve anything, providing you put in the hard work.

"Did you end up with a horse?" Tristian asks while touching my hand.

My smile turns into a sad frown. "Yes. My parents used to take me horse riding every Summer after I turned eight. I had to learn how to care for a horse, including mucking out the horse stall, feeding, and grooming. Just before my parents died, my parents presented me with my very own horse. Sadly, I had to leave her back in Australia after my parents' death. Aunt Hazel continued to pay for all the upkeep and expenses for my horse Mystic, and we agreed that other little girls should have the chance to ride her. When I was nineteen, I returned to Australia and rode my bay horse for the last time. She died two days later. The center thinks a snake bit her."

"Oh, Izzy. I am so sorry."

"Thank you. Mystic was nearly fifteen. I still miss her." It's time to change the subject. "What else did mini-me say?"

"What, apart from marrying only you..."

I nod. "Yes."

"Well, when you're all grown, I was to ask..." He pauses, staring straight into my eyes.

"Ask what...?" I urge.

He smiles, flashing his straight white teeth. "So, the question is, Ms. Heartson, will you marry your prince?"

Chapter Thirty

IZZY

*I*s he serious? My memory of all those years ago from my childhood is vague.

"From your facial expression, Bella, it seems you believe I am not serious, possibly considering me crazy. But I can assure you. I am one hundred percent serious. Marry me. Make me the happiest man on the planet."

All I can do is to laugh.

"You know that your reaction isn't good for a man's ego, correct?"

I continue to laugh. Only Tristian would say something like that.

"Izzy, I think you should give my brother an answer," Mel announces. My laughing stops, and I turn to look at her. "At least put him out of his misery."

From the corner of my eye, Tristian smiles and nods at his sister's words. "Yes, what she said," he announces.

I shake my head at the two of them. Great, two against one.

"No comments from the peanut gallery, thank you," I laugh.

"Oh, come on, Iz. My stupid brother seems to be honest. Why is this the first time I've heard about your prince and princess story?"

"Mel, if you had been listening, you would know the answer. Plus, if you had mentioned who Izzy was, I would have presented her with this ring long ago."

Tristian turns, his eyes focus on mine. My eyebrow rises. "If I were to agree, how can I trust you won't become controlling?"

"Izzy, without a doubt, we have a lot to talk about. Please remember that I love you and want us to be equals." My breath catches as my heart speeds up. Finally, the words I've been waiting for.

Now, what am I to say?

He confirms two things I'm looking for in a relationship.

"Even though I believe you can make a better choice. It would be fantastic for us to become sisters legally," Mel says with a smile.

My eyes meet hers, and we both smile. Well, there is that. She might be my best friend, but I've always wanted a sister.

Hazel mentioned the paperwork I requested is in the side pocket of my satchel. *The prenup.* Gotta love that woman. I asked, and she delivered — fast.

Let's see if Tristian clicks when he reads it.

I turn enough to face my friend's brother. "Tristian, can you pass me my satchel, please? Something for you to read is inside."

He frowns, nods, and stands. "Sure."

He passes me the satchel. I slide my hand into the side pocket, reach for the documentation, and pass it to him. "Here, you need to read this, and if you agree, fill in your details."

He frowns again, carefully holding onto the sheets of paper and scanning the wording. His eyebrow rises as he glances up. His eyes meet mine, and he smiles.

"Does this mean you'll marry me?"

With a nod, I reply, "If you agree."

"Is there a pen in your bag?" My heart flutters. I take that as a yes.

I pass him a pen with a smile. "Here you go?"

"What's going on? What's with the paperwork?"

"A prenup," I say with a smile.

"A what? What in the world for?"

I glance towards Tristian as his eyes meet mine. He turns and faces Mel.

"Because, with our family fortune, you marry no one without having something legal in place, or your so-called partner will strip you of your assets and money. A safety measure. That is why I am annoyed you married Corey without one."

Mel shakes her head. "I didn't know. Is it too late for me to have one?"

"I've arranged for my solicitor to meet with you tomorrow."

Her face turns pale. "What are you thinking?" By her look, she was not expecting Tristian to have something organized.

"Mel, I know it is personal, but since you married

Corey, have the two of you had sex? Have you consummated the wedding?"

She shakes her head. "No. Why?"

"Thank goodness. We can go from there. I'll let my solicitor know. Mel, if you are willing, we'll confidently have the marriage annulled."

"Oh, Tristian. I'm so sorry about everything. But I love him and would prefer to remain married to him."

Oh, Mel. Lust blinded the girl. Her brothers should have had a serious conversation with her years ago regarding prenups.

"As much as I think of Corey as a brother. I wouldn't trust him. He's had financial trouble over the last couple of years. That is why he left. That is why he traveled overseas. To work some of his debts off and hide from certain people after him, demanding money that he owes them."

"What are you talking about? He has never mentioned he has had financial trouble. Why haven't you said anything earlier?"

"Why would he? It was not my place to say anything. Sorry, Mel, but I think Corey only saw you as a means to pay off his debts by using our family money."

Shit. Corey now knows Mel has been banking her family allowance. He knows she has money.

"I'm sorry, Mel," I say. "He knows about the money you've put towards Trinity's schooling," I murmur.

"We'll work something out," Tristian says. "Now, the next question is... When are we going to get married, Izzy?"

Chapter Thirty-One

TRISTIAN

*S*ince when did Izzy think about getting a prenup? I couldn't help but wonder if it's because she was contemplating my earlier proposal or she was thinking of her future.

Regardless, I am thankful she was wise enough to prepare for the future. Our future. As the heir of the Heartson family empire, it carries both a substantial fortune and significant responsibilities.

As Mel and Izzy banter with one another, I take the time to read the prenuptial agreement. Pleased with what I see, I proceed and enter my personal information. Now, all that is left is finding a witness for our signatures.

"Hey, I'm heading to the nursery to spend some quality time with my daughter. You two might as well talk." Mel slides out of her bed, grabs the robe from the end of her bed, and slips it on before leaving.

I shift my attention to Izzy, only to discover that she is observing me. "What do you think of the prenup?"

she asks with a straight face. "My aunt had it prepared for me. I intend to be well-prepared."

With a nod and a smile, I place the documents down, sit on the edge of her bed, and reach for her hand. "Thank you for agreeing to marry me. The prenup looks to be in order. I've completed all the blank sections I'm required to fill in. All we require is to have our signatures witnessed."

She nods. "I wasn't sure how you would react."

"Surprised but relieved. At least I know your thoughts on a marriage between us are real, and you're ready to proceed."

"When would you prefer to have the ceremony?"

"Izzy, if I could marry you right now, I would."

"Why the rush?"

"Apart from the fact that I think we have waited long enough ...I have a feeling. There is something not right. There's an urge to have everything completed. The sooner, the better."

She nods her head and moves her hands as if she were counting on her fingers. "Well, I nearly crashed my car. At the last second, I changed my mind and decided not to travel in that elevator. Then there is my friend, whom I was supposed to have dinner with, who is now in intensive care."

*H*ang on. What friend? Intensive care? "What do you mean, your friend is in intensive care? Who?"

"What... are you going to become all caveman on me?"

"No, Izzy. Too many things have happened. Too many to be a coincidence."

"Simon is my friend and business partner. We own and operate a security firm. We had a business meeting at his house the other day. The meeting ran longer than we realized, so Simon recommended I eat with him before leaving. He's as protective as a mother hen. With the food order delayed, my exhaustion set in, and I decided to leave, grabbing a quick bite to eat on my way home."

He's not much of a friend, neglecting her, I thought. "He should have driven you home, Izzy, picking something up for the both of you to eat on the way to your house."

"He suggested taking me home and grabbing something else to eat. It was at that moment that an alert was sent to our cells. One of our client's systems had gone down. Simon urged me to leave and assured me he would handle the emergency."

"Do you know if he had taken care of it?"

"Yes. But then, the following morning, Simon phones me, asking me to take his place at the meeting scheduled later that day. It had to do with the emergency from the night before. He said he felt sick, and I told him to make a doctor's appointment. The only thing, Simon, is one of the healthiest people I know. Something was not right with my friend."

My instincts say something bad is happening, and Izzy is the target.

"Izzy, when was the last time you spoke with Ms. Raiker? I think she should speak with you again."

"My last text was to inform her I was in the hospital. She messaged back saying she was sending over a bodyguard — Jackson — and that she's looking into a few different things on my behalf and would notify me as soon as she has answers."

I nod. "When morning comes, you better have her come in and speak with you."

"Yes, I agree," Izzy says before yawning.

"Izzy, try to relax and sleep a bit more. I'll stay here over by the window seat."

She yawns again and nods. "Okay." She closes her eyes.

I stand and kiss her head. I wait several minutes, making sure she's asleep.

It's time to see my sister and niece in the nursery.

Chapter Thirty-Two

IZZY

*S*omething or someone wakes me, and I'm not impressed.

Once I open my eyes, I'm greeted by an unfamiliar nurse. Who's this?

What happened to Nurse Fiona? I glance towards the window seat and notice it's empty.

Where is Tristian?

My attention moves to the person beside me. A flicker of surprise, or perhaps fear, shone in the new nurse's eyes as they widened when they met mine. I glance towards her hand and I'm startled by the long, sharp syringe clutched in her hand. A hand which does not belong in the medical field with long decorated fingernails, each finger circled with a gold ring. Don't even get me started with all the bracelets wrapped around her wrist. A cold prickle runs up my spine as she injects an unfamiliar blue substance into my IV.

A bad feeling washes over me; my instincts scream

danger, so I hit the call button to alert the nurses. Where is Nurse Fiona? Where is Tristian?

With an urgent, decisive fourth press of the call button, she lunges for my pillow, her fingers closing around the starch cotton before I can react. As my brain comprehends what she's about to do, I scream for help at the same time, pushing the pillow away.

She lunges towards me, her height giving her the upper hand. The pillow lands hard on my face, its soft bulk stuffing my mouth and nostrils, cutting off my breath. If I don't act quickly, I'll suffocate. Despite hitting her with all my strength, the bitch refuses to let go of the pillow.

My heart is a frantic drum against my ribs as it hammers with a terrifying intensity. Any attempt to remain calm evaporates with each second that races by. My air supply is running dangerously low. My lungs scream in protest as a cold grip of dread fills me as I feel my life slipping away. In these last moments, my thoughts drift to my baby, a wave of bittersweet love washing over me.

Sorry, little man — I love you. I tried to save us.

Knowing that my time is running out and fighting for my life, my determination fills me one last time to save my baby. I struggle to locate the cannula on my other hand and yank. My lungs burn, I need to breathe, my strength all but gone. With one last tug, it comes free just as my ears catch the distant sound of someone yelling as I descend into a void of darkness.

*M*y senses inform me I feel like crap. There's pain in my lower body, and I'm unable to determine the cause. It soon becomes obvious my eyelids do not want to open. What is wrong with me? Footsteps, then the sound of a door swishing closed reaches my ears.

Who's there?

Is there someone there?

After multiple attempts, my eyelids finally flutter open. My room emerges into focus as my eyes adjust to the dim lighting. When I turn to look towards Mel and notice she and her bed are missing. It is then I realize I'm in an unfamiliar room, and look to my other side and see Tristian peacefully sleeping awkwardly in a chair next to me.

Ouch comes to mind, knowing when he wakes, his neck is going to be in pain from his head and neck being in an uncomfortable position. Then I do a double take. A baby hospital cot rests next to Tristian, and something seems to be inside.

No. And shake my head from side to side.

All thoughts go to my baby.

No.

I reach for my belly. A belly I soon discover is no longer as prominent, round, or hard as it had been the last time I had seen it. Only soft and spongy. What in the hell has happened? Where is my baby? I glance at the baby cot again.

Is my baby in there?

Did I give birth to my son?

Before I can say anything, movement catches my attention from within the baby crib, followed by strange little noises. My focus remains on the movement, watching and listening until a baby's cry fills the room.

Tristian startles awake and stands immediately at the sound.

"Hey, little guy. Do you need changing?" he says in a soft voice. He carefully picks the swaddled baby up, placing it against his shoulder, and continues whispering to the baby. "It's okay, little man. Momma will wake up soon." His eyes then meet mine and grow wide. "Hey, you're awake. Hang on, I have to alert the nurse." He presses the buzzer several times before walking over to a table and placing the baby on it.

"I have to change our boy's diaper. He's wet." All I can do is nod. I'm lost for words.

My attention moves to the door as it opens. In walks a nurse. She smiles as soon as she sees me awake. "Hello, Ms. Delany. It's great to see that you're awake. Could you please share your first name and whereabouts with me?"

I glance back to Tristian, then back to the nurse, and frown. "My name is Izzy, and I think I'm in a hospital."

The nurse nods. "Yes, you are Izzy. My name is Susan, and I will be your nurse for this shift." Susan checks my obs and enters the information on the electronic chart. "Were you in here just before?" I ask.

The nurse frowns and shakes her head. "No. I'm on my rounds. I've been with other patients."

"*Strange.* I'm sure someone was here before," I murmur.

The nurse glances at the door, then to my I.V. with a frown.

I turn back towards Tristian and ask, "What happened to me?"

He stands and turns with the baby to his front. He glances towards the nurse, then back at me, and smiles.

"Izzy, I would like to introduce to you our son," he proudly says. My arms lift as Tristian lowers the babe into my waiting arms.

My boy's appearance holds me captive; I observe every detail, from the dark, delicate silken strands of hair to the subtle shadows playing across his face. His dark, perfectly sculpted eyebrows arch above his striking, inquisitive eyes, which are framed by incredibly long, dark lashes. One of his tiny hands emerges from his blanket as if he's trying to reach out to me.

With my opposite hand, I lovingly touch my infant's tiny fingers. Taking note of his minuscule fingernails. Aww, they're gorgeous. I feel overwhelmed with emotion. My love for this little guy has already grown. Leaning in, I inhale the delightful aroma of his baby scent and lovingly kiss his little head.

My baby is here. He's alive.

"Tristian, I love Rowan so much. My heart melts looking at him. How did we get so lucky?" Thank goodness my boy is safe. Tristian didn't even blink or respond when I mentioned our son's name. I glance up and once again ask, "What happened, Tristian? The last I remember, I was on bed rest."

Sadness fills his eyes. "The doctor had to perform an emergency c-section."

Huh? "Why? What went wrong?"

"Babe. Someone went into your room and tried to kill you."

What the hell? Why? With a frown, the image of a stranger fills my mind. "There was a nurse. She was injecting something into the IV line. I tried to stop her. A pillow... She tried to smother me," I murmur.

"That's right. A fake nurse attacked you with a pillow while injecting a deadly toxin."

What the hell? That bitch with the syringe. I glance down at my son. Is he hurt? And look back at Tristian. "Our baby...he is okay?"

He nods. "Thankfully, you pulled out the cannula before the toxin reached your shared bloodstream."

At least, that is something.

"Has the staff had background checks?" I demand.

"Essy has her team on it. Keep in mind, several staff members need to be checked."

"I need to be safe. I want our son safe."

"Yes, I agree. Thankfully, Jackson was returning from the bathroom when he heard your buzzer and noticed no nurses were answering it. He sensed trouble and hurried to your room."

With my next breath, the weight of the world presses against me. I feel exhausted. As much as I want to keep my son snug within my arms, my eyelids droop.

"Make sure to thank him for me," I mumble with an enormous yawn. "Why is my body not responding to me?" Did someone give me a sedative? My fingers refuse to move. I try my feet...Nope. "Something is wrong, Trisitian. What is in my I.V.?" I mumble again. "Tristian, the baby," I slur before everything turns dark.

Chapter Thirty-Three

TRISTIAN

"What in the hell is happening?" I wonder as I recall the two serious incidents Izzy experienced while I was in the hospital. As I stand outside Izzy's room, holding my son in my arms, I can't help but feel a sense of unease.

The doctor continues to monitor my girl, while my little guy fusses and I try to comfort him by propping him against my chest. It's baffling how no one noticed that someone tampered with Izzy's I.V. again. Just then, the sound of my cell chimes, showing an incoming call. "What have you found out?" I greet the caller, making sure my son is safe in my hold.

The voice on the other end informs me, "Astor, I'm still searching. This is a courtesy call to let you know I've sent three extra staff to guard Izzy."

I breathe a sigh of relief, grateful for the additional security. However, I can't help but question, "No offense, Ms. Raiker, but why didn't you have more guards on Izzy? Two attacks within a short amount of time..."

There's a hint of frustration in her response as she explains, "Listen, Astor. Depending on the event, clients usually find that one bodyguard is sufficient. While Ms. Delany was hospitalized and on bed rest, I requested Jackson to keep me updated about her condition. Your sister specifically asked Jackson to protect the baby upon his birth, so I immediately arranged for another bodyguard to guard Izzy. I want to know what happened to Samson?" Ah, that explains why Jackson was not in my wife's room.

Curious, I inquire, "What do you mean? Are you missing a bodyguard?"

"Yes," Ms. Raiker confirms, her tone still frustrated. "I have two other staff members at the hospital searching for him." Ms. Raiker will be quite busy. I can't imagine the difficulty she's facing with an MIA employee.

The million-dollar question is: who is after Izzy?

Trying to gather more information, I ask, "Ms. Raiker, with your background with the FBI, have you completed a full history on Izzy and the people around her?"

She assures me, "Yes, I know exactly who Izzy is. Her parents. I've been looking over information and reports from their deaths and that of her cousin and uncle."

"Izzy believes their deaths are related."

"Yes, I agree. The devastating events of the gala, the poisoning of her business partner, and the damage to her car all seem to be related. I have contacted one of my old buddies who still works in the FBI, as they should be able to dig deeper than me. I have requested that they do a complete search for this Gavin person. As well as several Board of Directors at Heartson Industries."

"Is Izzy still in danger?"

"Yes. Whoever is after her wants her dead. This means both Izzy and your son require full-time protection."

What am I to do? My family cannot live in fear. My fiance and sister arranged protection. And what did I do? Somehow, I allowed non-medical personnel to attend to my fiance. I've failed to look after Izzy's safety.

"Look, Astor. The bodyguards Smyth, Handson, and Johnson should arrive any minute. My two other staff members are Flints and Ashworth. If anyone else arrives by a different name, inform Jackson or myself immediately."

"Will do. I want these criminals caught and dealt with and for my family to be safe."

"So do I, Astor. So do I."

Just then, I notice two men walking towards me, their footsteps echoing in the deserted corridor. Their eyes scan our surroundings, noting the people and rooms they pass.

"Hold on a second," I murmur to Ms. Raiker. I place my cell in my pocket and reposition my sleeping boy.

The two strangers turn, and their attention focuses on me.

Both men, dressed in smart casual clothing, smile.

The guy on the right with fair, short, cropped hair lifts his hand for me to shake. His grip is firm as he eyes my son before his eyes focus on mine.

"Hello, you must be Astor. My name is Ashworth, and my partner is Flints." I shake the other man's hand. "Essy Raiker sent us here. We are currently searching for one of our colleagues." Ah, the missing guard, Essy, mentioned.

"I hope you discover what happened to him. What was his name again?"

The first man, named Ashworth, gives me a smirk and replies, "Samson. Are you speaking with Essy on your cell? May I speak to her briefly?"

I slip my cell clear of my pocket and place it near my ear. "Did you grab all that?"

"Yes. Their voices match Flints and Ashworth. Pass your cell to Ashworth."

From the corner of my eye, I notice Jackson. He nods and encourages me to approach him.

"Izzy, how are you feeling?" my doctor asks as she enters my updated medical details on the computerized chart. Each time someone goes near my I.V., I take an extra interest.

My eyes meet hers. "Still weak. What did you place in my I.V.?"

She smiles and taps the I.V. line. "Ah. Medication to boost your system and the other is a drug to continue to counter-react to your last I.V. mishap." Seriously... How much medication can one person have? I think. The doctor continues speaking. "We are concerned about the events you've experienced. This was inexcusable. The hospital board has overhauled our security."

I give a small nod. She doesn't have to tell me about it. If the hospital had better security in the first place, I would have been safe. But then, someone is after me. All I can think of it's to do with my father's company. Everything points in that direction.

How can I trust anyone?

Is my doctor a person I need to stay away from? Can I trust her?

Where is Tristian and my son?

"Izzy, your obs are better than I'd expected."

"Why? What were you thinking they'd be?"

She walks around the bed towards the door. "Izzy, after everything you have been through. You have survived. Remember that you're a fighter."

I'm unsure what to think regarding the doctor. I can only nod.

"Doctor Hamlin. When can I leave the hospital with my son?"

"How about we wait until the afternoon and re-evaluate? If you're both medically cleared, then you can leave."

"Until this afternoon." And I glance towards the clock on the wall. Twelve more hours to go.

"Izzy, are you ready to leave?" Mel questions, standing by my door. She pauses when she notices Helen Trents, my female bodyguard. Jackson mentioned earlier that it would be best to have Helen protect Rowan; she was a trained medic from her days in the army.

"Mel, I want my son safe. That is the only reason I agreed to stay at your family's home," I explain.

My best friend and soon-to-be sister-in-law smiles.

"All I can say is you and I create gorgeous babies." Trust Mel to say something so silly. It's true, but still silly, as she gently rocks her baby in her stroller.

"Remember, Benny has the car organized for us. We can travel anywhere with Trinity and Rowan," I remind Mel, noticing her uncertain expression regarding my female bodyguard. Essy arrived earlier with Helen, ensuring that she transferred Helen's bags and equipment to Astor Manor earlier.

"I still can't believe you named your son Rowan," Mel comments.

I look up, surprised. "Why do you say that?" I ask.

"I thought you would have named him similar to or after Tristian," Mel explains.

Not in this lifetime.

Tristian's treatment of me should have been better over the years.

"Sorry, Mel. With all my hassles with your brother, I named my boy after my father. Rowan is a family name passed through the generations," I clarify.

"I thought your father's name was Philip?" Mel questions.

"It is. In the public eye, people knew him as Philip Heartson. When, in fact, his birth name is Rowan Philip Heartson," I reveal.

"Oh, I never knew that," Mel admits.

I zip my case and respond, "Now you know. Come on, it's time to go. Benny is waiting for us." I nod to Helen, and she nods to another guard who acts as the luggage carrier. Poor man, he's probably annoyed acting as our luggage handler. He picks up my case and carry bag and heads out the door.

"When did Benny find time to install two baby carriers in the car?" Mel wonders.

"This morning, in case we happened to leave together," I explain.

"I haven't told Corey that Trinity and I are leaving today," Mel confesses.

After the attack, the staff moved Mel and Trinity to a private room under complete protection. She has her own bodyguard, who is waiting just outside the door for them.

Helen lifts Rowan's carrier and steps forward. My little man doesn't seem concerned about moving about in the carrier, he just continues to sleep.

"Don't sweat it. I haven't updated Tristian either. I feel it's best to keep our leaving quiet," I assure her.

She nods as she reaches for her carry bag and passes it to the guard. Then, she pushes the stroller towards the door, saying, "After everything you've been through, I agree. Come on, let's go."

With a nod, I smile at the nurse before I gingerly sit in the waiting wheelchair. "Thank you," I murmur.

"It's my job, Ms. Delany," the nurse says, releasing the brake.

She wheels us through the doorway, and I notice Jackson to my right and we give one another a nod before he moves into position.

Then, I glance to my left and notice the other two bodyguards. Jackson agrees with me regarding keeping my leaving quiet. They found his colleague unconscious in an empty room with a severe head injury. The man is lucky to be alive.

Essy's team continues to review video footage to apprehend the two remaining attackers, including the one who tampered with my I.V. for the second time with the deadly toxin.

Turns out Tristian did not think the fake nurse was strange when they walked into the room. He kept on working on his phone. The same person came back in when Tristian fell asleep and tampered with my IV. Now, he's beside himself with guilt for not taking more notice. Not my problem. He was in my room to watch over me. He kept working on his cell instead of asking questions, as I had when a nurse came in.

See how that worked out?

Chapter Thirty-Five

IZZY

*A*ll set up in my room. My son is down for a nap in the Astor Manor. Rowan will remain in my room, sleeping in his crib beside my bed.

Since arriving here with Mel, Tristian did not appreciate discovering two strange vehicles entering their secure garage. Thankfully, Mel had pre-organized with her staff to allow us through the gate into the multi-vehicle garage. Our security people have their own rooms with full internet and computer access to keep on top of surveillance.

Tristian's recent tantrum made it clear to me I will not be sharing a room with him anytime soon, even if he apologizes repeatedly. I'm still upset about his actions and how he let me down by not keeping me safe.

With tea and coffee sorted, I savor another sip of my tea and watch Essy arrange her laptop and papers on the table. "Essy, how is everything going with your investigation?"

She taps several keys on her laptop and meets my eyes. "We have several leads at this stage. My friends in high places have been a tremendous help." That's good. Though she's still not answering my question.

"In what way?" I ask.

She takes a sip of her coffee and opens the folder beside her. "We have several suspects. Four of them had connections to your parents before their deaths."

Okay. Could they be my father's Board of Director members? "Who?" I calmly ask as I take another sip of my tea.

"Izzy, how well do you know your family tree?"

Unsure of Essy's question, I place my cup on the table and sit up straight. "I don't understand. What relevance does my family tree have?"

She pulls a printout from her folder and opens the document, which appears larger than the poster size. "From what we have discovered, your father had several relations on his father's, your grandfather's side of the family, who wanted their share of the family business," she explains, placing the large white paper down on the space of the table.

Uncertain, I respond, "I don't understand. As far as I know, my father had no living relatives."

Essy shakes her head and says, "Izzy, I have discovered you have distant relatives." Huh? Since when? She indicates at the paper. "Check the names to see if they seem familiar. Through extensive detective work, two names appear on your company's board. There is someone who also calls you a friend. Here, look for yourself," she points to the names.

I scan over all the names, and a tear escapes when I read my father, mother, mine, and baby brother's names. Memories flood back as I recall the last time I had seen them alive, the day my baby brother was born.

Standing in the hospital car park, my parents said goodbye to me, urging Aunt H to take me back to her house, promising to pick me up the following day. Little did I know, a drunk driver would hit my father's car, killing all three of them several minutes later.

After several deep breaths, I pull myself together and continue reading over the names where Essy pointed until... Huh?

What the...? You have to be kidding me.

I re-read the name — Franklin Goodwin Davis. No, it can't be Franky.

What are the chances of Simon's assistant being one of my relations? I read the following name and shake my head — Edward Brown, who had been on the Board of Directors for Heartson Industries, the annoying person from the elevator who got himself blown up.

Reading further down the family tree, I discover another Board of Directors member. "You have to be kidding me," I mutter to myself, not surprised by the trouble he's been causing the company — Ted Davis.

The next name beneath his has me pausing. What the... It couldn't be. Surely? Ted's son, another name that is far too familiar — Gavin Davis. He's my distant cousin! Why didn't he say anything? How could he manipulate me like that?

Why didn't I click with Gavin having the same surname as one of the Board of Director members? It's probably because he never once mentioned his father worked for Heartson Industries.

The more I look over the family tree and continue to read the names, the harder it's to fathom that Franky and Gavin are first cousins to one another — my distant cousins.

I glance up. "Essy. I don't understand. I have never seen this family tree. How did you discover all these people?"

She replies, "Izzy, I have excellent resources and contacts. The best in discovering family trees with hidden history."

"How can Franky and Gavin be my distant cousins?"

She shakes her head. "I'm sorry. I wish I had better news."

"Why do I sense you're about to say something else I won't like?"

"Probably because you're correct. From what we have gathered, including different video surveillance, we discovered Franklin Davis had intercepted the takeaway food on its way to Simon's address. My people found the takeaway containers at Simon's apartment and had the contents tested. We are applying for a search warrant to search Franklin's property for the poison used in the takeaway food."

Someone had poisoned the takeaway food. Poor Simon. What made Franky do that?

"But why poison him?"

"From what we have so far gathered. We think Franklin thinks you have been in a secret relationship with Simon, and your child belongs to him."

"I still don't understand why poison my business partner. We've never been in a relationship."

"Izzy, you were supposed to eat the food. Without you and your son, the ownership of your family company will be transferred to another family member. I have seen the Will. I have had my solicitor go through it with a fine-tooth comb."

Oh, shit. Why didn't Aunt Hazel mention any of this? Perhaps Aunt Hazel was unaware that these people were related.

"But why try to kill me? Why not let me know I have family?"

"Because you are the missing Secret Heiress. Throughout your life, your identity has remained hidden from the world. Your absence from the next AGM in two weeks will allow your so-called distant relatives to seize control of the company legally, leaving you powerless."

"What?" Well, that confirms why they kept Aunt Hazel from the last meeting. And say, "No. They will not be taking over. How did they know I was the missing heiress?"

"That I cannot tell you. Maybe we'll discover the answer sooner rather than later."

"Thank you so much. Keep looking, keep searching. Gather as much evidence as you can. These people need to be stopped."

Time to call Aunt Hazel and work out a plan to protect my son and my father's company.

Chapter Thirty-Six

TRISTIAN

"What will we do regarding Mel and Izzy?" Alex mumbles, taking another sip of his drink and leaning back on the dark leather armchair.

"Well, brother. As for Mel, our sister will continue to live here until she officially moves out. If you didn't already know, Izzy is my fiancé. Which means I want her and my son under our roof."

"Huh? Since when did you have a relationship with Izzy?"

Meeting my brother's gaze, I focus all my attention on him, determined not to avert my eyes. If he stops vanishing without a word, he would understand what was happening to our family.

"Alex, Izzy, and I have been seeing one another for some time. Our family will cherish, protect, and look after my son. We have a lot to sort out."

"What do you mean? What is there to sort out? Open your eyes, brother, she's after our money."

How stupid is my brother? "Alex, explain why you have been after Heartson Industries."

He pauses, frowns, and then turns to face me. "How did you know about that?" His eyes narrow. "Oh, I get it. Izzy's aunt, she blabbed, didn't she?"

"Are you serious right now, Alex? You have taken steps to take over Heartson Industries, New York branch. A heads up. You will never get it."

Alex frowns, and then his eyes narrow at me. "Why? Because you say so."

I shake my head at my brother. "Oh, little brother. My son will one day inherit Heartson Industries."

"Huh? How?"

"Alex, get your head out of your ass. You must know all players in business."

"What are you going on about, Tristian?"

"Do you know who Izzy is?"

My brother shakes his head. "Tristian, you need to stop drinking. Izzy is a nobody. Remember, her aunt raised her."

"Alex, when you dealt with the Heartson Industries Board of Directors, had they mentioned anything regarding their missing Heiress to the Heartson Industries?"

"Tristian, what is going on? Why would they mention such a thing?"

"Alex," we both turn to Izzy's voice, "as your brother said to you. *'Get your head out of your ass.'* You will not take over my company. Remove that thought from your mind and stay away from my family company."

"Izzy, why would you even say that?"

"Alex, why is it so hard to believe?"

"You are dreaming. You have nothing to do with Heartson Industries."

"Where is your proof?" Izzy demands.

"Why? The Board of Directors said there is no Secret Heiress."

My brother can be such an idiot. "Alex, who approached you?" I demand. "Who have you been in contact with?"

"Are you serious, Tristian?"

"Serious as a heart attack on steroids. Now answer the questions."

*O*nce we're all seated, I know our sister has something important to say. As for me, I'm dreading it. Conversations have been moving around the table for the past five minutes.

"Maybe, brother, you should be more observant," Mel states louder.

"What's that supposed to mean?" Nick asks.

With a serious face, Mel turns and looks at each of us. "Thanks to Izzy, I have a better understanding of our family business, including its operations and your roles. You never once sat me down to discuss meetings, takeovers, or anything else. What kind of business partners are you?" I cringe at her words. She has a point.

"Mel, why would you want to know? It's not like you'll be sitting behind a desk working." Alex gloats.

My brother's comment is foolish. I couldn't help but shake my head in disbelief. "Alex, shut it," I say, trying to contain my frustration. He is a stupid, selfish fool. "Do you even have any knowledge about our sister and her business?"

Alex's head snaps around to face me, clearly caught off guard. "What business?" he grunts. "All Mel does is spend her allowance on shopping every week."

I can no longer contain my disappointment. "You're such a clueless fool. As her older brother, you know absolutely nothing about our sister," I say, glancing at Izzy, who seems aware of my recent discovery. I only recently realized how little I knew about Mel, and since then, I have made it my mission to learn as much as possible.

Alex smirks, disregarding my words. "And what about you, big brother? You don't know much either," he retorts.

I quickly correct him, wanting to set the record straight. "No, Alex. That's where you're mistaken. Our sister is incredibly intelligent. She doesn't just spend her money, she saves it for her child's education," I explain.

Alex seems skeptical. "If that's true, how has she managed without any money?" he questions.

"Oh, you foolish boy," Mel casually interjects, shaking her head in disappointment. "And yes, that's exactly what you are. You've all been taking me for granted all these years. You've treated me like a naïve girl. Well, guess what, boys? From now on, my name will be legally included in every document for any future sale or purchase. My signature is essential for any deal to go through, or the contract will be void," she asserts.

Alex starts spluttering, clearly overwhelmed by this revelation. Nicholas sits there, stunned and speechless.

It dawns on me that I have underestimated Mel far too much. My lack of faith in her abilities had motivated her to dig into our family business, where she discovered that we had been signing documents on her behalf.

Hazel had sent the necessary documents, stating that Mel was to move into our mother's office and be present at all meetings. Including — Mel signing her own name on all legal documents, and her seat on the board reinstated. It was our responsibility to ensure that Mel, as the female representative of Astor's International, sat on the board after our mother's passing — a duty we neglected. Now, we will have to face the consequences of our mistakes.

"What makes you think you can boss us around, little sister?" Alex demands.

With a raised brow and a straight, determined face, she replies, "Since I am family, we all have equal shares in our family business." Bugger, she's pulling the equal share line. This conversation will not end well.

"You know nothing about business," Alex states.

Mel leans forward with her hands spread on the tabletop, her voice fills with frustration. "Seriously, Alex. What makes you think I don't?"

"Well...well..." Our annoying brother looks between me and Mel, stuttering. "Well..."

I lift my hands and shake my head, signaling for him to stop. "Alex, close your mouth before digging your hole any deeper."

"What do you mean? What are you not saying?" Alex presses, clearly sensing that there's something more to the situation.

"What I had not been saying is that our sister has an extremely successful business in IT. She owns and runs her own consulting business, building and creating apps. Our little sister is wealthy all on her own."

"What the hell, Tristian? What are you talking about? When did Mel start knowing about computers?"

As I glance towards our sister, her face conveys her disappointment before her eyes narrow with anger at each word Alex says.

"Alex," our sister demands, her voice firm. "Have you heard of the company MeBe Tech?"

Alex frowns, then slowly nods. "Yes," he says slowly before his eyes widen towards Mel. "Are you saying that is your company?"

She nods sarcastically. "Give the boy a stuffed toy. Yes, brother. MeBe Tech is my company. What did you think I was doing while studying for my bachelor's degree in software engineering and app design, graphics, and layout? Ha... Spending my time shopping? Maybe...sleeping around, oh, hang on, that was you?"

I cringe, not wanting to know about my sister's sex life. It's bad enough she slept with my so-called friend.

"I was busy attending university for my degree, Alex. To make a future for myself," Mel explains, her voice a mixture of frustration and determination. Alex shakes his head, his silence sparing him from our sister's wrath.

Chapter Thirty-Seven

IZZY

"My darling girl, how are you feeling?"

What do I say...? I'm nervous, scared, emotional, annoyed, impatient, maybe — second thoughts? Tired. My lower belly has pain. I could go on.

Today, well this morning, I will marry Tristian. I can't help but wonder what there is to be nervous about. Last night, Aunt Hazel brought over all the paperwork, including my amended Will to include my son. It had been signed, witnessed, and lodged before she arrived half an hour ago, with her good close friend Owen Statesman and his partner James Western. I'm grateful to have unbiased witnesses. Aunt Hazel also arranged and picked up and delivered the Celebrant who will be performing the ceremony today. And thanks to her, she also has my new Will for after I marry Tristian to be signed.

Avoiding her question, I decide to ask one of my own. "Hazel, is everyone here?" A strange feeling filled me earlier when I was feeding Rowan. I'm not sure if it was just my nerves or something else entirely.

She lifts her sharp brow and rolls her eyes. "Everyone, that is important, yes. I even have the ring in my pocket. Now, Izzibella, let's check Rowan's diaper and head downstairs. Your groom is waiting."

Ah, yes. My groom. Tristian. He was my long-time teenage crush, the one who broke my heart as an adult. But just twenty minutes ago, he whispered that he loves our son and me, assuring that he would see us downstairs soon.

My best friend, Mel, is beyond excited to become my sister and she can't wait for it to be official. However, last night, after she boldly announced her position in the family business, Alex and Nick swiftly departed, dismissing any belief in Mel's business intelligence. They still haven't returned home.

Tristian and I decided that if the boys went out without informing us of when they would return, we wouldn't inform them of the ceremony this morning.

A few minutes ago, Mel left my room with her daughter, leaving a trail of her floral fragrance behind. It doesn't take Aunt Hazel long to change my son's diaper and put him in his onesie tux.

"Come on, Izzibella. I'll carry Rowan while I walk beside you. Let's go," she says with a smile.

*W*ho's bright idea was it to take the grand staircase?

My focus goes to my side, where my aunt stands. I don't know about anyone else, but I'm ready to sit down and rest. I've pushed my body too far, too quickly after the emergency cesarean procedure. *We should have taken the elevator.*

"It might be best to rest before proceeding," Aunt Hazel suggests as she leads me to a seat near the grand staircase. "We should have taken that elevator. It was silly thinking you could make a grand entrance in your condition." *Gee, you think, Aunt H. Bit late now.* I think. Yes, we should have taken the small elevator — my lower belly aches. I should have popped more painkillers before venturing out of my room.

"Izzy, what's happened? Are you okay?" Tristian's voice captures my attention as he approaches and kneels before me. Concern fills his features.

My eyes meet his. "My lower belly is a touch sore," I mumble.

"Izz, I can see it is more than a touch sore." He stands and smiles. Oh, no, that cheeky smile indicates he's about to do something he should not be. He leans down towards me and lifts me in his arms against his chest. "Place your arms around my neck and hold on," he urges.

"What? No... I'm too heavy, Tristian."

He glances at my aunt, not bothering to comment

on my announcement. "Come on, Hazel, let's get these two downstairs and become a family."

She smiles and carefully proceeds us down the grand staircase.

"Remember, Princess. I will always be there for you. Let me be your knight in shining armor."

I hold my breath with each step he takes. I hope we can stay upright and avoid any unexpected tumbles.

"Bella, please forgive me for my past stupid, obnoxious behavior. I have loved you for a long time. My idiocy was not declaring those words to you a long time ago. Today, I want to make us official and give you my heart. Please, my princess. Please marry me this morning," he pleads as we stop before the patio. Tristian must have sensed my thoughts. "I want you and our son by my side. We belong together, Izzy."

I squeeze around his neck, hugging him tightly. "Yes. I'll marry you," I whisper.

*M*usic tickles my ears and has me turning my head as the sound of the Righteous Brothers - Unchained Melody escapes through the open doorway. It sounds from hidden speakers leading out to the gorgeous decorated patio and spectacular gardens and pool.

Everyone turns as one with matching smiles. Mel,

James, and Owen quickly get up and carry a chair before the Celebrant for Aunt Hazel, Tristian, and me to sit on.

"You can put me down now, Tristian," I mumble with embarrassment.

My groom carefully places me on the chair, straightens his suit before undoing the buttons on his tux jacket, and then sits on the other seat. He leans forward and places a gentle kiss on my lips, sending erotic sensations through my body and straight to my core. Damn the man. I slowly open my eyes to see Tristian smile with desire-filled eyes.

"Our last kiss as single people, Izzy. I cannot wait until our next kiss, our first kiss as husband and wife," he says in a husky voice.

The sound of someone clearing their throat has me turning. Then I remember where I am. Shit, we have an audience and focus on the man who will be our celebrant today with a smile.

"Right now, if everyone is ready. Let's get this show on the road, shall we?" he says with a smile. "Now, do we have the rings?" I glance at my aunt. She smiles and retrieves a ring box from her jacket pocket.

"Here you go, the bride's ring for her groom." I roll my eyes as she passes the box to the Celebrant. He opens it, removes the ring, and places it on the crystal stone dais Mel organized for the rings to rest on.

A male's voice. A voice I have not heard for a long time announces, "Here is the groom's ring for his bride," Tristian's grandfather. Oh, my... I haven't seen him in two years or more. The man had always opened his arms, welcoming me to the family since I was a teenager. Plus, there was a vague memory of him visiting my father. He had once said when I'm all grown, he'll be there for my wedding day.

He remembered.

Tears fill my eyes, looking into his elderly, watering ones. "Hello, little Princess. I'm here to watch you marry your prince."

I blink several times with a huge smile. "You remembered," I manage through happy tears.

He nods. "Of course, young Bella. I promised your mother I would look after you when marrying. Unsure if Tristian is the right man for you," he says with a cheeky smile resembling Tristian's.

I glance at my groom, and he shrugs. "It had taken a lot of convincing to this old man why I should be allowed to marry you." I laughed. Joshua was like a grandfather to me. Now, he's going to become my legal grandfather after all these years.

"Why didn't you tell Tristian my true identity?"

He shook his head. "Not my place to say. How will he learn anything if he is not smart enough to ask the questions? And then, if he does not remember…"

He has a point. Tristian should have been more assertive.

"All right, everyone. We are here for a wedding. You can all catch up later," the Celebrant announces.

At that moment, our gazes connect, and we exchange nods and knowing grins. Tristian mouths, *I love you* and I mouth it back. We then turn our attention to the man who will officiate our union.

"Now that both rings have arrived, we can continue. Now... Do you, Tristian, take Izzibella Bethany Rowena Heartson to be your wedded wife, to hold, cherish, protect, and love until the day you die?"

I turn to look back at Tristian. He meets my eyes with his and smiles. "I do."

"Do you, Izzibella, take Tristian Drake Astor to be your wedded husband, to hold, cherish, protect, and love until the day you die?" the Celebrant asks.

"I do," I reply with a smile.

"Here, we stand in front of your family and friends to witness you place the wedding band on one other's ring finger and, from your heart, declare your vows to each another," the celebrant states as he picks up and passes Tristian a ring, and nods his head for him to proceed.

"My little Princess. I have loved you since you wrapped your little five-year-old fingers around my heart." I let out a laugh and look up to see Grandpa Joshua chuckle with a smile and turn to focus back on Tristian. He lifts my hand slightly and slides the diamond-studded platinum wedding band along my ring finger. "With this ring, I will become your prince forever. Allow me to be by your side. Together, we will have one another's backs and be there for our son and other children. We will raise them as best as we can, teaching them right from wrong, compassion, and love. In front of everyone today, I vow to be the best man I can be and become your forever husband and father to our children. I love you, Bella." As he pushes the ring to its final resting place on my finger, and says, "With my ring and heart, I give freely to you. I wed you, my love, my princess, my Bella, for the rest of our lives through good times and bad, sickness and health, until we sadly part and gain our angel wings."

Tears make their way down my cheeks. Caught up in the moment, I mouth. *'I love you,'* back to him. Turn and face the marriage celebrant and pick up the ring I had chosen for Tristian.

My groom lifts his hand towards mine, and I place my fingers around his as I slide the ring on his finger, pass his first knuckle, and say, "With this ring, I sit here today in front of our witnesses and son to marry my prince. To stand by your side as you stand by mine through good times and bad, sickness and health."

I struggle to ease his white gold and platinum band past his bigger middle knuckle. After a hard push, it finally slides the rest of the way along his long finger. I continue, "Today, I give you my heart and body freely as we become one until we gain our angel wings." I release his hand and turn towards the Celebrant.

"Now you have both declared your vows in front of your witnesses in the state of New York. I now pronounce you as husband and wife." Tristian and I both smile at one another. "You may now kiss your bride, Tristian," the Celebrant declares.

"Now, the part I've been looking forward to," my husband announces, making our guests laugh. He leans forward. "As for my gorgeous wife, our first kiss!" He gently presses his lips against mine, caressing my lips in a sensual tease until his hand reaches up and cradles my jaw, increasing pressure and changing the angle of his mouth. I return the pressure as our kiss deepens, feeling our passion erupt through my body and curling my toes. Now, this is what I call a kiss.

We gradually pull apart, and our eyes meet. "Well, Mrs. Astor," he says in a husky voice, casually adjusting the front of his suit pants.

My eyebrow rises as my lips twitch.

Before he could continue, I cut him off, "We better try that again, my husband, just to make sure it was good for a first kiss!" I cheekily say.

With a growl, Tristian wraps his arms around me and plants his lips firmly against mine. Instead of a gentle kiss, he urges my mouth open. Thrusting his tongue into my mouth, dueling with my own, until I thrust mine past his lips and into his mouth, where he snags it, sucking on it as his hands slide along my back, moving up and down. All common sense leaves me as I moan into his mouth, pushing myself into his body until the sound of a baby cry alerts my ears. We are not alone. Then reality hits. And I freeze before pulling away from Tristian, refusing to meet his eyes with embarrassed, burning cheeks.

Instead of looking at everyone, I focus on my son and lift my arms for him. Aunt Hazel steps forward with a big smile and shakes her head.

"Now, I think we can call that a good kiss," she says with a cheeky wink, placing my baby in my arms.

Rowan soon calms and snuggles into me. "Hey, little man, it's okay. Did you miss Momma?" He made a little mewing noise and pushed his face into me again. Ah, he's thirsty. I glance up at everyone. "Rowan needs feeding." I glance at Tristian. "Can you lift us and take us into the lounge area so I can feed him, please?"

He nods. "Sure. Hold on tight," he says as he stands and leans down, carefully lifting Rowan and me.

I then look at my aunt. "Hazel, can you escort everyone to the pergola for refreshments? We shouldn't be long." She nods.

"I'll ensure all the documents are ready for signing and witnessing."

"Thank you, H. We'll be out in a few minutes."

Tristian heads back inside, towards one of the armchairs, and gently places me down. "Here you go. Do you need anything else while I'm here?" Rowan becomes fussy and demanding. I've learned so far when my little one is hungry, he also requires a diaper change. There is not one without the other.

With a nod, I reply, "Yes. Rowan's change mat with his diaper bag from out of my room. He'll need changing once he's fed."

"Okay, I can do that. Be back soon, Mrs. Astor," Tristian says with a smile.

I smile back and say, "See you shortly, Mr. Astor, my husband."

He leans down to kiss my lips and says, "I like the sound of that, wife," then walks through the door.

As soon as Tristian leaves the room, I make quick work of unclipping and lifting my clothing to gain access to my aching breasts. Rowan fusses, searching for my nipple. It doesn't take me long to place him in the correct feeding position. I'll give it to my son, he is a quick learner. He latches on and begins guzzling down his milk.

As I watch over my boy nursing, I still cannot believe I am now married, and also a mother to a handsome little boy.

"Right, James, Mel, and Joshua, I require you to witness Izzy and Tristian's signature along with the celebrants on the documents for today's ceremony," my aunt says over all the chatter.

The room quietens. Joshua, James, and Mel all beam, their smiles wide as they cheerfully agree. "Sure, we can do that." And proceed to the decorated table containing the documents.

With a repeated motion, the celebrant indicates the specific areas on the documents where our signatures are required. The group watches as Tristian steps forward, eager to take the first step, and picks up the fancy white pen Mel got yesterday with a large long white curling feather at its end. As I glance to the side, I first notice Aunt Hazel engaged in a discreet conversation with her friend Owen, then she converses with James after he finishes signing, making me question whether she's discussing my Will requiring to be witnessed.

"Now for Izzy, we need your signature," the celebrant requests. My fingers cradle the elegantly designed fountain pen. Its curling plume tickles my hand as I quickly sign each document, ensuring they are all for the marriage license certificates. The last thing I want is to sign my legal name on any fraud documents. Joshua, James, and Mel sign as my witnesses, and Mel hugs me after she finishes.

"Welcome to the family, sis. Wow! I finally have a sister," Mel laughs as reality sinks in. My family of three has grown. I've always considered Mel my sister, and now she is legally part of my family.

Once everyone has signed and witnessed each document, the celebrant hands over our copy of the papers for Tristian and me to keep. Celebrant Michael is eager to leave with his copies to be submitted and processed.

"One moment, Michael," Aunt Hazel says. "I'll say goodbye, and then we can leave. I also have paperwork that requires lodging. What's that saying? Two birds or something? We can submit everything today," Hazel adds with a straight face. Michael, the celebrant, nods. From the look in his eyes, he was not expecting my aunt or anyone to leave with him.

"That's fine. I'll just use the bathroom first before we go." The look on his face was anything but fine.

Joshua speaks up. "I'll show you the bathroom to use." Grandpa Joshua is quickly beside Michael, touching the man's back. "This way." They left the celebrant's briefcase on the chair. As they walk through the doorway, Joshua winks over his shoulder.

As soon as it is clear, Aunt Hazel quickly opens Michael's briefcase and photographs several pictures of today's documents before carefully closing it. She left the celebrant's briefcase where he had left it on the chair. Then she slips her cell back into her pocket and wraps her arms around me.

"Now for you," she whispers. Extracting and placing my new Will in front of me, pointing where to sign. Both James and Owen sign as witnesses. Having these complete is a relief. "I'll lodge everything without delay."

The things my aunt does... Trespassing into someone's case and taking photos. In our world, we have to be careful. It's hard to know who we can trust. Did they know her intentions? That might explain Joshua's wink upon their departure. Come to think of it, they should be back here by now.

"Thank you, Hazel." I turn to James and Owen. "Thank you, guys, for coming today and acting as legal witnesses."

Both men hug me. "You're more than welcome. Hazel here," he points and says over his shoulder, "is a goddess. A day spent with her is always fabulous," James announces with a laugh, and my aunt and Owen laugh along with him.

"It is a pleasure to meet you both and being here with us on this special day." Giving them both a hug in return.

As Hazel hugs me, I whisper, "H, is James or Owen a lawyer or solicitor?"

She nods. "Yes, they are both. That's why I asked them to be here. Everything has to be legitimate." She takes a step back. "Now, I hear Michael and Joshua approaching. I best not keep him waiting." She turns to Tristian, Mel, and Joshua. "I'll see you all later for the bridal dinner." She then turns back to me. "Love you, darling girl. See you soon"

"Thank you again, Hazel. Love you, too."

a sense of relief washes over me as Hazel's text arrives.

Hazel:
Glad I accompanied Michael to lodge the documents. He wasn't going to lodge them today. Everything is now submitted and legal. Welcome to the family, Tristian.

Thank goodness. At least I am now legally wed to Izzy. And I quickly reply back.

Me:
Thank you. I'll let Izzy know. Thankfully, you had the man sign the NDA. He seemed shifty.

I wonder if the man realized that he had signed the NDA documents.

Sometimes, I feel grateful that the woman is on my

wife's side, protecting her. It's not surprising that Izzy stayed hidden for so long. But what if a few of the Heartson Industries Board of Directors were to uncover her true identity? It would explain the mysterious occurrences involving her car.

Three dots appear, and another text silently comes through.

Hazel:
That is why I went with him to lodge the paperwork.

Me:
Thank you, Hazel, for everything you have done. See you soon.

*M*y brother's voice intrudes on my thoughts as I scroll back over the text messages from forty minutes ago with Hazel. She should be here by now.

"Tristian, what's going on?" Nicholas asks, his frown deepening as he surveys the grand dining table. "What's the special occasion for this dinner?"

"I agree with Nick," announces Alex. "What is the reason for us eating in this room?" He glances around. "We eat in the family dining room as it's closer to the kitchen." The serving staff move around the table and fill each of our glasses.

With a smile and wink at Izzy, I turn towards my two brothers. My lovely wife and I decided to break the news to Alex and Nick at dinner.

We were not taking any risks regarding our marriage. After the ceremony, Izzy's doctor arrived at the house for a home visit to perform her daily medical check-up. We also asked if the doctor could acknowledge that we had consummated our marriage.

After discussing with the doctor, Izzy and I awkwardly and quickly consummated our marriage. I agree with the doctor's advice. After what I saw down there, I'm waiting several more weeks before jumping back into the marital bed. Izzy's doctor also gave us a signed document stating we had consummated the marriage.

"Alex and Nick," I murmur as I glance at my watch, then towards my brother's. "I wanted to let you know that Izzy and I were married this morning."

"What?" Alex explodes. "Since when?"

I glance at Nick. Frowning, he shakes his head, then redirects his attention to me. "Did you wait for us not to be here, Tristian?"

I shake my head. "No. I mentioned I had special plans today and asked if you would be here for breakfast?"

"Tristian, you know we don't eat as a family in the mornings," Alex says before looking at Izzy. "I suppose this is your doing, Izzy. What's with all the secrets?"

She shakes her head. "It wasn't a secret from either of you. It's up to the both of you if you show up. As you proved once again, you had better things to do."

She turns to Nick. "As usual, you never bothered getting home until two hours ago." She then faces Alex, "As for you... I can smell the cheap perfume on you. Then there were the lipstick marks on your shirt and neck. Just like your brother Nick, you didn't bother telling us if you would be home. You never said that you were staying out overnight. So don't turn this around on us," my feisty wife says. "Maybe next time, you might be courteous and inform us you'll stay out overnight. Then the cook will know how much food to prepare for each meal. By the way, we do eat breakfast together. It's not our fault if you don't bother showing up."

The look on my brother's face was priceless. Score one for my wife.

Izzy's aunt appears at the dining room entry. We make eye contact and nod.

"Thank you for the invitation, Tristian and Izzy," Hazel states as she sits down.

"You're welcome, Aunt Hazel," Izzy states.

"Thank you, Hazel. You are always welcome here," I say as she settles at her set place at the dining table.

My sister stands and says, "Tristian, Izzy." Everyone turns and looks at her. "Congratulations on your nuptials. May your future together be long and happy. Cheers," Mel says, raising her glass of non-alcoholic bubbles. Izzy and I follow with ours. Hazel lifts her freshly filled glass of wine. Nick and Alex sit there frowning before I stare daggers at my brothers, with annoyed looks, and they reach for their glass.

"Cheers," Hazel announces. "Here. Here."

"Thank you for everything, Hazel. Cheers," Izzy announces with a bright smile.

"Cheers and thank you," I say before lifting my glass to my wife in silent cheers.

Not one to allow the current topic to drop, Alex demands, "So, if the two of you are married, where's the certificate? Is the marriage even consummated?"

My hand hits the table. "Look, you little shit. My wife and I were married this morning. All the documentation was submitted, lodged, and processed. Hazel here can vouch for that. Even though marriage consummation is not your business, I'll answer you. Yes. We have consummated the marriage. A doctor witnessed it for anyone attempting to dispute the fact."

"Holy fuck. Where does this leave us with the family business?" Nick mumbles.

"Watch it, Nicholas. It is unacceptable to use profanity in the presence of guests." I sit straighter and glare at both my brothers. "To answer your question, Izzy acquired our company shares during the initial public offering on the share market. Besides that, Izzy and I had signed a prenuptial agreement. We do not have a claim to Izzy's family's money or company, nor does she have a claim to ours apart from the shares she previously owns."

Chapter Forty

IZZY

*I*f doo-doo is going to hit the fan…now is that time. Maybe I should sit back with a bucket of popcorn and watch the show.

"What the hell? Why would you purchase my family stocks, Izzy?" Alex demands.

Is he serious right now?

Should I even bother informing him or the others that Mel has also purchased twenty percent of stocks? Or that Hazel purchased fifteen percent of stocks. My percentage was forty-five percent for my son.

"Alex, get your head out of your ass. I ensured my son has something of his family heritage for his future. You're the one wanting to float Astor International, your family company, on the stock market." I met all their eyes with a raised brow. I remember how angry and disappointed Mel was. They left her out of the conversation and decision-making to float the family company despite being an equal partner. She now owns more shares than her brothers. "It was a foolish business mistake for flotation, but the three of you agreed. I want to know why you didn't discuss this move with Mel?"

*H*azel attempts to change the topic, "So, how is everyone this evening?" my aunt says as she scoops a spoon of mashed potatoes onto her plate with her roast beef, peas, and gravy.

The fantastic cooks created a variety of foods, including mashed and roast potatoes, roast beef, peas, carrots, and several other steamed vegetables, with two different gravies.

Mel answers, "It has been an interesting day. How was yours?"

"It was interesting as well, thank you."

I focus on my aunt. What really happened after she left earlier? "How? What do you mean?"

"Izzy, the celebrant, Michael, would have leaked today's ceremony to the press and not lodged the documents."

What? That is not good. "What happened?" I ask and glance to my husband, then back to my aunt.

"I was grateful to have James and Owen with me as they followed us into the building. In short, I ensured Michael submitted the documents." Oh wow. Thank goodness H escorted the man. My aunt takes a forkful of food and chews thoroughly before swallowing, leaving us in suspense for her to continue. "He found the non-disclosure agreement and other things in his briefcase." Holy cow. Not sure if that was good or not? "His reaction was shock, then anger as he uncovered the signed and witnessed NDA after taking out all the documents from his case."

"You still have it, Aunt Hazel. Well done."

Grateful, she smiles and nods. Next, she gives a stern gaze to everyone in the room. "We've gathered here to celebrate Izzibella and Tristian's wedding, correct? After dessert, we will discuss Izzy. Her past and current circumstances need to be addressed and resolved."

"What are you talking about? Alex spoke up as he reached for his drink."

"Alex." Hazel shook her head. "If only you could use your brain for good."

My brother-in-law's features change to a glare. "Why do you not like me, old woman?"

"Alex," I growl. "How dare you. You do not speak to my aunt like that."

Finally, Alex seemed apologetic.

I look at Hazel, our eyes meet, and she winks at me, then turns to Alex.

"Do you know who I am, Alexander?"

Alex frowns and shakes his head. "Is this some trick question?" And looks around the room.

Tristian then speaks up, "No, Alex. Just answer the question."

He focuses back on my aunt and replies, "Hazel Delany?"

Hazel shakes her head. "That is my everyday name, just like Izzy's. But what is my business name?"

Alex glances from Tristian to me, then back to Hazel. "Let's save some time, shall we? Just tell me."

"Unbelievable, Alex. Do you ever use your brain?" I demand, "Look, you three, and yes, I am including you, Tristian, because you have all been naïve for far too long."

Alex focuses on Tristian. "What is going on? What should we know?"

Chapter Forty-One

TRISTIAN

The urge to punch Alex and Nicholas in the face has never been this strong.

My fists tighten until I flex my fingers. Why are my brothers so selfish?

"Look, Hazel. I really do not care what your real name is. In our life, it comes down to family and connections. And from what we have seen, Izzy does not have these connections for family money," Nicholas annoyingly states.

My free hand grips Izzy's. If she had not had surgery recently, I would have let her punch the crap out of my pathetic brother.

"Nicholas, you are being an idiot. I protected Izzy the best way I could," Hazel says through clenched teeth.

"Why did you change Izzy's name?" My brother demands.

"Our lives were in danger, Alex. My primary

concern was for my niece. She just lost her parents. What would have you done?"

Alex shrugs his shoulders with a smug look on his face. "Had the culprits captured and stood my ground?"

My fingers clench. They ache to form a fist. "Are you serious right now, little brother? When someone made the deaths look like an accident, how would you know to have the authorities go after them?"

Before I can say another word, Izzy cuts in. "Alex, what my aunt is saying is that her husband, daughter, and also my parents and newborn baby brother were not just killed in a car accident. They had been murdered."

His smile drops, and he looks at Nicholas, whose eyes grow wide. He lifts his hands. "Hey, bro. Don't look at me. I never knew Izzy had a brother."

My brother straightens, sits a little higher on the chair, and considers his words. "Why move here to New York?"

Hazel shakes her head in disappointment. "At the time, I did the best I could, Alex. My sister, her husband, and my baby nephew had just died. I was still recovering from my own near-death experience and losing my daughter and husband. I had to keep Izzy safe. Remove her from the public eye. Plus, the legal side of Phil's Will had to be dealt with."

"Wait... Who is Phil?" Nick demands.

Hazel shakes her head. With a stern face, she glances around the table. Her sharp brow lifts as she announces, "Boys, officially meet Izzibella Heartson.

The owner of Heartson Industries. I am her legal representative and guardian. Plus, she also replaced her mother as owner of LaniD."

"Huh? LaniD, the big clothing, and cosmetic company?" Nicholas stutters. His gaze moves from Izzy to her aunt and back to Izzy again.

Alex nearly spits his drink out. "Izzy, the owner of Heartson Industries?" My brother places his drink down and wipes his mouth with his napkin. "I thought you were joking regarding that bullshit."

Hazel shakes her head. "No bullshit. Izzy legally is. Then there is my beloved sister and Izzy's mother. She was none other than Helanna Swits. Owner of LaniD."

"Holy shit," Nicholas murmurs. He looks in my direction, his brain busy thinking. "If what I am remembering is correct... that would make Izzy a what ...multi-millionaire?"

Hazel shakes her head. "Multi-billionaire, boys, and never forget it. She has more money than your family, as Izzy is the Secret Heiress of Heartson Industries. So who is after whose family money!" she states with a raised brow.

"Alex and Nicholas, don't forget Izzy also runs a security business. This is another item we need to discuss."

My brother's focus remains on Izzy. For once, their opinion of my wife has changed. She is no longer frowned upon as the poor kid from across the tracks, where we had sadly placed her all those years ago. My grandfather had always treated Izzy with love and friendship. Why did I behave and act the way I did? Maybe because I listened to my father and didn't make up my own mind.

Mel clears her throat. All attention moves to her. "I think you owe Izzy a big apology for how you have treated her over the years. Oh, and while discussing business, Izzy is also my business partner."

Both Alex and Nicholas yell, "What?" at the same time. "Since when?"

Mel continues talking as if her brothers did not interrupt. "Thanks to her, I've learned how to make my own money. Money that had nothing to do with the Astor family. You, my brothers, should have cared for me and helped me grow. To encourage me to look into and learn all about our family business. Instead, you, like Daddy, pushed me to the side and treated me like a nobody."

I watch Izzy give me the evil eye. It's not a good look to see on your bride on our wedding day. Rising to my feet, I walk around to my little sister's side. "Mel, honey," I gently say, grabbing the empty seat beside her, and sit down. "The treatment you received was dismal. Sadly, I followed Dad's way of thinking, and I am sorry for that. Never again will any of us take advantage of you. You are one of us; together, we are Astor International." I glance towards Alex and then Nicholas. Mel follows my line of sight and our brother's nod in agreement. Thank fuck, or I would have serious words with them.

Then Alex speaks up, looking at Izzy. "Just how many businesses are you involved in?"

I face my wife and watch her smile. Her brow rises as she replies, "A few." She leaves it at that, picks up her cutlery, and continues eating.

That was my cue to go back to my seat and eat.

Chapter Forty-Two

IZZY

$\mathcal{U}$pon Joshua's arrival, a wave of relief washes over me. All the family is finally here.

"Sorry, I'm late," he mutters, his way of addressing us, as he rushes into the room, wasting no time in sitting down. Then, he adds with a chuckle, "I may be retired, but I still keep myself informed about the latest business happenings." Tristian was on his feet, preparing his grandfather's dinner plate, which includes a ladle of gravy over his meat and vegetables. "All right, son," Joshua said, his hand resting gently on Tristian's shoulder. "That is enough food to sink a battleship."

Tristian smiles at his grandfather. "Gotta keep up your strength, pops. Tomorrow is another business day."

I nearly spit out my mouthful of food when I hear Joshua harrumph with attitude.

"Grandpa," Mel casually says.

"Yes, Granddaughter, what have your brothers done now?" The man may be old, but I must credit him for where it's due. He knows how to read Mel.

"Grandpa, would you like to join me next week when I see Momma's old office?"

He glances at the boys with a raised brow. He shakes his head and then turns back to Mel. "Certainly, baby girl. What do you have in mind?"

"I'm not sure, but I have to make certain the office is clean and modern enough for my daughter's visit. It is time the boys move over because I'll take my rightful position on the board and in my office."

Before breaking out into a full-body laugh, the old man's lips twitch with amusement. After he slows his laughter and takes a sip of his drink, he says, "You boys reap what you sow," before continuing to eat his dinner.

Tristian shakes his head. Alex's and Nicholas' mood changes. "Grandfather, why was Mel permitted to serve on the board?" Nicholas demands.

Joshua finishes chewing, uses a napkin to wipe his lips, and answers, "It's because she has equal rights and shares in the company, along with what your mother left her. The position belonged to your mother, which is rightfully Mel's. Your actions to exclude her were not acceptable. You will now have to face the repercussions."

"But...?" says Alex.

"No, Alex. There is no but. Your sister is intelligent and has a good head for business. I have monitored her with MeBe Tech. She is very talented and successful. It's a pity you, Nicholas and Alex did not follow her lead. You would have been better financially and know how to handle a business situation."

"What do you mean? I know how..."

Joshua shakes his head. "No, Alex. If you had, you would have purchased Heartson Industries New York branch. Instead, a woman who is yet to take her rightful position stops you in your tracks." He turns to my aunt. "Isn't that right, Hazel?"

She lifts her glass in solute and nods before replying, "Yes. Exactly, Joshua. That boy should return to school because he has demonstrated what not to do in a business situation."

Alex slams his napkin on the table. "How dare you, Grandfather... You are a retired old man. You know nothing about me."

Joshua places his napkin beside his plate and calmly turns to Alex. "That, boy, is where you are wrong. I know exactly what you have been up to. Soon, you will go on a business trip with me. You too, Nicholas. It is time you both learned how to run the family empire. Presently, I would not allow you to run a bath for me."

With outraged faces, Alex and Nick stand up simultaneously, about to cause a scene.

Joshua slams his hand on the table and with a growl, he commands, "Sit down, you two ungrateful little shits. Your incompetent father would roll in his grave if he knew how you have handled the family company." He turns his head and locks eyes with Tristian. "And as for you, my boy," he speaks in a tone that holds both firmness and concern. "Tristian, get your act together and start focusing on your family," his grandfather scolds, frustration clear in his voice. "You should have been aware of the ongoing events involving your siblings."

Shocked. Tristian looks at his grandfather. "So, I take it you knew about Mel being pregnant and what Alex and Nicholas have been up to behind our backs?"

Joshua nods and takes a sip of his drink. "Even though I'm retired on paper, I am still actively watching and dealing. And you, my dear boy, have a lot of work to do. I can still claim my granddaughter as the CEO. Never forget that." I nearly spat my drink out after hearing those words. My gaze instantly focuses on my husband, and I notice his knuckles turn white, wrapped around his napkin.

With his eyes focused on his grandfather, Tristian asks, "You wouldn't dare?" His voice is filled with disbelief.

"Prove to me you are in charge of this family and the company!"

Chapter Forty-Three

IZZY

*T*he scent of the miniature wedding cake hung
in the air as the staff cleared away the dessert
dishes. Mel left when Trinity's baby voice came through
the baby monitor, letting her know that my newborn
niece was awake, wanting to be changed and fed.

After yawning for what felt like the tenth time, as
exhaustion washes over me, I feel my eyelids growing
heavy and decide to call it a night. Glancing at the wall
clock, I knew it wouldn't be long before my hungry son
would wake again, demanding to be fed.

Speaking of my son. He makes his little grunting
sounds before crying.

Tristian gets up from his seat and walks towards the
small sunroom next to the dining room. "Hey, little guy,
you hungry? Once I change your diaper, you can go see
your momma."

I rise continuously, cradling my stomach, and slowly
make my way to the adjacent room, over to the cozy
armchair to nurse my son.

It takes Tristian only a short time to change Rowan and bring him to me.

"Here you go, Momma. One hungry little boy."

Once Rowan attaches, I watch Tristian walking back to the dining room. All the males began whispering, including Joshua, as his words were louder than a whisper. With my aunt still in there, she'll update me later on about their conversations.

The soft sound of knocking has me sitting up in my bed. Who is waking me? The bedroom door slowly opens, and Mel appears.

"Hey, Sis. I wanted to check on you and make sure you are okay," Mel quietly says.

"Come on in, Mel. You might as well sit with me."

Mel eyes me before saying, "Shit. Were you asleep?"

Duh. I nod. "Yes." What else would I be doing?

"Oh, I'm so sorry. I thought you would be full of excitement and wouldn't be able to sleep."

I shake my head at my friend and now sister-in-law. "Mel, I'm exhausted. Don't forget, I should still be in a hospital bed. Not walking about."

"Sorry, Iz. I wasn't thinking. I wanted to talk with you about a few things."

My tired eyes meet hers. "What's up, Mel?"

"Well... I've considered a life together with Corey. It is not what I truly want."

Either it is a bit late for her to be thinking of backing out... or. "Okay. As you have not consummated your marriage, Tristian is certain you can get out of it. Just let your brother know. He's there for you; remember that."

She nods. "Yes, I know that. Tristian's solicitor has contacted me and asked me several questions, which he explained a few things to me in return."

Ah, so that is why she wants out of her marriage. I recently learned this via Essy; they discovered some terrible things about Corey. When she explains to Mel, my new sister will be furious. "What is the other thing you wanted to discuss with me?"

She examines her short nails before locking eyes with me. "Knowing you're busy, I'll assume more responsibility at MeBe Tech." She should, because I know she can handle it.

"That is a good idea," I agree.

"You do?"

"Yes." I smile, and she smiles back. "What else do you want to talk about?" Knowing my friend, she would have something else to discuss.

"Um, Izzy. What do you have planned for Heartson Industries?"

Good question. "Take my rightful place at the helm. Fire certain employees and make several others happier with a promotion. Oh, and I'll be hiring a few more people. Compliments to Essy and her detailed list of ex-FBI, Navy Seals, et cetera, who are looking for a change of direction."

"What about the security business with Simon?"

Ah. Now, that one is a wait-and-see. "With Essy's assistance, she has provided me with competent staff. They will run things until Simon has recovered. If he ever recovers fully."

"Have you heard from Vicki?"

Just then, my cell chimes softly. I glance to my right and notice the screen. Vicki's name appears. I wonder if Simon is okay.

Mel passes me my cell, its screen illuminating the dim room. With a swipe of my thumb, I answer the call with a calm voice, "Hello, Vicki. How is Simon doing? Is he awake?"

"Hello to you too, Izzy," a male greets, his voice carrying a comforting warmth.

It was a voice that didn't belong to Vicki or Martin.

No, it couldn't be... could it? My heart races as I consider the possibility. "Simon?"

"Hey, Izzy," he replies in a cheerful tone. "What you up to?" Tears welled up in my eyes, blurring my vision.

"Oh, Simon. It is so good to hear your voice." My throat clogs up with emotion. "You have had me so worried."

A snort reverberates through the cell phone, catching my attention. "I scared myself," Simon murmurs, his voice barely audible.

"Simon," I ask, "how are you feeling?" Concern filling me. "What are the doctors saying?"

"Currently, I feel like shit. The doctors report I am lucky to be alive."

I nod. "Yes. I was told it was a miracle that you survived."

"Yeah. That is what I've been told."

"Ah, Simon. Did they tell you that the takeaway food poisoned you?"

"The doctor mentioned it before. It's hard for me to comprehend someone would poison me."

"Simon. It was Franky. He was seen on surveillance tampering with the food."

"I cannot believe that," he says with a mixture of astonishment and disbelief. "Why would Franky do such a thing?"

"He was getting back at me. Wanting me and my son dead. Franky had no qualms about taking you out, too."

"But why?" he asks, his voice filling with confusion.

"Simon, you won't believe this, but Franky mistakenly believed that you and I were in a relationship and that my son was your child."

"Are you serious right now?"

"As a heart attack."

"Shit."

"Simon, I have had Tereasa take over the business until you are well enough to return. I also have hired more staff."

"Why are you not there in the office?"

"Simon... I had been attacked. Nearly killed several times in the last week. Plus, I had to have an emergency cesarean."

"Shit, Izzy. I'm sorry. How's your baby?"

"My son was born early. He's okay. But it will take me several weeks to recover."

"Holy shit."

"Yeah, you can say that again," I murmur. "At least our business is being taken care of while we're away."

"Thank you, Izzy."

"Simon, if Franky stops by, call for help. Don't be fooled by him."

"Do you really think he is that dangerous?"

"Yes," is all I can say. I would never trust Franky again.

*T*he small interior elevator to the kitchen provides the only means of transitioning from the upper bedroom floors to the sun-filled ground-level kitchen without using the stairs. I take slow, careful steps, my hand pressing against my lower belly, as I make my way to the kitchen table for my meeting with Aunt Hazel.

Relief washes over me as I finally have a nanny to take care of my son while I recover. Last night, Suzie Stalt arrived, full of anticipation for her first day as a nanny to my boy this morning.

With my son's full-time bodyguard and Essy's imminent arrival in the kitchen, I'm carefully checking off my post-hospital to-do list, including security.

Tristian walks into the kitchen behind me. "Hey, babe. Why is Essy walking around our home with a strange woman?"

With a smile, I turn. "Hey, snuggles," I say, fluttering

my eyelashes. "Because I'm in the middle of organizing security and a full-time nanny."

"Huh? Why do we need a nanny?"

"Are you going to remain home for five weeks while I heal?"

He shakes his head. "No." And reaches for a coffee cup before saying, "Why?"

"Did you miss when the doctor said to avoid lifting for six weeks? No driving for two weeks or more."

He fills his cup from the coffee machine. "I'm sorry, Izzy. I didn't think."

And there you have it. He doesn't think.

Tristian's problem was not thinking things through. Despite being one of New York's wealthiest businessmen, he often overlooks the little things in life. He has a habit of being blasé about them. "Yeah, well. I require help. Suzie is the new nanny. The woman who is with Essy is Rowan's bodyguard, Helen."

"Why a bodyguard? We have enough security around the house."

I shake my head. "No, Tristian. I am not taking any chances with Rowan's safety. Plus, Helen has already protected our boy previously and been here the day we left the hospital."

"Oh." He glances at his watch, and his eyes widen. "Sorry, Izzy. I have to go. I have a meeting in forty-five minutes." He steps up, engulfs me in his arms, and kisses my head. I turn, our eyes meet as I lift my lips to his. Our kiss starts slowly and deepens until Tristian pulls away, breathing heavily and leaning his forehead against mine. "I'm going to miss you and our son. Don't overexert yourself."

"Good morning, Izzy, Tristian."

Ah. Aunt Hazel has arrived.

"Good morning, Hazel," Tristian says against my lips. "I'm on my way to the office. I see you later." He kisses me. "I'll miss you. Bye, Mrs. Astor."

I smile and reply, "Bye, husband."

Aunt Hazel waves her fingers. "Bye, Tristian."

My husband turns and heads toward the garage. He should have a driver, but he doesn't. See what I mean about security.

"Where is my gorgeous nephew?"

My lips twitch at the thought of my son. I struggled to leave him this morning. I could watch my baby boy all day. "He's fast asleep. His bodyguard will watch over his security and the new nanny, Suzie, is starting today."

"Ah. How does it feel to have someone else watching your child?"

A frown forms on my face as I contemplate her words. "Strange. However, I need to overcome this. Now, it won't be long until Essy arrives. What about Joshua, James, and Owen?"

"I'm expecting them any minute now," she says, glancing at her watch. "Let me fill the kettle with water and switch it on. I'll make us a cup of tea," she adds, reaching for several cups and a variety of tea bags.

"*S*o, with the unscheduled meeting happening tomorrow instead of the following week, I think we have everything sorted." All I can say is thank goodness for my business-savvy aunt.

"Hazel, I have all the documents for Izzy, including proof of ownership and her identification. What else do I need to bring?" James takes a sip of his coffee and adds, "Ah, the perfect way to wake up in the morning."

Hazel smiles and rolls her eyes at James' behavior while drinking coffee. "Can you have certified copies made for each of us before the end of the day? I do not want to leave anything to chance."

James nods. "Can do. Leave it with me."

"Good idea for us to hold a copy," says Grandpa Joshua. "Also, it would be best to avoid mentioning that Izzy is married to my grandson. That will only cause a box of problems." I agree with Grandpa Joshua. The last thing I want or require is for my marriage to become public knowledge.

"Agreed," murmurs Hazel.

"What time is the meeting tomorrow?" Owen asks.

"From three o'clock. But knowing what the main Board of Directors thinks, we will arrive by eight-thirty. I can guarantee the meeting will begin at 9 a.m. sharp."

James, Owen, and Essy pause and look at Hazel.

"Is that normal practice with these men?" Essy questions.

Hazel nods. "It is the way they have proceeded. You never underestimate the main Board of Directors. They have been ruthless over the years," she announces.

"They had changed the time and day of the last meeting to avoid Hazel being present," I say from behind my cup of tea.

The men look from me to Hazel and back to me again. "Are you serious? No wonder you said for us to arrive at eight-thirty."

With a nod, I go on and explain part of my plan. "I have had Essy do a security sweep of the building. My father's private elevator still works with the passcode he gave me when I was young. As far as I know, none of the directors have discovered my father's secret room and elevator beside his office."

"How can that be?" Joshua frowns. "Surely, someone must know of its existence."

I shake my head. "My father's secretary is the only one, and she had signed several NDAs, which are still valid today. I spoke with her a couple of weeks ago, as she knew me from when I would visit my father." My lips twitch, and a laugh escapes at the memory of the day I had scared her half to death when I was ten. "My mother had shown me how to enter Daddy's building unnoticed. The standard blueprints do not show the elevator and secret room. My father made sure of that."

"But how? Wouldn't the other rooms near his office hear the elevator?" Owens asked.

"No. My father had spent a small fortune in soundproofing the area."

"So you will enter via the presidential elevator to his secret room?" James asked.

"Yes. Essy and Jackson will accompany me. Hazel, Owen, and James will arrive together. As for you,

Joshua, I understand you have slipped through the unexpected nets of the directors and become a silent member yourself."

Joshua frowns. "Yes. How did you know that?"

Smiling, I reply, "I am my father's daughter. Not much gets by me. I know exactly when you started the process and when you officially became one of the silent members."

Joshua smiles and winks at me. "You will give my grandson a run for his money. He needs you in his life."

I nod. "Thank you."

The sound of a notification fills the pause. Grandpa Joshua glances around and then realizes it came from his pocket. "I better look," he says.

Hazel perks up with interest. "Is it them?"

I frown. Who would she be talking about?

He reads the message and nods. "Yes, you are right. The meeting is now at nine in the meeting room beside the president's office."

"Why change the time and room?" James asks.

"The directors are scared. They think we do not have access to that area."

Just then, a notification chimes on my cell phone. Everyone's attention focuses on me.

"Hold on, I better look. That notification is for security."

I lift my cell and activate the screen. The first notification is for my father's office. That is interesting. No one should be in there. I tap my app to access the video and audio files.

"What is it?"

I glance up as I tap the file. "I have video and audio set up in my father's office, the secret room, and the elevator. My app notifies and alerts me when someone has gained access to those areas."

"Oh shit. Are you serious?" James says.

"It's my office and spaces. No one should be in those areas."

James and Owen nod to one another and then to me. "This could change how you enter the building," Aunt Hazel announces.

"What I would like to know is how you placed your equipment, et cetera, in there," Joshua queries.

"Have you forgotten that I run a security business or that I have been working in that very building for four years?"

"But how did you..."

"My niece has been working undercover. Learning about the staff and different aspects of the Heartson Industries."

With a nod, I continue the conversation. "Yes. As an unknown person, I gained the trust of the original staff members and became one of the hundreds of workers. It is amazing what you discover."

"What did you learn?" asks Joshua, as he picks up his cup and takes a slow sip of his coffee.

My brow rises at his question. "Many things." And make eye contact with each person at the table. "Especially employed under a false name. It is interesting what you discover is amazing."

*R*esting on my king-size bed, I hear the creak of the connecting door as Tristian enters my room. Low around his hips, he has a towel wrapped loosely, revealing his toned physique. He vigorously rubs his scalp with another towel in his hands to dry his hair.

My lips twitch as my body reacts, seeing his six-pack and chest. The temptation to wipe my chin and check to ensure I'm not drooling down it as my eyes rove, taking in every inch of his muscled beauty. Admiring his glorious body. I'm a lucky girl. The knowledge that I can look and touch his sexy body when I want and knowing he's now all mine — fantastic.

"How was your day?" Tristian asks.

My brain and mouth are slow to respond to his question as my eyes continue to rove over his glorious body.

When my brain and mouth function as one I say, "Ah, I caught up with Aunt Hazel. I'm making plans to attend the general meeting at Heartson Industries."

Tristian pauses, "When is the general meeting?" He stands with his damp towel in one hand.

"It depends on whose information you use. The official meeting is next week. Otherwise, there are two different times for tomorrow."

He walks towards our shared bathroom doorway, casually tossing his towel onto the floor. "Huh?" He turns and takes a deliberate step closer to me, his gaze locks on mine. "What do you mean tomorrow? You're not in a condition to physically travel into the office. The last thing I want is for any harm to come to you."

With a sigh, I reply, "Tristian, if I don't attend the general meeting, I will lose my company. I have no choice."

He sits on the bed beside me. "What do you mean? How has that happened?"

"A legal technicality."

"Say what?" He focuses on my eyes and shakes his head. "A legal technicality. I don't understand."

"Look, Tristian, tomorrow morning, with Essy and Jackson at my side, I will attend the meeting."

He shakes his head. "I don't know, Izzy. Will you be safe?"

Tomorrow fills my mind. Would anyone be safe in this situation? I can still see the worry etched across Hazel's face this morning, a clear indication that she knew about my plan to enter using my father's secret elevator.

"Tristian, time will tell. I plan to use my father's elevator."

His eyes meet mine, full of concern. "I didn't realize he had one."

"It's more of a secret elevator. It's not common knowledge."

"You kidding me?"

My father wanted to be safe. He has one in each of his buildings. "No. I'm serious. My mother used to take me up to my father's office." A giggle leaves my lips. "I even scared my father's secretary one day. She couldn't work out how a child was in her employer's office. I was playing on my father's computer."

I watch his lips twitch. "What would you do on his computer?"

"Different files and spreadsheets. My father noticed how I detected the small details which he had missed."

"So, your journey into the business sector began when you were young."

"Yes." I nod and smile, remembering that my father was looking forward to the day I would be by his side as an adult.

"Izzy, please be safe."

"Tristian, my mission is to attend the meeting and announce my name and rightful place as owner and CEO. Essy said she would accompany me personally with Jackson as my bodyguard. Our son will remain here with his bodyguard. His safety is my concern."

"What about Hazel?"

"Ah. My aunt will arrive with James and Owen." Thoughts of Tristian grandfather fill my mind. "There is something you should know."

"What? Tell me what it is."

"Your grandfather is also on the Board of Directors."

"What?"

*a*s I watch the numbers change on each floor we pass, my voice fills the elevator space when I say, "Thank you for being here, Essy." Leaning against the side wall, I observe Jackson, his gaze fixed on the closed doors, while Essy lingers slightly behind him.

She looks at me and replies, "You're welcome. I'm not about to let you go up there alone." She turns and watches the numbers, then shakes her head. "As a member of the Board of Directors, I will be addressing why the female board members didn't receive the updated meeting time, as Joshua had," Essy announces.

It would explain why she made several phone calls yesterday after our little meeting.

I had no intention of mentioning her board membership in front of everyone yesterday, but Hazel, who was aware of it, also remained silent.

"My husband will meet us there," Essy informs us, surprising me with the revelation that her husband was accepted as a member of the Board of Directors two months ago. I did not know that the company was considering candidates for a new role. Essy, although a silent member, has influential friends, which can be advantageous.

We decided to take additional precautions today due to a sensor activating in my father's office yesterday. Suddenly, the elevator stops with a jolt, and the doors slide open, revealing darkness. This is unexpected, as this area should be lit up.

I tap Essy's back and she glances at me, understanding my concern. I shake my head, signaling that something is not right. Jackson notices and pulls out a gun, stepping out into the darkness first. I had shown him and Essy the plans, and according to them, there should be a light switch directly to our left.

Suddenly, a loud bang echoes, causing Essy to move and push me against the elevator wall. An oomph rushes out of my mouth as my shoulder and back hit the wall as she demands in a hushed voice, "Stay out of sight. Phone Ashworth for backup now." Thankfully, Ashworth, Flints, and several others had previously entered the building and stationed in different parts until required. With my cell in hand, I quickly swipe my finger to the pre-programmed number.

After two rings, Ashworth answers the phone. "What do you need?" he barks.

I whisper, "Backup at Essy's location."

Essy calls out, "Jackson?" Essy stands against the wall beside me with her gun raised. The small portion of the elevator door and wall gives her little protection.

"Got one, boss," he replies.

Ashworth replies through the cell, "Roger that. Sending now."

A second bang sounds followed by an oomph and an agonizing cry. "Drop your weapons and show yourselves now," Essy demands before the lights fill the room. At the same time, Essy somehow forced me down as she fired her gun.

The loud sound echoes inside the small elevator, including a thud against the wall. My lower belly screams in protest at the unexpected movement. A grunt and the sound of something hitting the floor have me looking up. Only to have Essy blocking my view.

"Search for any others, and call in the police and request for a medic. Also, let the EMP-Ts know that people have been shot."

"Roger that, Essy." Relief fills me. Jackson is okay.

"Izzy, I'm sorry about that," she says. "Are you hurt?" I flinch at the sharp pain. Geez, of course, I'm hurt. I shouldn't be here in the middle of danger. I'm recovering from surgery. My thoughts freeze as I spot something from the corner of my eye and notice a small hole in the wall where my head had been.

Then my brain registers what I'm looking at. Holy shit! "Essy, you saved me from that bullet. Thank you." She nods.

"Izzy, I need you to keep focused. We are not safe yet. Are you able to walk? It's time to get off the elevator."

I nod. Well, I think I can get up and move. "We'll soon find out. Let's move," I say, my voice shaky to my ears. I take a small shuffled step, followed by another one. We need to access my father's safe room. His secret room, now before we are discovered.

I hear another gunshot coming from the direction of my father's office. "Izzy, come on. You're doing well. Just a few more steps."

The pain is almost unbearable as I breathe heavily through my flared nostrils with every step. I focus on moving one foot in front of the other, determined to open the door to safety. I reach up against the dark tile on the wall, which is actually a secret palm reader. I feel a slight buzz under my palm, and then the sound of the door lock clicks, and the door partially opens.

Essy pauses me with her hand as she pushes the door fully open, and the lights turn on automatically. Finding the room empty, we both step inside, shut the door behind us, and activate the door lock.

I sit in the swivel office chair behind the desk. Essy glances around the room, taking in the queen-sized bed with a side table against one wall, a kitchenette on another wall, an office desk with a computer, desk phone, a control box, and a filing cabinet at one end, which overlooks several wall-mounted monitors, and a second doorway near the bed leading to a small bathroom. The room still resembles a hotel suite, including a computer desk.

I reach for the control box, entering a code that

activates the monitors on the wall. They flicker on to display the interior of the elevator, the foyer we were just in, and my father's office with a split screen of the secretary's office and the door to the foyer, which leads out to the hallway to the other office and meeting rooms and the public elevator.

"Wow. Did your father spend much time in here?"

"Yes, also with me and my mother." I used to sleep in here with my mother while Daddy had long meetings. My father used to have a TV with a video player, including an ATARI console, with several games. The memories of me beating my father when we played and how he would say *'he needed more practice.'* makes me smile at the little things I remember.

Rising, I cautiously approach a hidden wall panel— one of several in the room. I press the wall a certain way, remembering how I used to keep my things in this hidey hole. Inside, it reveals several items remain inside. I pull out a framed photo of me with my parents. My rainbow-colored toiletry bag. I unzip it and see my old toothbrush, comb, and hairbrush. Some used cracked dry soap in its container and a small shampoo bottle and conditioner. My DNA would be on those items.

Next, I pull out my old notebook with its hard cover covered in pictures of fairies and other enchanted characters. I shared my special book with my father. I flip through the pages to discover several pieces of folded paper tucked in between them.

Not sure who could have placed the unexpected

pages inside my book, I slowly pull them free, opening them carefully, and scanning them.

Tears form. It's a letter from my dad dated six months before my family's death. I cannot believe I haven't looked in this secret compartment.

My father wrote to me.

Pain forms in my chest, and the ache increases just thinking about my parents. I miss them so much.

With my next breath, I slowly expand my lungs, focus on the paper, and read his handwritten letter.

To my dearest daughter, Izzibella.

Hey gorgeous, Bell,

If you're reading this, either we are back in the States, or something has happened, and you have sneaked into my office.
If it is the second option. Well done. But I need you to be extra careful.

Why?

There have been several death threats, my darling girl. There are bad people in this world who want us dead. Your mother said I should write none of this to you, but I know better, for you are strong and intelligent. It is important for me to warn you so that you know what needs to be done.

Last week, I discovered two of my board of directors are, in fact, related distantly to us. At the moment, I am looking at a way to have them removed from the company, for I do not trust them. But if I cannot, I will urge you to take caution. For I believe they mean us harm.

Tonight, we board a plane for Australia. Your aunt Hazel has been in a tragic car accident. Sadly, your uncle and cousin died. For your mother's sake, I hope Hazel can pull through. I still cannot believe my best friend and right-hand man, your Uncle Shane, is gone. I'm lost. He was my sounding board, and he made sure I worked my butt off every day to provide for you and your mother and to succeed in this harsh world of corporate business.

With everything happening, you and your mother will remain with your aunt until I can make it safe for you to live back in New York again.

If anything should happen to your mother and me, I pray you grow up and remain safe. I have named your aunt to be your guardian. She will also act as your legal counsel. My girl, you will legally take over Heartson Industries when you turn twenty-five. Until then, you have legal say via your aunt. I will have to make other arrangements if she does not survive.

On the last sheet of paper, you will find the names of our distant relatives, who will demand that you give them the company and family fortune. If the worst-case scenario happens, I have had your mother deposit funds into your offshore bank account. Keep safe and do not give in to these thieving people.

Always remember, my precious girl, that Daddy loves you.

You are my special and extremely talented daughter. You will prosper and go far in whatever you choose to do.

And if you didn't know, you will soon have a baby brother to look after and cherish. Teach him about the business, make sure he studies hard, and look after him.

I just hope if anything happens to me, your mother is still there to be with you, but on the chance we are both gone — don't trust the main Board of Directors.

NEVER ALLOW THEM TO RAILROAD YOU INTO GIVING UP THE FAMILY COMPANY.

APART FROM A MAN FROM YOUR PAST. I DON'T KNOW IF YOU REMEMBER GRANDPA JOSHUA, BUT I HAVE MADE HIM A SILENT MEMBER OF THE BOARD AS OF TODAY. HE WILL LOOK OUT FOR YOU.

I HOPE THAT WHAT I AM SENSING DOES NOT HAPPEN, BUT THERE ARE A LOT OF GREEDY PEOPLE OUT THERE, BELLA. I HAVE ALSO WRITTEN A LETTER TO YOUR AUNT, AND I WILL TAKE HER DOCUMENT AND GIVE IT TO HER BEFORE I LEAVE FOR THE STATES. THERE IS NO POINT IN WORRYING HER FOR NO REASON IF I DON'T HAVE TO. YOUR MOTHER HAS ALSO WRITTEN A LETTER TO HER SISTER IN CASE ANYTHING SHOULD HAPPEN TO HER. I THINK WE HAVE OUR BASES COVERED FOR NOW.

IT IS GETTING HARDER TO KNOW WHO TO TRUST.

MY PERSONAL SECRETARY HAS JUST SIGNED ANOTHER NDA. I HAVEN'T INFORMED HER I WILL LEAVE THE COUNTRY. I'LL PHONE HER LATER. THE LAST THING WE REQUIRE IS FOR OUR WHEREABOUTS TO BECOME PUBLIC KNOWLEDGE.

We might remain in Australia for the duration of your mother's pregnancy. For now, I'll wait and see what happens. Plus, with your momma's company growing, she can expand and increase her business. It would be easier for her while in Australia.

Something you might not know about your momma is that she's been having sleepless nights and has started drawing. Her sketches look beautiful and professional. By the look of them, I think she will expand into clothing. I hope so, as your mother is exceptionally talented. I guess that is where you got your creativity and ambition from.

I have been writing long enough, but I need to say more at the same time.

Always remember, Izzibella, both your mother and I love you. Make us proud.

Give us gorgeous grandchildren who will one day take over the family company. Turn it into the empire I have inspired for it to become.

I better go. It's time to meet you and your mother at the airport.

WITH ALL MY DEVOTION, LITTLE ONE. REMEMBER THAT I LOVE YOU MORE THAN ALL THE STARS IN THE UNIVERSE.

YOUR,

DAD.

Tears continue flowing, landing on my chest and dampening my blouse. I cannot believe I'm sitting here with a letter from my father, which is over twelve years old. In his grief, he wrote even though his concentration was not there. A shuddering breath catches in my throat. If I had more time, I would have a good cry. Instead, I swap the last page to the front and focus on the writing again.

NAMES OF PEOPLE TO BE WARY OF.
DISTANT RELATED PEOPLE.

- IAN HASLOW — WIFE ~ SHARNIA HASLOW — DAUGHTER ~ BEVERLY HASLOW
- EDWARD BROWN — WIFE ~ SUSANNE BROWN — SON ~ WESTERN BROWN
- TED DAVIS — WIFE ~ JULIA DAVIS — SON ~ GAVIN DAVIS
- MARTHA GOODWIN — SON ~ FRANKLIN GOODWIN DAVIS, UNKNOWN FATHER (DECEASED?)

According to the saying, you can choose your friends, but you cannot choose your family. Essy's research into my family tree indicates that Franklin Goodwin Davis is the same person as Franky Davis. He likely changed his name following the passing of our parents. As for the others, I wonder who they are and where they fit into the scheme of things. Are they known by another name, just as Franky had changed his? It seems people in my life are not always who they appear to be.

"Essy, my father left me this letter. He wrote it six months before their death. My father warned about distant relatives he discovered and the Board of Directors not to trust."

I pass the pages to Essy. She leans against the desk and begins reading as I watch the monitors. I soon notice Gavin enter my father's office with a handgun.

"You have to be freakin' kidding me," I growl. How did Gavin gain entry into my father's office? "Essy, look at monitor two. Gavin is here with a gun."

Essy looks up from the pages to the monitors. She reaches for her cell, and within seconds, she is speaking with someone.

I watch the other monitors, and two men with half their faces covered, enter the foyer. One sits behind the secretary's desk and runs his hands over it. What is he searching for?

Then, it occurs to me. "Essy, where are your people? Because our location is about to be revealed."

Essy continues to speak into her cell. "Get the fuck in here now and bring reinforcements."

She listens to the other person and shakes her head. "Busy! We've all been busy. If I'm shot or end up dead, my husband will make sure you all die. Now move your ass." Okay. I would not like to be the person she's speaking with. "Three hostiles, moving in," she pauses, then replies, "You have less than two minutes." Then, she shoves her cell on the table.

"So...What happened to your backup people, Essy? They should be here by now."

Essy stands. Her focus is on her gun as she checks it. "Busy, it seems." She looks up. "Izzy, is there another way out of here?" And Essy is only asking that question now... As she slips her gun into her holster and glances around the room.

"Yes," is all I say.

Her eyes dart around the room. "Where?" she asks as her eyes meet mine. "Because we need to leave. Bring your letter and place your things back where you got them."

I swiftly follow Essy's instructions, closing the small door and beckoning over my shoulder, "There's another way." If I recall correctly, a small switch should be inside the kitchen drawer. With a push of my finger, it moves to the side. "Yes!" After pushing the drawer back in, I explain, "Turn off the monitors via the control box on the table. Then follow me." Essy does what I ask.

Another control panel appears before me, and I tap in the sequence to another secret door. Even though we are standing in my father's secret room, he made sure the room has a secret exit. Always have a plan C, he would tell me.

I love my dad and his contingencies.

"Why didn't you inform me of the secret way out of your father's secret room?" My eyebrow rises in reaction to her statement, I turn, and step through the doorway, with Essy directly behind me.

"Essy," I reply quietly. "I listened to your advice and followed your lead and trusted your team, and we ended up trapped inside my father's secret room." The door behind us shuts as I approach the wall box, placing us in darkness. Shit! My hand reaches out until I feel the side of the box. My fingers touch a small switch and tap it. A small light globe functions and radiates enough light to see around us. I open the wall box, grab two glow sticks from inside, and activate one. "While within these walls, I suggest you speak more softly."

Essy reaches out, and I pass her the glow stick. "Thanks. Where are we headed?" she whispers, turning her head in the direction we need to go.

"Along this passageway for now." She nods and allows me to lead the way.

After several meters of treading carefully, the narrow passageway widens by a foot. Finally, what felt like forever, I recognise a section of wall containing a peephole. Sliding the panel to the side, I look.

Several strange people in dark clothing and facemasks stand around talking in an office. I shake my head and slide the panel shut. "Come on. We aim for the next one," I whisper.

"Why? Who was in there?"

"I'm not sure," I hiss over my shoulder. "They had guns. Me and guns do not mix." The sound of Essy snorting stops me long enough to glance over my shoulder.

"You noticed I have a gun, right?" she says with a smile.

With a nod, I reply, "Yes. But I trust you. I don't trust those people in the room back there."

Thank goodness for the dusty passageways my father had installed. When my father married my mother, he had an extra ten floors built in this building with all these secret rooms and passageways. He had contractors come in who he could rely on and secretly trust.

We bypass the people with guns. My so-called

money-hungry relatives have taken things too far. No wonder my father was concerned. He had every right to be.

Essy wasn't sure about taking a shortcut, but she gave in when I started descending a ladder to a lower level. How I descended in my condition, I don't know. Finally, we come across an empty room. Relief fills me. I close the peephole and push against the panel to release the secret door. And voila, we enter a small office.

I close the door panel behind us. Essy heads straight to the doorway and carefully peers through the small gap before joining me on an office chair near the wall. "Where are we?"

"A floor below, my father's office." With my butt resting on the seat. Regretting my choice of footwear, I lift one of my feet and slowly rotate it. "We'll need to leave via the office door," I quietly murmur.

"Why?" Essy whispers. "Can't we go back into the passageways?"

I shake my head. "No. I don't remember how to open the door from this side."

"Now, what will we do?"

My eyes meet hers, and my brow rises. "Leave via the office door," I reply.

Essy's lips twitch as she scoffs and shakes her head. "No wonder why I like you. You remind me of my sister." She gets up with her gun back in her hand, approaches the door, and once again peeks through the small gap. "Come on. We might as well find the others," she says over her shoulder. Then, as an afterthought, she asks, "Where would the others be if they couldn't gain access to the presidential floor?"

Instead of answering her, I send a text to my aunt.

> **Me:**
> How are you?

Three dots appear and begin to wiggle, indicating she's reading my text.

> **H:**
> Why? Where are you?

I glance up. "Essy, I think we have a problem?"

"Why do you say that?"

"Because someone else just answered my aunt's cell." And show Essy the message.

"Are you sure?"

I nod. "Very."

"I was afraid of that." Once again, Essy has her cell to her ear. "...What is going on? Update me." She nods, then shakes her head and nods again. "Have the medics and the police been called?" She pauses, then replies, "Do it now."

Different scenarios travel through my mind. What has happened upstairs?

hanks to Essy's tactical special forces team, they successfully neutralized the armed individuals on the way to the presidential level.

According to the information, Joshua, James, Owen, Hazel, and a few other board members, including Essy's husband, Declyn Bianchi, are sitting at a conference table three rooms away from my father's former office.

"Is there a way to reach the top floor undetected?" Jackson asks as he studies the building's blueprints. I glance back at the plans, and then it clicks. These blueprints are not up to date.

"Look," I point at three walls. "This area is a secret passageway."

Jackson shakes his head. "Are you sure?" I nod.

"Yes."

"Where did we walk through when we escaped?" Essy asks as she looks over the plans.

As a child, I felt disoriented the first couple of times I walked through the passageways.

"Here and here. You must know how to enter those areas."

Jackson looks over the architectural drawings before making eye contact with me. "Can you tell me what I should do?"

I shake my head. "It's not that easy. My hand is the key to entering these areas. It was a safety feature my father installed."

"Darn it. Now, what are we going to do?" Jackson states.

The sight before me confirms my worst fears — my aunt, helplessly tied to a chair, unable to speak because of the gag in her mouth. Her head turns, revealing the bruising on her face. My hands clench tightly into fists as anger wells up inside me. The person responsible for hurting my aunt will pay.

"After releasing the door panel," Essy whispers near my ear, "Izzy, remember to step back and keep yourself safe. My people will take care of the rest." Nodding in reply..

Surprisingly, my father never expected that people would use his hidden passages like this. Thankfully, he had the foresight to have them installed.

My focus remains on my aunt. We have to save her.

I follow instructions and use the hand signal while placing my other hand on the reader. A light click sounds as I step to the side, allowing the others to quickly pass me.

Shouting and the sound of gunfire fills the air.

Right as I reach the peepholes, Essy touches my arm, making me pause. With her gun prepared, she guides me deeper into the passageway for added protection.

She shakes her head and says, "Don't look until we are given the all-clear." Our eyes meet, and she gives me her *'don't mess with me and do what I say look'* which has me pausing. As hard as I try to understand what is happening, I nod and shuffle further down the passageway to wait for the unknown to finish.

Chapter Forty-Eight

TRISTIAN

*W*hat is happening?

Izzy and Hazel do not answer their cell. The calls go directly to their message bank.

The Heartson Industries building is on lockdown, and I am thinking the worst.

"Bryan, organize a car to take me to the Heartson Industries building," I firmly state. The man likely assumes I have gone insane. Given the volume of calls and emails he has made for me today.

With Bryan speaking on his cellphone, I have no idea who he is speaking with and miss his conversation. After what felt like hours, even though it was most likely a minute, he turns towards me. "Sir, your brother has taken the company car."

"Pardon?" My voice hits a deeper tone. My brother had no plans to go anywhere in the car.

"Alex has taken the company car. I can track it to see where it is?"

I was not expecting this. Since when can we track the company car?

I nod and reply, "Do it. And contact the driver. We require the car back here."

"Yes, boss."

I turn the volume up on my wall-mounted television. A reporter is standing on a busy street with police and emergency vehicles behind him.

"In breaking news, there has been a reported shooting at the Heartson Industries building. At present, information is sketchy. We'll bring you more details when they come to hand. Over to you, David."

"Thank you, Gerry. Keep us posted," the news desk reporter says. "Now, on other news, five fishermen had to be rescued this morning."

I mute the television.

I need to be there. What can I do, though? I think of my son, so I pick up my cell and dial home.

"Astor residence," our housekeeper, Mrs. Fraser, states.

"Mrs. Fraser, this is Tristian. Is everything okay at the house?"

"Yes, Mr. Astor. The electrician Mr. Alex ordered has arrived at the front gate."

Huh? What electrician? We don't need one. Something is not right. "Mrs. Fraser. We don't require an electrician," I blurt out.

"Mr. Tristian, they are through the gate."

Oh, no... "Do not let them into the house. Find the nanny, have her watch the baby, keep him safe, and speak to Rowan's bodyguard and let them know. Family

Lock Down," I say before my housekeeper's voice blasts through my speaker.

"Emergency alert, people. We may have intruders pretending to be electricians. Place the house under lockdown immediately."

The woman is like a general in her own army. "Mrs. Fraser, I did not authorize an electrician. Alex has not left a message. Let the female bodyguard know she might require backup."

"Mr. Astor, I have ordered the maids to lock the doors and place the house in lockdown. I'll find the nanny and the bodyguard. No one will enter this house without my permission."

Just then, I receive a text from a number someone has programmed into my cell under the name — Rowan's bodyguard. Thank goodness for Izzy, thinking ahead.

"Thank you, Mrs. Fraser. Protect my son."

"I will, Sir."

I end the call and tap on the message.

ROWAN'S BODYGUARD:
Mr. Astor, I cannot contact Izzy. I have contacted my office for reinforcements. We have intruders on the property. At present, we are watching them on the monitors. Your sister has now informed me that there is a panic room. I have urged her to take her daughter and the nanny with your son there for safety until we know more.

The last thing I need is for my family to be in harm's way. At least Mel remembered the panic room.

Now contact the bodyguard. What was her name again...? After several names, I finally remembered — Helen Trents.

> **Me:**
> Helen, thank you for the update. Keep my son, niece, and sister safe, please. The news has stated there has been a shooting at the Heartson Industries building. That's all I know of the details.

I then send a message to my sister.

> **Me:**
> Helen just texted me. Keep safe. Have plenty of formulas and nappies for the kids. Remember, little sister. I love you. Protect my son.

I watch three little dots move about, indicating Mel is reading my message. It then dinged, and her message appeared.

> **Mel:**
> Trist, I know the procedure for intruders. Mother drummed it into my head plenty of times.

My cell dings with another message from my sister.

Mel:
Have you contacted Izzy? She is not replying.

Shit... Now, what do I say? And tap out...

Me:
I think Izzy is a little busy at the moment.

And leave the message like that.

My new assistant knocks on my door. "Mr. Astor, I have located the company car. It is currently at the Heartson Industries building."

"What?"

Why in the world would my brother be at Izzy's company? What is he up to?

Chapter Forty-Nine

IZZY

he echoes of shouting and gunfire fade away and I watch Essy busy speaking to someone on her cell.

Animated and emotional, she commands, "Send another task force immediately. Protect the child and capture the intruders." My focus zeroes in on Essy's words, and I wonder, who is the child she's referring to? And who are the intruders? Essy nods and glances at her watch, saying, "Okay, that's good to know. Keep me updated. All right, notify the authorities." She then turns to me and remarks, "It's a busy day where you are concerned, Izzy."

I can't help but wonder what she means by that.

Suddenly, thoughts of my son flood my mind. *'Protect the child and capture the intruders.'* Oh, my... I lock eyes with Essy and urgently ask, "What has happened? Is my son safe?"

She nods and taps another text on her cell. "Izzy, my people have your son, niece, and sister-in-law inside the panic room at the Astor manor." She glances up and our eyes meet. "The house is in lockdown mode. My team can handle the situation."

Just as I'm about to respond, a voice yells down the passageway, "Essy, we need you up here now."

"Shit," Essy exclaims, turning her head. "We'll be right there." She then faces me again and says, "Izzy, I want you to be on alert. Remember, people out there have suffered gunshot wounds. It will not be pleasant. Do not rush off. Stay near me at all times, please." I nod, feeling helpless as my son's safety hangs in the balance. Essy offers me some comfort, placing a warm hand on my arm and saying, "Come on, we'll take it slow."

"Thanks, Essy," I mumble.

As I step into the conference room, I immediately regret my decision upon seeing the splattered blood. People are scattered around the room, slumped either on the floor, against the large conference table, or in their chairs with blank expressions.

Part of my brain refuses to acknowledge that they are dead. My thoughts turn to Hazel, my aunt. Where is she? Worry fills me with dread until I spot her with Joshua, sitting on the floor, quiet and haunted. Jason is there too, with Owen's head in his lap. Just as I start to process this scene, a noise to my left captures my attention, and I notice someone familiar lying on the floor in a pool of blood.

Alex.

His arm moves, and I rush over to him. "Alex, are you okay?" Then I feel a hand on my shoulder.

"Izzy, Alex is one of the masked gunmen."

I shake my head. "No. That cannot be true." I turn and look at Essy. "Why would he do that?"

I turn and face a man I thought I knew and hit him in the chest and face. "Why, Alex? Why would you do this?" Blood coats my hand, and Essy grabs my arm, preventing me from striking him again. "You bastard. You think so little of me."

His eyes flutter open and narrow. "They intended for you to be dead. My family was going to take over this company, and we'll become one of the richest families in the world." He coughs, and blood bubbles out of the corner of his mouth.

"You stupid fool, Alex. The people behind this would have had you killed as well. You were their pawn."

He tries to shake his head. "No." He coughs again, and more blood leaves his mouth. "They were my business partners."

How stupid and naïve my brother-in-law was. "Oh, Alex, you're living in a fantasy world. I feel so sorry for your family. They had trusted you."

He coughs again, then swallows, his blood filling his mouth. "My family did not appreciate me."

I shake my head. "No, Alex. Your family loved you. Now you leave behind a niece and nephew who will never get to know you."

"My nephew will be lucky to see tomorrow," Alex mumbles before his eyes glaze over and turn blank.

"Essy, did you hear that? Send the police now to protect everyone at the Astor mansion, especially my son."

Essy slips her cell back into her pocket. "Izzy, Alex was delusional. The police are there now. Someone just informed me that several masked men were shot at the manor. Two others tried to escape and have since been captured." I turn away from Alex and look at Essy. "My people are taking photos of every person and matching them against the video surveillance. We have to make sure we account for everyone. There at the manor and here at Heartson Industries. Izzy, can you hear me? Your son is safe."

I nod. Why did Alex raid the manor and do this to his family? I want my son in my arms. I need Tristian.

Oh, no...

Tristian, Mel, and Nicholas will be devastated when they hear about Alex.

There is not much I can do about it right now, and I glance towards my aunt. She's wrapped in Joshua's arms, her head on his chest.

Essy helps me to stand. On autopilot, I walk to my aunt and drop to my knees.

"Aunt Hazel?" I murmur as I reach for her. "Are you okay?"

She nods and faces me. "Izzy, I thought I would never see you again. Those crazy, savage men. What they did. They brainwashed Alex. It is a miracle that we have survived."

My focus moves to Joshua. Sadness fills his features. My fingers gently squeeze his arm. "I'm so sorry, Grandpa Joshua. Alex is gone." His eyes meet mine before filling with tears.

"I couldn't stop him. He wouldn't listen. When I saw

the gun in his hand, he pointed it at me and Hazel. I knew I had lost him. Thank goodness for Essy's team. They saved us. But I still cannot work out how the special task force got in here. The door was locked."

"Thanks to my father, we could."

"What does that mean?"

A slight twitch dances across my lips. "I'll explain another day," I reply, my voice tinged with a hint of mystery.

The police and medics rush into the room. Essy and her team display their identification. Then, Essy takes charge and directs the medics to the injured individuals and the police to the people who had been captured and bound.

More people fill the room. I need to get out. I need to see my son.

But first, the reason why I am here today. I look at Aunt Hazel and ask, "What do I need to say before I leave?"

My aunt shakes her head and smiles. "Be yourself and declare who you are." She turns her head toward some of the Board of Directors.

I stand and announce, "My name is Izzibella Heartson. And I am the Heir to the Heartson Industries empire. And I hereby take my seat at the head of the company, for I am the legal daughter of Philip Rowan Heartson. If you need to speak with me, contact Hannah. As you know, she is my legal representative."

Essy and one of her staff assisted Hazel and Joshua in standing. Together, they announce, "We second that.

Izzibella Heartson is now officially in charge of Heartson Industries."

My shoulders feel relieved, as if someone has removed a heavy weight from them, even though I know it will be challenging in the next few days, weeks, and months.

The medics lift and remove Owen quickly from the room with Jason on their heels. At least we know they are both alive. From the corner of my eye, I notice Essy in a man's embrace. That must be her husband.

I slip my cell phone from my pocket and turn it on. Notification after notification sounds. I have missed calls and texts from Mel, Tristian, and Helen.

My emotions are too high to speak to them on the phone. It's best to send a group text instead.

> **Me:**
> I am safe with Aunt Hazel and Joshua. Once the police finish with us, we will return to the Astor Manor.

Within seconds, Tristian and Mel both call me. Not wanting to speak to either of them, I switch my cell to do not disturb and turn to Hazel.

"Come on, we'd best go to my father's office." It is going to be hard to walk in there without seeing my father behind his desk. My dad has left me to fill some big shoes. He wanted me to take over, so now I have to pull my big girl panties up and claim it for myself. "I mean my office. We have much to discuss before we can leave."

Hazel nods, and we slowly walk out of the conference room and towards my office.

Right as my hand is about to grasp the door handle, a hand on my shoulder stops me in my tracks. "Don't open that door," my old bodyguard says, his voice filling with urgency. "We have not checked it for explosives." I glance over my shoulder and see Jackson's concerned face.

With a nod, I reach for my cell, turn it on, and go straight to the security app for my father's office and secret room.

"Here, look," I say to Jackson. He moves in closer and watches the screen as I bring up the different files throughout the day and open the ones that had been activated.

With the audio up loud, we can see and hear Alex and Gavin break into my father's everyday files. Not finding what they want, they pull everything out of the drawers and throw them on the floor. They search the rest of the room, again not finding what they want, and then I watch Gavin remove something from his backpack.

"Jackson, it might be wise to use the secret entrance to take care of Gavin's little object."

He nods. "I think you are right. I'll have our bomb expert meet with you, and you can take him through to the office."

It looks like I won't be leaving anytime soon.

The million-dollar question is — if it is a bomb — is it scheduled to go off or activated when the office door opens?

Jackson shakes his head. "I better let Essy and the police know we must evacuate and search the building." I frown at Jackson's words. Can the man read my mind?

Chapter Fifty

IZZY

The Astor manor comes into focus as Benny drives toward the multi-car garage.

Benny wastes no time as he drives straight into the building, taking advantage of the rising roller door. Before the vehicle has even stopped, Tristian eagerly swings the car door open while Mel rushes to pull me out and wrap me in a tight embrace.

"Thank goodness you're safe. We have been so worried," Mel says near my ear. My leaking, enlarged, painful breasts become squished between us.

"Ow. Take care, Mel. I need to feed my boy. I'm leaking milk here," I mumble beside her face. She releases me. But before I can take a step, Tristian wraps his arms around me, pulling me close as he showers me with kisses on my head and neck, gradually making his way to my lips.

All the pent-up emotions that have been building between us fill our kiss. Tristian's love comes through. The moment his fingers graze my skin, my hormones go into overdrive. I must take control of my actions and force myself to pull away. Even though I long to be in Tristian's embrace, my desire to see my son is stronger.

"Hey, can we take this inside? I need to see Rowan." Tristian nods. I turn to make sure Aunt Hazel and Joshua have exited the car. "Come on, guys, let's go in."

I head straight to my room via the elevator. The nanny and Helen sit around my small table, drinking tea and relaxing. As soon as they see me, they stand.

"It's good to see you, Ms. Delany. Rowan is asleep at the moment, but I sense he will wake once you go near him," Helen says with a smile.

I nod and reply, "It's good to be back. Thank you for everything, Helen."

"It's part of my job, ma'am."

I glance towards my son's baby bed. The temptation to go to him is strong. But first, I need to clean up and shower to remove the dust from the passageways and the traitor's blood from my hands.

*F*eeling relieved and clean after my rushed shower, my clean clothes feel soft against my skin after I dress and head straight to the nursing, rocking chair, putting my feet up with a sigh of contentment.

The smiling nanny arrives with my boy and places him in my outstretched arms. Rowan attaches right away and guzzles his milk. One of the friendly maids carries in a cup of tea and a couple of cake slices and places them on the little table beside me.

"Thank you, Sara. Thank the chef for the delicious goodies."

"You're welcome, ma'am," she says and smiles before leaving.

My boy eagerly gulps down the milk, providing instant relief to my engorged breast. He pauses intermittently, his small fingers exploring my breast with gentle taps and presses. His curious eyes fix on mine, and the warmth of his touch captures my full attention.

"Hey, little man," I whisper, my voice barely above a hushed murmur. With our gazes connected, I feel an immediate connection. His intense gaze pierces through me, reaching the depths of my heart and soul. "Guess what?" I excitedly say, "I found a letter from your grandfather today! He wants me to teach you all about our family business empire. I miss him and my momma so much. I wish they could be here to meet you." My eyes fill with tears, and I try to blink them away. "Remember, I love you, and I always will, more than all the stars in the universe."

With my little boy content and fast asleep in his bed and the nanny staying close by, I take the elevator to the kitchen. Like Mel, I purchased one of those baby monitors. Hearing my little boy via an app on my cell while I am elsewhere in the house is a relief.

Mel, Tristian, Grandpa Joshua, Aunt Hazel, and Nicholas sit in silence around the kitchen table, each holding a drink with a stoic expression on their faces. The question lingers in the air: are they waiting for me or for someone else? Suddenly, the housekeeper takes a step forward, offering me a cup. The scent of coffee prompts me to shake my head and force a small smile. The last thing I can stomach right now is coffee.

In an attempt to distract myself, I focus on preparing my drink, keeping my hands busy and my mind occupied. I grab a cup, make my tea, and settle into a kitchen chair. As I glance at Hazel's concerned, bright green eyes and Joshua's eyes reflecting loss and heartbreak, they both give a slight shake of their heads.

The absence of any mention of Alex makes me realize it's best to keep quiet about my traitorous brother-in-law. After swallowing a mouthful of tea, I place my cup on the table, feeling the grating quietness unsettling my nerves. It's time to break the silence.

"I discovered a letter from my father dated the day I flew out of the States with my parents for Australia thirteen years ago," I announce, my gaze sweeping across each person at the table. Hazel's face reveals she knows exactly which day I'm referring to.

Curiosity fills her eyes as she croaks, "What did it say?" Instead of answering, I reach into my pocket, retrieve the letter, and pass it to her.

Giving me a raised eyebrow look, she nods in understanding. "Read it," I urge.

Hazel takes a moment to focus on the writing, and as she finishes, tears stream down her cheeks. She then passes the letter to Joshua, who reads it and passes it to Tristian. My husband's gaze meets mine, and I give him a nod of confirmation. After reading the letter, he shakes his head, lowering it in disbelief. "I'm sorry, Izzy. Your father was a great man."

I acknowledge his words with a solemn nod, and a barely audible, "Yes, he was," passing my lips. Before turning my attention to everyone at the table, finally settling on Joshua.

"Has Essy been?" I inquire, my voice fills with concern. Joshua shakes his head, his expression mirroring my worry.

"Izzy, can you join me in the office? I have something private to discuss with you." Confusion furrows my brow, but I agree, nodding in response.

I glance at Mel, seeking any clue from her, but she shrugs and shakes her head. It becomes clear that even Mel is unaware of what is unfolding.

*J*oshua sits behind the large stained oak desk while I relax in the swivel armchair. I stare at him and ask, "So, why are we here, exactly, Joshua?"

His lips twitch before smiling, and then he replies, "Just like your mother. Straight to the point. I knew why I liked you. Now, the reason for this private conversation." He pats his jacket, checking for something. "While your parents were in Australia, Phil phoned me and asked for his call to be recorded. The call was for you."

For me?

My eyes widen, and my jaw drops slightly as I demand, "Do you have this recording?" My shock is most likely palpable on my face. "And why did you wait so long to inform me?" Joshua reaches into his suit pocket and places a small device on the desk.

With a questioning glance and a hint of nervousness, he asks, "Are you ready? You need to prepare yourself." Confused, I frown at his words but nod in response. I watch Joshua press play on the device; I hear a man mumbling and rustling in the recording's background.

Then, as if someone turned up the volume, a man's voice begins to speak, "Alrighty, Joshy... I'm ready. Start recording now."

Joshua replies, "Philly, I've already started."

The voice on the recording continues, "Okay, then. This recorded message is for my daughter, Izzibella Heartson." My breath stalls in my lungs as I realize it's my father's voice. Tears fill my eyes. He addresses me, saying, "Please, Izzibella. Listen to my words. What I have to say is important. Bell, half an hour ago, your mother informed me she had gone into labor. Which means time is running out."

I look up and meet Joshua's eyes, then wipe my face free of tears and focus on the recording device. My father's voice continues, "There have been many death threats against our family. I have requested your aunt to look after you and become your legal guardian. Few know you as my daughter. I want it to stay that way until you're announced as the legal owner and CEO of Heartson Industries at twenty-five. Until then, if anything happens to me, your talented aunt will be your legal representative. Don't get me wrong, you're still in charge, but for safety reasons, you will go via your aunt. Protect our family empire, Bell."

His words fill my mind. Oh, Daddy, I will do my best and make you proud.

My father's voice continues, "I have since discovered

we have distant relatives and written the information down. There is also a letter in my office. You know where to look. Names of these so-called relatives. I have more details in correspondence in the usual spot. Be careful when you turn twenty-five, kid. Watch your back."

I nod at my father's words. A bit late now. At least we survived. I lean forward and switch the recorder off.

"Joshua, what's the reason behind the delay in delivering this recording to me?" I inquire, holding back my anger. "You knew I had to find the letter." I'm not impressed. It could have saved me time. If proper actions had been taken, the outcome could have been different, and Alex might be alive.

"Izzy, regarding the letter. Someone searched for it."

Seriously! "Joshua, if only you had let me know. You knew who I was. Why didn't you approach me?"

"I said to your father, if anything happened to him, I would not contact you until you turned twenty-five for your own safety."

I shake my head at the stupidity of the whole situation. But when I thought about his words, he admitted he had searched my father's office.

"You never discovered his letter. How would you when my father made sure I was the only one to have access?"

He shakes his head. "Izzy, have you checked all his secret compartments in your father's secret room?"

I smile and lift my brow at his words. I don't care who he is. My father drummed into me. When it comes to his secret rooms, I was not to reveal his compartments to anyone.

"My search resulted in empty compartments apart from mine," I say with a matter-of-fact face. "I found his letter. You just read it."

Joshua nods and reaches forward and turns the small recorder back on.

My father's voice sounds again. "Something I need to discuss before I finish. Grandchildren. One thing I did was to take care of my future potential grandchildren. When you give me a grandchild or grandchildren, I have real estate and money set aside for them. Joshua Astor will speak to you and present to you the full details and documents when the time comes."

I glance up and look at the man contemplating my father's next words. Unsurprisingly, Joshua hasn't been eager to discuss the details. His great-grandchild is the Heartson Heir, the new owner of said real estate and money, and my husband's grandfather has the paperwork. My eyes meet Joshua's, and I lift my brow.

He breaks eye contact and looks down at the small box.

My father's voice fills the void. "My, Bell, remember baby girl, I love you. Don't trust anyone." The sound of a door opening in the background causes my father to pause. "Rowan, it is time. We need to leave," a woman grunts.

Was that my mother? I glance at Joshua. He nods. "Your mother, Izzy." My eyes fill with tears once again.

"Rowan, who are you talking to?"

"Darling, say hello to our daughter. I'm recording a message for her."

The sounds of pain emit in the recording, followed by rushed panting. "Rowan," my mother gasps. "As much as I love my baby girl. You need to get your ass moving. Or your son will be born here at home." I smile at my mother's words. When she wants something done, she doesn't muck around. Pity she didn't have my brother at home. They might all be still alive today.

"Don't give me that look, honey... Oh, what the heck. Hello, Izzy Bell. Your baby brother is demanding to be born today. I know how much you have been looking forward to him arriving. You are going to make a fantastic big sister. I can't wait for you to meet him."

Oh, Momma. I loved him as soon as I laid eyes on my baby brother. You allowed me to pick his first name. James.

"Izzy Bell, remember my baby girl. I love you so much. Rowan, come on. We need to leave. Another contraction is starting." She makes grunting and groaning noises again.

"Bell, you heard your mother. It's time to leave. Remember to finish your workbook with all your designs." If I wasn't mistaken, I swear my father was talking in code. "Now baby girl, I better go, your mother has waddled out the door. I will always love you, and may our family empire prosper."

Silence fills the air. For several seconds before I hear Joshua speak, "Take care, Philly. Give my best to Helanna."

"Look after my little girl, Joshy. Until we see each other again."

Joshua switches the device off.

My eyes meet his. "That is it. I'll leave the recording with you."

I nod. "Thank you, Joshua. It is a treasured gift to hear my parents' voices again."

"We better go back to the others."

Is he serious right now?

"Ah, Joshua, are you forgetting the little thing my father spoke of regarding the real estate and money for his grandchild? I want all the documentation on my desk by the end of the week."

If his brain catches on, he only has one day to produce all the documents.

Chapter Fifty-Two

IZZY

*E*veryone around the table watches us walk into the kitchen and sit down. The housekeeper, Mrs. Fraser, is by our sides, placing a hot drink in front of us, and I nod in thanks.

As I take a sip, I notice Essy has not arrived.

"Why did you need to speak with Izzy privately, Grandfather?" Tristian asks.

Joshua replies with, "A private business matter. Nothing for you to be concerned about."

Tristian shakes his head. He is just about to speak again when the sound of footsteps has our heads turning towards the hallway. Essy and Jackson walk through the kitchen door. Her straight face does not give away what has happened.

"Izzy, Hazel, and Joshua, how are you feeling after everything today?"

We look at one another before turning back to Essy.

"What do the police say? Were the ones who

remained alive taken into custody?" I demand, avoiding her question.

Then Mrs. Fraser passes Essy and Jackson a cup of coffee. They nod in thanks before taking a sip.

She looks at everyone before focusing on me. "Does everyone know about Alex?"

"No," I reply. "We have been waiting." I would have thought Tristian and Joshua would have informed Nicholas and Mel by now. When I broke the news to Tristian, he sobbed in my arms back in my room.

Essy glances at everyone and then nods. "Okay, I'll start with — after investigating too many computer files, we learned Davis introduced Alex to the organization. From reading through several files and notes, Davis had promised Alex that if he joined them, he would become the owner of Heartson Industries."

How naïve Alex was to believe such BS. "Yes. Alex thought he would become the owner of my company and the Astor family would be the richest in the world. He refused to listen when I told him he was only their pawn and they would have killed him." My attention moves to Tristian. His head is down, and he shakes his head. He's probably thinking he's failed his family.

"What are you all talking about?" Nicholas demands, his voice echoing through the room. "Where is Alex?"

With a worried look, Joshua shakes his head slightly in response to Essy's glance. She then turns to Tristian, and then me. How can I break the news to Nicolas and Mel that Alex has passed away? Unable to complete the task, I shake my head, a wave of defeat washing over me. With a slight nod of understanding, she then turns around to face Nicholas. Her eyes lock with his and fill with sadness. "Your brother died today, Nicholas."

Mel gasps, her eyes widening in shock, and shakes her head in disbelief, mirroring Nicholas. "No. That can't be true."

I glance at Mel. Her bottom lip trembles and her eyes fill with tears. She meets my gaze, and I nod, place my hand over my heart, and then point to her. Our way of saying *'Love You'*.

As I glance at Tristian, he lifts his head, and our eyes meet. His eyes are hollow and empty, and heaviness fills my chest.

Somehow, I force my lips to move. "He died in my arms," I explain. "One of Essy's men had removed the gun from his hand."

"What gun? Would someone care to explain what happened?" Nicholas demands.

Essy sighs, places her coffee cup on the table, and stands. She removes her cell from her pocket, taps on the screen, and walks around where Nicholas sits.

"Nicholas, there is no easy way to explain. Sometimes pictures can explain more. Today. Your brother Alex and a group of armed men infiltrated Heartson Industries, determined to kill Izzy. They wanted to take over her family's company. These men convinced your brother to join them. Witnesses saw Alex shoot a board director, and he was about to shoot Hazel and your grandfather when a group of special task force men gained entry to the locked conference room and shot him before he could pull the trigger again."

Nicholas kept shaking his head. "No. It cannot be true." He turns to his grandfather. "Tell them, Grandfather. Tell her she's wrong."

Grandpa Joshua shakes his head and replies, "I'm sorry, my boy. Alex had turned into a traitor. He would have killed me and Hazel if he had not been stopped."

"But why would he want to kill you?" Nic mumbles.

Joshua shakes his head and shrugs. "I was a witness. I was on the directors' board. Maybe there are many reasons. Otherwise, I do not know what was going through Alex's head. He refused to listen to me to put the gun down."

"No. I don't believe it," Nick screams.

Tristian gets up and goes to Nicholas, wrapping him in his arms. Nicholas weeps and screams before Tristian turns to Mel and wraps his arms around her.

"I have several photos of the conference room as evidence to show you what those people did. The people they had killed in cold blood."

Nick looks at Essy. "Show me."

Joshua shakes his head. "No, Nicholas. You do not want to see those pictures. You do not want the last visual memory of your brother as a murder."

My aunt remains silent and sips her tea, staring at the table.

Then I remember the explosives and turn to Jackson. "What about my father's office? Was it rigged to explode? Was a sweep of the building for explosives done?"

Jackson nods and looks at me. "Yes, Ms. Delany. Thanks to you, we could dismantle the explosive device and remove it safely from the building. After completing a thorough search using a trained dog that can detect explosives, we came across three other packages." My aunt makes a sound and covers her mouth. Her eyes, wide and shining with unshed tears, say everything she couldn't put into words.

Unbelievable. Those traitors had everything planned. If they couldn't kill me and take over, they would have blown my building up, killing who knows how many people.

"Do you know if the explosives match those from the gala last week?" I ask.

This time, Mel gasped.

"Yes, they did. We just got word as we arrived here," Jackson replies. So, it is true. The traitors had planned to kill me at the gala. Several people lost their lives that night.

My eyes meet Essy's. "Is Ted Davis, Gavin, Franky, Ian Haslow alive? Are they in custody?"

She shakes her head. "Izzy, most of the men were killed, including Gavin and Franky. Haslow and Ted Davis were escorted to the hospital under police guard with critical injuries. The doctors don't hold out hope they will make it through the night."

"Have your people had the chance to identify the other family members amongst the dead?"

With a firm nod, Essy says, "We have identified Western Brown." Essy pauses and turns to Tristian. "Mr. Astor, I would advise you to change all passwords and key locks as soon as possible. We recently discovered that your secretary, Ms. Shirly Wine, was employed under a fake name. She is none other than Beverly Haslow. Ian Haslow, an organizer and one of the Board of Directors, is her father." This time, it is me who gasps. No wonder the woman never liked me.

A sudden realization hits me: the truth. Some Board of Directors members knew my true identity. But how is that possible? And how long have they known?

Chapter Fifty-Three

IZZY

*I*n the wake of the tragic shootings, the funeral for Alex was held the following week, a somber affair attended only by close family and select friends.

We're all grieving in our own personal ways. Tristian is having the hardest time with this. Alex's death and decisions weigh heavily on Tristian's conscience. I hold their father responsible, as he was not a role model for any child. We've successfully kept Alex's death out of the media. The ceremony concluded with a somber burial of his ashes beside his parents' graves. Tristian, Nick, and Mel will install a commemorative plaque in the future.

My focus goes from my computer screen to the framed photo of myself with Tristian on my wall taken on our wedding day. We look so happy. Since the attack on Heartson Industries, my relationship with Tristian has been strained. We've hardly seen one another since the funeral service and he keeps me at arm's length, and I had enough of being treated as an afterthought.

The sound of my desk phone captures my attention. I've been busy reviewing spreadsheets for the last hour and need a break.

"Yes, Blade," I casually ask, as I save what I am doing and focus on the phone call. "What's up?"

My new personal assistant is one of Essy's ex-military personnel. Qualified, and if I need a last-second bodyguard, I have one.

"Ms. Delany, your husband is on line three. The four o'clock appointment confirmed the meeting, and has scheduled to arrive fifteen minutes before to set up a slide presentation. And Mel is on line two."

"Thanks for letting me know. Oh, and obtain a picture of the person who's scheduled to attend the four o'clock meeting," I request. "It's best we're well-prepared and avoid any unexpected surprises." Plus, if Essy is correct, the FBI will visit my building in the next hour or so. They have been targeting the boss of the individual who is supposed to be present today. "Also, Blade, you can call me Izzy."

"I know," he says before ending the call. My lips twitch at the man. I'll get him to call me Izzy yet!

I push the extension for line two. "Hello, Mel. Have I missed a meeting today?"

Over twelve days ago, I left Astor Manor and moved back into my beach home. Mel and her daughter moved in a few days later.

Mel has taken her position on the board of Astor

International and is settled in her stylish, modern designed office with her daughter.

Mel also discovered Corey had been seeing another woman for several months and requested an annulment. The man failed to get a dime out of my best friend.

I hear Mel giggle along with a happy baby gurgle noise. "No. I've taken care of it. I just wanted to confirm dinner for tonight." Yes, we girls are still together. It's been so long since we've been anywhere, just the two of us. My son is thriving every day. He's growing so fast. My body is slowly healing, and I have my next doctor's check-up in a few days. I need some adult time with my bestie.

"Yes. I have the nanny all set, and Helen will watch over them," I say with a smile.

"Great. I can't wait to have some girl time." She pauses and whispers something to Trinity. The sound of Trinity feeding makes me miss my son even more. I made the hard decision and switched him from breast to formula. Our feeding time and running a family empire do not mix. "Have you heard from my brother?" she asks.

A sigh escapes, and I glance at the desk phone, seeing Tristian is still on hold.

"Kind of. He phoned me today."

"Really. What did Tristian say?" Trust Mel, wanting to know the details.

"I don't know yet. He's still on hold."

"What?" she screeches. "Why is my brother on hold?"

I chuckle. "Because you both called me at the same time."

"Oh. Well, I better let you speak to the pain in the butt, then." Mel fought with Tristian regarding where she was going to live and the family business, which is another reason she left the family mansion.

"Yes, I better. See you at home. Travel safe." I say.

"You too. Ciao."

Before starting a conversation I'd rather avoid, I pause and take a deep breath while looking at a beautiful picture of my son, and then I press the blinking number three button on the phone.

"Hey, Tristian," I say nonchalantly, despite my longing for him.

"Hello, wife. It's been a while. How are you and our son?" Even though I moved back to my home, I have never informed Tristian he couldn't see his son.

"We are both well." I made the room beside my office into a fully equipped nursery for my boy. It's more like a small apartment. I would not leave him at home. The nanny and bodyguard go everywhere with my son.

"When can I see my son, Izzy?" It amazes me that Tristian hasn't made an effort to see him since we left. Following Nicholas and Joshua's departure, Tristian became more distant. I hope Joshua can penetrate the emotional barriers Nicolas has erected, allowing him to grow and heal, just as Tristian has become lost within his own emotional barriers.

"Tristian, I have not prevented you from seeing our son."

"Yes, you have, Bella. You moved out of my home."
And there you have it. His home. Not our.

"Tristian, you can come to my office and see Rowan
or when we are at my home. The choice is yours."

My feelings for the man have dimmed. Don't get me
wrong — he will always be in my heart — but we have
separate lives. We run our own family companies.

"Do you know I have never seen your new place?"
he says, and I shake my head in annoyance.

After he shut me out regarding his brother's death,
and considering the information I recently discovered,
frankly, I don't have time for his behavior.

It shows how blasé he was in the past, as far as I was
concerned. "Seriously, Tristian. I have lived in my
beachfront home for several years. What is so new
about it?"

The line goes silent until I hear his sigh. I remain
quiet, waiting. It is time for Tristian to man up. "Bella, I
don't know what to say to you anymore. I want you in
my bed and my son under my roof."

Yeah, that is not happening anytime soon. Images of
him at a bar flashed through my mind.

"Tristian, I think you need to see your son first. But I
am staying in my home with my son."

"Our son and you're my wife."

"That's right, I am. And you seem to forget I was
under your roof when Rowan and I stayed there."

"I had been busy, Izzy."

"Seriously, Tristian. So was I, but I still was at the
manor for dinner. Mel and I would eat at the family
dining table. Hazel would join us when she was back in

New York. Where were you?" Before he could provide a stupid reply, I said, "Don't forget, I run Heartson Industries. A security business, and the IT business with Mel. Plus, I have my charity AngelStar organization to keep running."

"Huh? Since when have you had an organization called AngelStar? Hang on... Aren't they the ones who organized all those housing units for the bushfire victims?"

Give the man a prize!

"Yes. I organized for the families to have housing, even if it was only temporary. See, Tristian, something else you do not know about me. You didn't bother to get to know me at all. Look. You can come to my office this afternoon and spend time with Rowan. Just don't expect me to be in the same room. I have an important business meeting."

A meeting depending on what the FBI discovers first.

"Is he left by himself?"

If the man were in front of me, I would slap him. "Seriously, Tristian. Rowan has a full-time nanny and bodyguard. I also have a mobile baby monitor so I can keep a watch on him. Plus, his room has full surveillance. I am not taking my son's safety for granted."

"Okay, Izzy. I get it. I failed our son's safety several times. I failed yours."

"At least you acknowledged it," I mumble.

"You don't have to rub it in, Iz."

"Look, Tristian. Stop by. Make sure to sign in at the

front desk downstairs. I'll let them know you have an appointment."

"Seriously, Izzy. I have to sign in?"

"If you want to step inside my building, yes."

There is no way my staff will become vulnerable again. Since I acknowledged my position as CEO and owner, I have made many changes. I have upgraded my security with more cameras, patrol guards, and eye and hand scanners for the staff, including the cleaning staff.

I have since turned that conference room into a welcoming relaxation room for the staff. A widened archway replaces the double doorway. Tiles replace the carpet, and new colors are on the walls. Comfortable chairs to relax in, with several small tables nearby. The room features strategically placed large, tall, and medium-sized plants that offer privacy. There is an extensive drinks fridge for the staff to enjoy. Next week, I have arranged for a small plaque to be revealed in memory of those who died.

Chapter Fifty-Four

IZZY

y patience is wearing thin. My 4 p.m. has only just arrived. He's already running over ten minutes late. I'll give them five minutes to set up before I walk in for the meeting.

My phone buzzes.

"Yes, Blade."

"Ms. Delany, we now have a photo of the person who arrived for the 4 p.m. appointment. We will have their identification shortly."

"Thank you, Blade."

An old foe of my mother's organized this meeting, wanting to speak with me regarding a business opportunity. As far as I know, one of his assistants is taking his place. But knowing this scrupulous man, he'll most likely show up unannounced. Thankfully, I have organized extra security with Essy and have a smaller special task force in place. I do not trust this man. Where he's from, he's a prince. Here in the States, he's a ruthless businessman you do not want to cross. Plus, he's wanted by the FBI. A man who I have avoided at all costs.

An old journal of my mother's helped me remember how, as a little girl, he tried to proposition my mother until my father walked in. Daddy had wondered why momma's meeting was running overtime.

Let's just say things did not end well. My father got into a physical fight with that horrible man. Callas did not believe my mother was married to my father. Callas was determined to have her for himself at any cost.

"*M*s. Delany, your husband is with your son in the nursery."

Trust Tristian to arrive early. "Thank you, Blade. Lock the external door after he goes in."

"Will do, Ms. Delany."

"Blade, any word of the person's identification in conference room four?"

"I'm reading the information as we speak... Ms. Delany, the person who arrived for the meeting, identified himself as David Trunch. The information on the facial scan has confirmed it is indeed Mr. Costos Callas in conference room four."

CC. Shit. I was afraid of that. "Blade, have extra security brought up and notify them we may have a breach in the building. And contact Essy."

"Are you in danger, Izzy?" Wow. It takes me being threatened for Blade to call me by my first name.

"Maybe. I do not trust CC. Be prepared for anything. Oh, and have my husband and son moved through to the sleep room."

We call the secret room the sleep room for safety reasons.

"Will do, Ms. Delany."

With a small earpiece tucked carefully inside my ear, I can communicate with Essy's special task force team, who also work for the FBI when required.

"Izzy, can you hear me?" Jackson says.

"Yes. What about me?"

"Loud and clear. We have eyes on the suspect. Proceed with caution."

Jackson does not need to tell me that. I don't trust CC in the first place. At least I know I have agents behind the wall with guns trained on CC.

"Can someone explain to my husband he needs to remain calm? He could place Rowan's life in danger if he does not."

"Roger that. Helen is explaining things to him now. He will see you on the monitors."

Great. I was afraid of that.

"Okay. Let's get this show on the road. Going in now."

"Roger that," Jackson states.

I pause long enough beside Blade's desk. "Please bring the satchel bag with the notebooks in it and ask for refreshments to be brought in," I request as I pause beside Blade's desk. "Thank you, Blade."

My assistant knows the satchel also contains a hidden handgun if required. With the phone receiver beside his ear, he orders the refreshments to be brought up.

He stands and places the satchel under his arm, and with a nod, he says, "Ready, Ms. Delany."

That is my cue. Everyone is in position. Let's go.

With my back straight and a fake smile plastered, we walk into conference room four. We proceed to the opposite side of the table where CC sits and pretend I do not know his true identity.

I place my notes in front of me and sit. "Hello, Mr. Trunch. You have ten minutes to state the reason for this meeting." I meet Callas' dark eyes. "As previously mentioned, I do not know why you are here. We do not do business together." And I have made sure of it over the years.

He smiles and raises his eyebrow at me. "Come now, agapOUla mou," he silkily says. I know exactly what he called me, and I do not appreciate it. I am no one's little love.

"Mr. Trunch, I am not your little love. My husband and I do not appreciate any man calling me such intimate names."

His smile vanishes. "Since when are you married to someone else, Izzibella?"

"You have no right to call me that name. As for my marital status, it is none of your business, Mr. Trunch. You requested a business meeting. Why? What did you want to discuss?"

"I have not heard of you marrying another man." Before he continues, I lift my left hand to glance at my watch to display my wedding ring.

"You have eight minutes, Mr. Trunch," I announce as he notes my hand. I might not be living under Tristian's roof, but we are still married and wear his rings.

"No. That cannot be."

"Mr. Trunch, I have another meeting in fifteen minutes. You have wasted enough of my time. You can inform your employer that I am not interested in doing business with him."

"Why are you acting this way, Izzibella? You know exactly who I am. Your mother promised me you."

Shocked at his blatant lie, I shake my head.

"Excuse me. My mother never promised me to anyone. How dare you come into my building and state such lies? This meeting is over. My security will escort you out." I nod to Blade, and he stands.

"Mr. Trunch, it is time for you to leave," my assistant says.

CC shakes his head and slides a folded document across the table. His calm façade crumbles. He becomes panicked. "Read it. Everything is in there."

I shake my head. I know for a fact my mother would never say or do such a thing to her only daughter.

"Mr. Trunch, leave my building and take your fabricated document with you."

"Why do you insist on calling me Mr. Trunch? For you know exactly who I am."

"If so, why would you enter my building under false pretenses?" I state.

"Read the document," the annoying man demands.

Blade reaches forward, picks the document up, and begins reading it.

"How dare you? That is confidential. Only Izzibella is to read it."

The door opens, and three security guards enter. "Ms. Delany, is this the gentleman?"

I nod. "Yes. Escort this man out and deny him entry ever again."

"Certainly, Ms. Delany."

As Blade read the document, the tiny camera in Blade's reading glasses allows Jackson to see and hear everything, even though the room has full video and audio surveillance.

"Get out of there now, Izzy," Jackson yells in my ear.

I turn to look at Blade. His eyes meet mine. His skin tone turns pale as his lips change color. Shit.

I don't wait around and take off for the door. One of the security guards steps between CC and me, and the annoying man narrowly misses my arm as I rush by him.

"Jackson, what is happening?" I say as I keep moving and head for one of the secret passageways.

I turn a corner and see a strange man heading my way. "Who in the hell is that man coming towards me, Jackson?"

"Izzy, get to the nearest room with access to the passageways."

"What do you think I'm doing!" I hiss as I rush into an empty office. Slam and lock the door and press against the secret panel to gain access to unlock the mechanism for entry to the passageway. With a snick, the door panel releases. Just as I shut the secret door behind me, the office door explodes inwards with a massive bang. Shit that was close. I don't wait around and lock the secret entrance and take off.

Chapter Fifty-Five

IZZY

hank goodness I remembered this room.

Jackson said I had to remove my clothing and shower as quickly as possible. Whatever was in that folded document was dangerous. When I watched Blade change color, then he went stiff as a statue. It was terrifying. I've seen nothing like it.

Wrapped in a big towel, I sit on a chair, drying my hair before placing the earpiece back in my ear.

"Testing. Can you hear me?" I say, hoping Jackson is still there.

"Izzy, where are you?" Concern laces his words.

I glance around the room. If I remember correctly, my father built it as a panic room. "I'm not exactly sure, but I'm safe. I've showered and placed my clothing inside a bag first."

"Good. The last thing we need is for you to become paralyzed, like Blade. We would never have found you if that happened," Jackson says, his words full of concern.

I kept thinking it would have been me if not for Blade. He saved me.

"Jackson, is Blade alive? Will he be okay?"

I hear Jackson sigh. "Look, Izzy. The FBI transferred Blade to a special facility. They know how to handle the situation." Huh? What situation?

"Jackson, what happened back there?"

"Callas wanted you. He had people in place to remove you from the building. They coated that document in a toxic chemical." He what?

Goose bumps form as I turn cold from within. "Is my son safe?" I demand.

"Yes, Izzy. Your son and husband are safe." Relief fills me until I remember... Tristian.

How did I forget Tristian? "I need my son removed from this building and to be kept safe. Callas and his people should never have been able to enter my building." And think, where did I go wrong with my safety?

"We are looking into everything," Jackson states. "So far, we've discovered Callas had several people working from inside the building. We have taken two people for questioning. We are still looking for the third."

"What about Callas? Have you gotten any answers from him?"

"The FBI now has him. They've been after him for a long time."

"You didn't answer my question. Why do I feel something else is going on, Jackson?"

"Because where Callas is, there is always trouble, and the FBI is keeping the whole situation under wraps.

Before they had taken him away, I extracted some information from him."

"Why do I feel he did not give his answers freely?"

"Because you are clever."

"Jackson, answer me," I demand. "As I was leaving the room, I'm sure someone shot him."

"See, you don't miss much."

"Jackson. Answer me now."

He sighs. "The guns contained darts, not bullets." Huh? "Truth serum, for one." Ah. Now, that would make sense. "Before the FBI came rushing in, I demanded he tell me the real reason he wanted you and what your mother had to do with it and your company."

"What did he tell you?" I've never liked Callas. Even from a business point of view. He made my skin crawl.

"He mentioned he was in love with your mother. If he couldn't have her, then he would have you and all that your mother held precious to her, including removing your father from the picture all those years ago."

What? Does that mean he…

"Izzy… His people who had killed your parents had stuffed up." Oh, gods, no. "They only intended for your father to be in the car, not realizing until it was too late that your mother was also in the car with him." *He killed my family.* "Callas was behind the current takeover of your company, as well."

Tears well up in my eyes.

My emotions are a blend of different feelings. I feel sadness for my parents. Disappointment. The loss of human lives. Next, there was anger towards the man who orchestrated everything.

I am extremely furious at the moment.

And demand, "What else did you get out of him?" I want that man to pay for what he did to my family.

"Izzy, we had given him more serum to keep him talking until the FBI arrived. They will continue to question him."

"What else did he say, Jackson?" My irritation is increasing.

"Izzy, the man, was unhinged. He demanded we hand you over to him. He kept saying you were his wife."

What?

Never. The man is sick. I've never met him before.

My body shakes.

"Jackson, make sure he never sees freedom."

"I understand, Izzy. The FBI has taken the man to a secret facility. Now they have him. No one apart from you and a selected group will know what happened here today regarding what he said."

"Are you saying it will be as if the man was never in my office building?"

"Yes, Izzy," was all Jackson said.

Chapter Fifty-Six

IZZY

*I*n one of the cupboards, I discover a pair of coveralls and other men's clothing, still sealed in their plastic packaging. After getting dressed, I roll up the long legs and sleeves before leaving the secure room and making my way back to my office. It is a surprise to see Tristian, something I wasn't expecting.

"What are you doing here?" I demand from behind my husband, causing him to let out a startled squeak as he jumps in fright, unaware of my presence in the room. Maybe he should take in his surroundings and not focus only on the office door.

He spins around to face me. "How did you get in here?"

I nearly laugh at his panicked expression. I'd frightened him for once, but his face changes, and he springs from the chair, engulfing me with his arms, squeezing the air out of my lungs.

"I've been so worried," he says, his voice filled with a mix of relief and concern.

"Can't breathe," I gasp.

"Ah, sorry." He releases me enough to allow air back into my lungs.

As Tristian holds me, his intoxicating scent fills my nose, heightening my senses. The sensation of feeling safe surrounds me until my senses come back online. "Why are you here, Tristian?"

I step away from the man to place a much-needed distance between us so I can think straight.

"Fear and worry consumed me, Izzy. You never answered my question about how you got in here. I was watching the door." He glances around the room.

"I returned to my office only to collect my cell phone, purse, and briefcase. My priority is to be with my son." Once I pick up what I need, I turn and face my husband. "This is my office, Tristian. Why are you in it?" Avoiding his question, I turn for my office door.

"Izzy, please talk to me." My heart pounds at his genuine-sounding tone. Stop it, I demand of myself. Don't turn around.

I pause near the door, can't help it, and glance over my shoulder. "Tristian, I know about your little friend at the bar. You should have told me you were with someone else." Yes, I had my private detective follow Tristian. I had been worried. When he started making excuses for not coming home...

His face changes to shock and then annoyance as he shakes his head. "No, Izzy. I am not seeing anyone else."

"Tristian, I've seen the photos of the two of you together."

As he shakes his head again, his eyes widen in

disbelief. "No, you've got it all wrong," he says, taking a hesitant step closer to me.

Without hesitation, I lift my hand, motioning for him to stop. "Are you serious?" I am so annoyed right now.

I had the Private Detective do a full background check. Before making any impulsive decisions, I needed to gather information and get some answers. The apartment he had taken her to was none other than the Astors' sophisticated luxury apartments.

"Izzy, what pictures? Where were they taken?" My eyebrow rises. I don't have time for this shit. And place my hand on the door handle. "Wait. I don't know what you think, but you're mistaken."

Releasing the door handle, I turn to meet his gaze head-on. "Instead of being at home with your son and wife, someone captured you on film with another woman in your arms several times."

He steps towards me, shaking his head. Pleading. "Izzy, I met up with a woman Alex had been seeing. She wanted to know where he was."

As if... "Seriously? You want me to believe you after the way you treated me? The way you refused to speak with me. You shut me out, Tristian. You pushed me and your son away. How do you think that makes me feel?"

*W*hat have I done? The weight of my actions now rests heavily on my conscience.

I have to admit, my wife is right. I've messed up everything, making one mistake after another.

"Iz, a woman named Sara Harrow contacted me. I had my people look into her. I wanted to know if she was telling me the truth regarding her relationship with Alex."

"I know her name, Tristian." I nod. Of course, she would if she had investigated the woman.

And reply, "I met with her several times. She said she needed to find my brother."

"What did you tell her?"

"I said he left."

"Why didn't you tell her the truth," Izzy demanded.

Good question and say, "The detective was still digging into her past. I needed to know if she had

SECRET HEIRESS

anything to do with Alex being manipulated and why he turned against us."

"Did you ask her if she knew what Alex had been up to?"

I nod. "Of course I did. And Sara denied everything I had asked her."

"So, what was her answer for contacting you, Tristian?"

"The woman said she was pregnant with Alex's child. She needed money or somewhere to live as her family disowned her."

"Was she pregnant?" Izzy asked.

With a shrug, I reply, "To be safe, I requested for Sara to do a DNA paternity test for proof that she was pregnant with my brother's baby. And if the results were positive, I would move her into the apartment Alex would use in the city's heart."

"Was she?"

I didn't think it was possible, but I had sent the woman to a trusted doctor to perform the required tests, discovering the new NIPT can be less invasive, and said, "Yes. And she is pregnant with my brother's child."

She nods and turns. "It still does not explain why you said nothing. You still kept your distance. Why did you marry me if you don't want to be with me?"

Shit. I have stuffed up so badly. I wrap my arms around her, pressing my front into her back. "Izzy, I love you. I have been an idiot. I feel as if I have failed my family and you. Everything has fallen apart."

"You should have spoken to me," my wife murmurs

softly, her words barely audible but still piercing through my heart.

"Izzy, I know. Look, I love you and our son, and I want you both back. I want to be a family."

She sighs. "Look, I have to think. Go back to your home, Tristian. When I am ready to speak with you, I'll phone."

That is when I realized I had never said our home. Oh, no, I've always said my home. I've stuffed up again.

Izzy pries my arms from her front and walks out of her office, leaving me watching her back.

Chapter Fifty-Eight

IZZY

*M*ixed emotions pulse through me. Damn, my husband. I want to believe him... it can wait until after I have my son in my arms.

My driver maneuvers through the evening traffic.

I remove my cell from my purse and dial Mel.

"Hey, Izzy. Did you see my brother?" I don't answer her question. Even though she is angry with her brother, she would still prefer us to be all under one roof as a family.

"Mel, sorry, I have to cancel tonight."

"Huh? Why? What has happened? Was it Tristian?"

I shake my head. "No, Mel. My last business meeting went downhill fast. I found myself in a dangerous position. My assistant Blade was seriously hurt."

"Oh my god, Izzy. Are you okay? Where are you?"

"Mel," I hastily say, "I'm rushing to see my son. They have taken Rowan to a safe house. Don't worry. I've made arrangements with Essy to provide additional bodyguards for your protection at the beach house. Mel, you should seriously consider returning to Astor Manor...for a few days at least."

"Izzy, what in the hell happened today?"

"Sorry, Mel. I cannot get into it right now. I want to be with my son and hold him. Once I know it is safe, I'll return to the manor."

"Okay. I'll start packing. Do I need to contact Essy?"

I nod. It might be best if she does. "Yes, Mel. Then you know exactly who will be at the house to protect you."

"Okay. I can do that. Do you know if Jackson will be one of them?"

I knew it. Mel has the hots for my old bodyguard. "Phone Essy. But I think Jackson might be busy." The last thing I want to do is get her hopes up.

"Iz. Please be careful."

"I will. Love you."

"Love you more," she says before ending the call.

"Excuse me, Ms. Izzy." Benny grabs my attention. "We should arrive at the address you gave me shortly."

"Thank you, Benny. Can you let your wife know it will be a late night? Don't tell her our whereabouts."

"I understand, Ms. Izzy."

"Benny... Until I know more... There's a possibility we might still head back to the Astor Manor."

"Until we know more, Ms. Izzy."

It is becoming increasingly difficult to determine who is trustworthy. Heartson Industries hired those unfaithful employees who were working undercover for the notorious Callas — But then the scrupulous man had several Board of Directors wrapped around his little finger. Controlling the situation.

My aunt crosses my mind. She'd want to know what happened today. It's time to call her before we reach the safe house. After three rings, she answers. "Izzy, how are you, my darling girl?" From her tone, she has had a few glasses of her favorite wine. The background noise indicates she is with several other people — where is she now?

"Aunt H, I had a situation at the office this afternoon. My assistant got hurt. I'm contacting you to let you know I'm okay."

I can hear the background noise fade. Aunt Hazel must be walking to another room. "Izzy, where are you?"

"Aunt H, I cannot tell you yet. You could always meet me later at the Astor Manor."

"Shit," she says. "Izzy, are you still in danger?"

Wise woman, my aunt. "I'm not sure how to answer that, Aunt Hazel. I'll find out more soon."

"Shit... Okay, my darling girl. I'll pack a bag later and stay at the manor."

"I think that would be wise. We have much to discuss."

"I better go, Z. We'll speak later."

"Will do. Love you."

"Good night, my darling girl. Love you more."

"Bye."

Chapter Fifty-Nine

TRISTIAN

"**G**randfather, we need to talk," I casually say as he fills his glass with more ice cubes and whisky.

He turns, lifts his brow, and points to the armchairs where I can sit. "What would you like to discuss? Woman troubles?"

Settling into my chair, I savor the taste of scotch as I lean back. "Grandfather, I want to talk about Nicholas. What are we going to do about him?"

"Let me just say Nicholas had been warned. His name has now been removed from the company. He no longer has equal shares." Oh, shit. Nick will not be happy.

"His behavior concerns me." If Nicholas does not change, he will become like Alex.

"My boy. If Nicholas steps out of line again, we will cut off his financial support and send him away for treatment."

"Do I want to know where and how?"

My grandfather shakes his head. "No. You don't."

Okay, it's time to change the subject.

"Speaking of women. We have a situation with a woman named Sara Harrow," I say before taking another sip of my drink.

"Oh, boy. I have heard you have been seeing her at the family apartments. What were you thinking?" he growls.

Shit. I shake my head to deny his claims. Grandfather thinks, just like Izzy, that I'm having an affair.

Bloody Alex.

"Before you work up a head of steam, Sara Harrow was sleeping with Alex. She contacted me looking for him."

"If that is the case, why would you take her to the family apartments?"

With a sigh, I shake my head, take another sip of my drink, and feel the burn slide down my throat. "The short story is that her family disowned her once they discovered she was pregnant. I had requested a DNA paternity test to determine if the child belongs to Alex. And yes, the test came back to say Alex is the father. That is why I placed her in the family apartments until we can determine what to do with her."

"Does she know about Alex?"

I shake my head. "No. I only said he left." I savor another sip of my drink, feeling the burn.

"Your bloody brother. I wonder how many women will come forward once it becomes known that Alex is dead."

"At least Sara is one of the nicer females my brother had been with. Sadly, he only used women for sex. Poor Sara is going to be devastated when she discovers Alex is dead. I think the only way her family would take her back — if she married the baby's father."

"Sadly, that will never happen." That is an understatement.

"Grandfather, the other reason I wanted to speak to you is that I have decided to work on my marriage. And to do that, I need to take a step back from the helm of Astor International. Or at least share the load."

My grandfather nods his head. "Yes, I agree. I think that would be a good idea. Plus, it will allow your sister to display her talents and improve parts of the business with fresh eyes."

I nod. At least I had read my grandfather correctly. As long as he thinks Mel is up for the new position and I say, "I also gave Sara one of Alex's credit cards. It has a set limit on it. I said she could purchase food, maternity clothes, baby clothes, and baby furniture with it. But if she makes any large purchases on the card, the bank will cancel it, and she will lose the apartment."

"Do you think that was wise?"

"We will soon find out." When I saw the last credit card statement, I soon realized she had been careful with her purchases. "Time will tell if she becomes selfish with the bank card."

"Okay. We'll monitor her for now. Make sure she is seeing a doctor and is in good health. After all, the woman carries the next generation of Astor blood — my deceased grandson's child." He throws back his drink and then looks at me for several seconds before asking, "What happened at Izzy's building today?" Boy. Word gets around.

My wife came close to being seriously injured. "Do you know Costos Callas?"

He nods. "Yes. Horrible man. He is not trustworthy. Why?"

"Izzy had a meeting with him today. He nearly killed Izzy's assistant, Blade. The nanny and bodyguard have taken my son to a safe house for protection. Izzy should be on her way to be with Rowan as we speak. I was not privileged to be given the safe house information."

It still stings knowing my son is out there without his parents, and I am being kept from him.

"Boy, your wife will bring your son back here before you know it. One other thing, for you to move forward, remove your head from your ass first," he says before smiling.

Seriously...

Chapter Sixty

IZZY

*W*ith Benny's help, he carries Rowan into my room in the Astor Manor. He leaves shortly after to go back home to his worried wife.

I'm still in shock. Today, someone could have killed my boy. I stare down at him, fast asleep in his bed. All I want to do is hold my baby and never let him go. Now, I am short of a nanny and bodyguard, until Essy can send replacements.

Medics transferred Helen and Suzie to the hospital. Two of Callas' evil people had followed my son to the safe house. They nearly got my boy. Thankfully, Helen protected my son and the nanny, only to take a bullet to her chest before shooting one intruder. The nanny had a bullet graze her arm as she protected Rowan. Thankfully, Jackson arrived in time to shoot the remaining henchman, saving both women and my boy.

"Izzy, what is going on? Where is the nanny?" Tristian says, grabbing my attention as I spin around.

"Tristian," I reply, my voice fills with relief. "Helen

and Suzie were shot," I say, my voice trembling as I rush to my husband and wrap my arms around him. "They rushed Helen into surgery."

"How? What happened?" Tristian demands and holds me tighter.

"They were followed, Tristian. Thankfully, Helen and Jackson shot the intruders." I step away from him and turn back to our son. "That bloody monster CC. What he did to my parents, to my family. If I had a gun, Tristian, I would shoot him. The man is no man. He is evil in personified."

Tristian steps beside me, keeping one arm around my shoulders, and squeezes. "After witnessing what the man did today in your office. I completely agree."

Then I think of Mel and Trinity, and ask, "Has Mel arrived with Trinity?" And turn to meet Tristian's eyes.

Before my husband answers me, a knock sounds on my door. We both turn and see Mel smiling and holding Trinity in her arms. I rush to my friend and hug her carefully around my little niece. "It's good to see you."

"Izzy, I saw your car arrive. Where is everyone?" Mel asks as she looks around the room. "Where are Helen and Suzie?"

"Mel, come on. We'll let my little man sleep longer while I catch you up on everything."

"*H*oly Batman Robin. Are they going to be okay?" Mel demands.

I shake my head. "Essy said she will keep me up to date. I'm hoping she'll phone soon with an update."

We sit at the kitchen table, drinking hot chocolate with our baby monitors. So far, our little ones are still fast asleep.

"Izzy, have you spoken with my brother?"

I shake my head. Informing him that the nanny and bodyguard are in the hospital does not qualify. Then I think about the last conversation back in my office. "Unless you're speaking of the heated conversation in my office earlier... Then no."

My best friend's eyes narrow. "Okay, missy. Something has happened. Tell me now and don't leave a word out."

Trust Mel to pick up on the extra tension. She had to sense there was something else going on.

Swallowing the last of my hot chocolate, I sit a little taller and take a useless breath. Here goes. "Today, I confronted your brother."

Mel frowns. "Why? What has the idiot done this time?"

My brow lifts. "Tristian had been seen with another woman."

"What? No... Surely not." Mel shakes her head.

"Oh, yeah. At a bar, then at your family's apartments right in the city."

Her eyes widen. "Seriously?"

I nod in reply before saying, "Look, before your

mind goes into overdrive, your brother states that the woman, Sara, was one of Alex's hook-ups. It turns out she had been looking for Alex. Sara contacted Tristian when she failed to locate Alex. Long story short, she's pregnant with Alex's child."

"What?" Mel says. I nod. Mel shakes her head. "Please tell me…"

I cut Mel off. "Sara's family abandoned her when they learned of the pregnancy. The poor girl is on her own."

"Holy Batman Robin. Alex let a little swimmer free. Now, he is not here to face the responsibility of his actions."

"Yep. You might have to speak with Tristian and your grandfather. Sara is carrying another Astor after all…"

"Bugger. Another mess we have to clean up after Alex."

Chapter Sixty-One

TRISTIAN

*W*hat in the world is going on? Why were we taken to a hotel-like room? My confusion increases — why we're moved to this room as I glance around me.

What's the reason behind Izzy having such a room in her building?

Curiosity fills me as I ask, "Helen, what's happening?" I glance around us. "Why are we in this room?"

The woman huffs, then replies, "Mr. Astor, for your safety."

Huh? "What is going on?" I demand. My attention follows her movements as she touches a small dark box on the desk. Okay, so the room is more than I what I first thought. A wall of TV monitors activates and Izzy appears on one screen.

My beautiful wife there in all her beauty. Goodness gracious I've missed her.

Wondering what in the world is going on, as we then

watch Izzy go from her office on one monitor to another monitor. Indicating that Izzy is walking into another area. From the corner of my eye, I can see Helen has her cell phone to her ear and is quietly speaking with someone.

Why does this room feel like a control room, with more than ten monitors on the wall? As I look at each screen, my focus goes back to Izzy as she enters what appears to be a meeting room where an unknown man is also present.

The situation becomes intense, and I realize that the man on the screen is none other than Costos Callas — a well-known crime lord and criminal, who also happens to be a prince. Why is that man in my wife's building and meeting with her? What is going on? My wife's personal assistant, Blade, a male of all things, stands beside my wife.

The conversation between Costos and Izzy becomes intense. The next thing we watch, Costos slides a folded document across the table. Then three security guards enter the room. Instead of Izzy, her personal assistant retrieves the document and reads it.

Why would she allow someone to touch... my thoughts freeze as I watch the look on Blade's face change. I can tell something is very wrong. My focus moves to my wife's. She is now concerned about Blade. Instead of helping him, she takes off out of the room.

"Helen, let me out. Izzy needs my help."

She shakes her head. "Sorry, Mr. Astor. For your and your son's safety, you must remain in this room until it is safe to leave."

I look at the monitor again and watch Blade collapse. What in the hell was in that letter?

*M*y stress levels climb sky-high because of the uncertainty surrounding updates on my wife. As I hold Rowan close, my little one falls asleep after finishing his bottle. It's remarkable how innocent he is, oblivious to the extent of danger we've faced. Before Helen turned off the monitors, I had already viewed a portion of the footage. What I saw was not pleasant. The people Izzy has working with her are scary. No wonder she handles her own safety.

My son makes a funny face in his sleep. How I have missed him. He has grown so much. Guilt fills me. Why did I shut my wife out? If only I went home each evening instead of remaining in my office or grabbing a drink at the bar just up from my office building, my wife and son would be at home instead of staying at a different location. A house I did not know my wife owned for several years.

My Grandfather confronted me again this morning. Informing me I'm on the verge of losing my position as the CEO of the family company and I've lost my wife.

His words regarding my wife still ring in my ears. *"Boy. You made a hash of things. How could you run your wife off? She was the best thing in your life, and now you have lost her and your son. What are you going to do about it?"*

What am I going to do about my marriage? From what I've seen so far, it might be too late. My wife's life is in danger. She's now missing. Chances are, I might never tell her again that I love her, and I'm sorry.

Recognizing the importance of our son's safety, my beautiful wife understood the need for additional security measures. Taking precautions, she had support during her recuperation from the emergency surgery. How can I run a multi-million-dollar company when I cannot look after my marriage or family? What can I say — I'm selfish. I failed my wife and son, as well as my siblings. I'm thoughtless when it comes to my wife's and son's needs.

If I have another chance, I will ensure I am there for Izzy and our son. I might step back and allow Grandfather to have Mel take over the family company. But first, I have to fix things with Izzy.

"Helen, have you located Izzy? I need to be with her." My son's bodyguard gives me a strange look. She frowns and then shakes her head.

"Are you serious right now, Sir? From my observation, you do not seem to place other people's needs before yours."

I cringe at her words. She's right. I need to change. I never thought I would be like my father.

"Helen, I want to change. I know I need to be a better man. I want to be there for my wife. My family."

She shakes her head again. "Sir, if that was the case... what would you do to change?"

Why do I feel my son's bodyguard is testing me? Maybe she is. Perhaps she has known where my wife has been all this time. Was I blind to notice?

"Helen. I need to see my wife. She needs to know that I love her."

She sighs before replying, "That might be what you think is required, but Sir, it will take much more than those three little words to convince her to allow you back into her life, which is coming from another woman's perspective."

What does she mean by that? Her foot taps the floor for several seconds before she turns, shakes her head, and then turns the monitors back on and focuses on them. Women and their points of view! What have I done wrong now?

Her cell rings. She speaks quietly and glances at me. Now, what is going on? Has something happened to my wife?

"What is it? Is Izzy safe?" I demand.

Helen lifts her hand to indicate that I should wait. I wouldn't tolerate her silent treatment if I knew the way out.

"I'll make sure he's ready. See you soon," Helen says to whoever is on the other end of that call. She slides her cell into her pocket and turns to the nanny. "Pack Rowan's things." Huh? What's going on? "Have him readied to leave in five." Huh? Why isn't she talking to me? What about me? Helen glances at the monitors as the nanny reaches for my son.

"Sir, it's time." Time for what? I meet her eyes with a frown. "Sir, you will leave shortly." Huh?

I glance at the bodyguard. "Helen, what is going on?" As the nanny Suzie removes my son from my arms, leaving me feeling empty and alone.

Without looking at me, Helen replies, "Your son is being taken somewhere safe. As for you, you will have your chance to speak with your wife. I'd suggest — don't stuff it up."

Chapter Sixty-Two

IZZY

"Izzy, Sara is at her second scan today. Did you know she's at twenty-two weeks?"

What? No...

When the Astor family allowed Sara to move into the manor, my insecurities came into play. Sara is a lovely girl, but I don't know her.

To avoid the question, I say, "I have a date with your brother this evening?" I pick Rowan off the floor. The cheeky little monkey has discovered rolling. I blow a raspberry on his belly, which makes him laugh, and then place him back on the floor mat beside Trinity.

"Really?" she replies. "If you don't want to talk about Sara, say so. Now, how many dates is this... ten?"

My lips twitch, and I reply, "Twelve, actually." But who's counting?

"Wow. My big brother is acting all romantic. He is being romantic, isn't he?"

"Yes, Mel," I say with an eye roll. "Since you decided to take on more responsibility in the family company, he has been less stressed and more focused on Rowan, and our time together has brought us together."

"Oh, my. Tristian is growing up."

My lips twitch again, and I restrain myself from laughing. "Yes, you can say that. Your brother has been so thoughtful and caring. He's made me laugh." I smile at the thoughts of him. "Tristian has made me feel things again." The man has wormed his way back into my heart.

"That's great. It is great, isn't it?" Mel questions with a raised brow.

"I don't know, Mel. It will take more than a few dates to improve everything again between us."

"Izzy, my brother has put you first. As you said, he has stepped back from the family business. He spends more time with your son. He's spending time with you. That is what you wanted, isn't it?"

Now my friend is making me feel bad. I nod. "Yes, Mel. That is what I wanted. But life is not a fairy tale. He will have to focus back on work, and that is what I am afraid of. He'll slip back into old habits."

"Izzy, talk to the idiot. You and Tristian need to communicate. If there is no communication, how will your marriage survive?"

Darn it, she has a point. Am I being selfish?

"Okay, Mel. I'll speak with your brother."

She smiles and winks. "That's the spirit. As the new nanny is already here to look after Rowan, take advantage of her, cut the excuses, and meet him early. When was the last time you both did the horizontal tango?"

Technically, the day we were married, and before that, the night Rowan was conceived back in March.

I nod. "Alright. Where would your brother be at this time of day?" I think it is time to blow some of the old cobwebs away. Today, my husband is going to get himself lucky!

*a*fter showering in my old room and changing into something a little bit naughty, I search for my husband.

The first place I check his room, only to find it empty, then I head to his office on the lower floor and lightly knock on his door before opening it. "What the hell is going on?" I demand.

A vision I want to bleach from my mind. Seeing Sara sitting in Tristian's office chair as she gives Nicholas a blow job. Nick spins around quickly, slipping his penis back into his pants.

"How dare you bust in here, Izzy? The door was closed," Nicholas screeches before zipping up his pants.

My focus moves to Sara. "Why are you in here, Sara? Are you in a relationship with Nicholas now?"

Sara glances up and shakes her head. Her eyes fill with tears. She looks at Nicholas, then back at me. "I'm sorry. ...Nick..."

Why do I feel Nicholas is abusing his status? "What did Nicholas ask you to do?" Sara shakes her head and looks at Nick. "Look at me, Sara. Are you in a relationship with Nicholas?"

She shakes her head and replies, "No. Never." She places her hands over her round belly. "I love Alex. But Nicholas threatened to have me kicked out to the street if I didn't give him the occasional blowjob," she sobs.

"Really!" My focus moves to my brother-in-law. "Nicholas, why would you do something so low? You disgust me. Get out of my sight."

"Are you going to tell Tristian?"

"I'll be speaking to my husband about your little stunt." I shake my head. "If I find you anywhere near Sara again, I will kick your butt."

Nick swears and storms out.

I turn back to Sara. "Are you okay?"

She shakes her head. "Am I going to be kicked out? Please don't. I've got nowhere to go," Sara cries. She wraps her arms around her rounding belly. "We have nowhere to go."

Nicholas. Why did he scare Sara like that and abuse the family's trust?

"No, Sara. Did Nicholas hurt you?" She shakes her head. I nod and say, "Okay, then go back to your room, wash your face, and rest. Most of all, stay away from Nicholas. What he did was uncalled for."

Chapter Sixty-Three
TRISTIAN

"What in the hell were you thinking, abusing Sara like that?" I demand. "Damn it, Nicholas. Sara loved your brother. She's carrying his child, and this is how you disrespect her and our family."

He smirks, not caring. "Look, brother. Sara is free to fuck who she wants. At least I know if I fuck her," he gloats, "she will not fall pregnant."

My fists ball at my sides. "Are you serious right now? You make me sick, little brother. How could you do that?" How I haven't connected my fist to his face, I never know.

"Easy. It's not like Sara is seeing anyone. Or in a relationship."

How did Nicholas sink this low? His opinion of Sara is sickening.

"Nick, you leave me no choice. I will suspend your allowance until you can demonstrate that you can be trusted. Grandfather is waiting for you. This time, you will leave with him. If you cannot improve your attitude towards women, you will not be welcome back in this house."

He shakes his head, and his smirk vanishes. "You cannot do that. I have equal shares in the family company," he growls.

"Ah. You forget one thing, little brother. Grandfather is still alive. He can change the dynamics of the company as he sees fit."

"No. Grandfather can't do that," Nic yells.

"Oh, but he can and already has, thanks to your failure to go with him the last time. You have been removed from the family trust — you no longer own equal shares in the family company."

"No. Grandfather would never betray me. He promised Father."

Our father never cared for us. Nick is delusional and say, "The only money you have is what you currently have in your bank account. You are also responsible for any debt you have. We will not be paying your bills. Now I suggest you pack your bags and meet Grandfather and the driver outside. Goodbye, Nicholas." I turn and walk back towards the room my son is sleeping in. I need to see him.

Chapter Sixty-Four

IZZY

*M*y only thought is how can two brothers spiral out of control and fall so far in this family?

First Alex and now Nicholas.

Watching Nicholas argue with Grandpa Joshua and the bodyguard was heartbreaking. Witnessing Nicholas storm toward Joshua, I thought he would hurt the old man. Thank goodness Joshua had the foresight to have the bodyguard with him. As I have since learned, that particular bodyguard is also a life coach — another of Essy's retired military personnel.

I wrap my arm around Tristian and lean my head against his chest.

"I'm sorry, Tristian. Your father and Alex influenced Nicholas' attitude and behavior towards women and business."

He nods and places a kiss on my head. "Izzy, I feel I have failed."

I shake my head. "No, Tristian. Your father was not a good man in life or business. Mel and I had seen him with another woman several times in this house."

"What?" Tristian steps away to stare into my eyes. "Mel has never said a word."

"Maybe your father threatened Mel if she did."

"Why would you say that?"

"Well…" Memories of a long-ago night come to mind, and say, "We arrived here late while on leave from college."

"Was this the first time you saw him with another woman?"

I nod. "When we thought about it, it was the first time in this house and several times at galas we had attended."

"Geez. My poor mother. Go on. I might as well hear it as much as it annoys me."

I nod again and take a breath. "Well, we thought everyone was out. It wasn't the case. After dropping our bags off in Mel's room, we decided to go to the kitchen for a late-night snack. With the lights out, Mel said she used to practice walking around the house in the dark in case of emergencies. While we were walking past your father's office, an out-of-place noise made us pause."

"His office. The same office I use now?" I nod. "Bloody hell…"

"Mel thought she'd investigate. She slowly opened the office door and witnessed your father fucking another woman against the desk. Mel must have made a noise because your father turned his head and spotted her."

"Oh shit. What did he do?"

"He continued fucking the woman and Mel shut the door. When we were in her room reading in bed and watching a movie, your father barged in. When he spotted me, he shook his head, gave your sister the evil eye, and asked if she had told me what happened in the office."

"He what?"

"Mel shook her head and said no. I had innocently asked your father what was going on. What happened in the office?"

"How did my father react to you asking?"

"He told me to butt out of his family's affairs. And he will speak to Mel privately in the morning."

"Now that I think about it, it explains why my mother demanded the desk's removal when she redecorated the room."

"The other time Mel saw your father with another woman was when she and your mother saw him with the same woman on a different night. He thought everyone was out, but your mother had a headache and cut the evening short. She walked in on them in the office."

"I wonder why she didn't divorce him?"

"Not sure? But then your father died later that year."

"Yes, sadly. And then my mother died not even eighteen months later."

"I'm sorry, Tristian. The whole situation is terrible and hard on you all," I say as I hug him tight.

The feeling of having no parents can be hard on your soul, especially when they love you.

"Izzy, about tonight... Can we stay in, please? I don't feel up to going anywhere in public."

I nod. "Sure, Tristian. How about pizza, curling up in the lounge, and watching a movie?"

Chapter Sixty-Five

IZZY

We spent the next week in a whirlwind of shared moments, from quiet evenings to exhilarating adventures. The passion and excitement of teenagers were ours as we kissed and cuddled, our bodies tingling with the thrill of it all.

One of our cherished moments was sneaking into the cinema, the hushed darkness broken only by the rustle of popcorn bags and the occasional giggle, the buttery scent filling the air as we settled into the back rows.

The thrill of sneaking into the movie theater and acting like horny teenagers was fun, until we later slipped back out to enjoy a delicious dinner in a warm, inviting restaurant.

We are closer to one another than ever until doubt creeps in as Tristian holds himself back when it comes to sex, leaving a lingering sense of frustration and unfulfilled desire within me. I wonder if his lack of interest in sex was a sign that he was no longer interested in me that way. Can a man be turned off from sex after his partner has had a baby?

Now I know how it feels to gain a pair of blue balls! It has been so long since we've had sex together.

Tonight, with the nanny looking after Rowan, Tristian leans on a pile of pillows against his headboard. Our bodies intertwined in our usual position, with one of his legs straight out and the other bent at the knee. My head resting on his chest, feeling the gentle rise and fall with each breath he takes. The credits roll on the large flat screen, signaling the end of the hilarious and action-packed comedy movie.

All night, I have been fighting the urge to touch him sexually. His scent fills my nostrils, causing my hormones to go into overdrive. The question is... will we only kiss tonight as every other night? Will Tristian send me back to my room?

Or will we both be lucky and spend the night tangled in the sheets?

It's time for me to take charge because I am sick of waiting for Tristian to make the first move. Before my husband says anything, I sit up, strip off my T-shirt, and straddle my husband's legs.

"Izzy, what are you doing?" confusion lining my husband's voice.

Seriously... His words nearly have me pausing before deciding to keep going. "Now, Tristian. If I have to explain things..." I say as I rub my core against him. "It should be obvious that I want more than kissing and cuddling tonight if you do not want to have sex. Let me know, and I'll leave!"

He shakes his head. "Iz, I don't want to have sex." What? I frown and go to move off his lap when his hands grip my thighs. "Wait. Let me explain." My frustrated gaze connects with his. His eyes pleading. "I want you, Izzy. Never doubt that. Sex is sex. I prefer to make love to you for the first time as husband and wife."

Relief fills me, and I nod and smile.

Is that all?

My husband might be romantic after all. "Well...as you asked so nicely, sit up." He does and smiles as I lean forward, kiss his lips, and reach for his T-shirt. "You're wearing far too many clothes, husband." He lifts his arms, and I yank off his t-shirt, throwing it over the side of the bed.

Next, I crab crawl back over his legs to allow him to lift his butt enough for me to remove the rest of his clothes between heated kisses.

"Babe, I have missed you," he says against my lips. "I didn't know if you were up to making love."

Tristian rolls me over and removes my pants and underwear, leaving me naked before him. He smiles and surveys my body. Liking what he sees, he then leans over me and begins kissing the side of my neck, savoring it with his mouth before making his way down my body.

"Ah, huh," I nod and smile, feeling his lips sweep across my flesh.

The tip of his tongue circles my nipple before taking my flesh into his mouth and sucking, pulling on my breast before allowing it to slip from his mouth with a pop. His gaze moves to the other breast, and he pays it the same attention, causing my core to weep and pulse.

His teeth take little nips here and there, leaving a blazing trail heading south. Butterfly kisses dot my skin, causing goosebumps to form.

Eager for more of his touch, I remember how talented he is with his mouth. It has been so long since I have had the luxury of such a delight.

My hips rise, feeling the warmth of his tongue sliding between my eager inner lips, gliding up, down, and around before circling my little bundle of nerves, nipping me, and sending me toward the edge.

I never expected to be so sensitive after all this time. He continues his ministrations, causing a delicious sensation to travel through my body, building, increasing velocity. I'm a powder keg ready to detonate.

One hand reaches for the sheet beside me, hoping to ground myself. The other reaches for his head. My fingers sweep through his hair before gripping it, pulling his face closer to my core.

"You like that?"

His muffled tone reaches my ears as the vibrations of his voice against my clit send my butt higher towards the ceiling.

I think I'm floating. Maybe flying or having an out-of-body experience.

Pressure increases within me. My core muscles tighten, demanding to hold his fingers in place.

"Yes. Faster," I plea. "Suck harder."

As a good, obedient husband, he does what he is told.

The explosive orgasm has my body losing itself in the utopia of orgasm bliss as it explodes into hundreds of pieces, shattering my self-control. A scream rushes up from my throat. I think my toes just flew off my feet before Tristian leans over me between my thighs. My pulse races with each panting breath, my chest rapidly rising with my nipples hard and erect.

He gently skims his nose along mine before his lips zeroes in, brushing against my swollen, wet lips and kissing me again. Each sweep of his mouth is longer and more electrifying, right down to my toes.

He barely pulls away with a smile and asks, "Did you like that?" All I can do is nod. I'm left without the ability to speak. "Good. Now for the main course of this evening's activities." My orgasmic smile increases as I nod, agreeing with his words.

Yes.

Bring it on.

I want more!

He leans towards my lips once again, taking possession of them. What started as a hungry-for-more kiss turns frenzied, leaving me dizzy and breathless, eager for more of his mouth.

The touch of his hand runs under my thigh, urging my leg up, and I wrap it around his hip; before my brain can process his actions, he thrusts forward. Filling me. I scream into his mouth. I'm not sure if my body is ready for his large intrusion. He patiently pauses as I feel his length pulse within me. The brush of his fingers repeatedly against my clit nearly short-circuits my brain.

He lifts my leg higher and slides nearly all the way

out before thrusting forward again. His pubic bone meets mine before pulling almost out again and thrusting again, filling my body. Just like a steam train, he pistons back and forth, harder and faster as I scream.

He captures my lips, hungry for my mouth, and seeks my tongue and sucks it into his mouth.

With a swivel of his hips, he slides back and forth before filling me whole — his girth and length pulse within me. My muscles are unsure whether to squeeze him tight or relax and enjoy the ride.

Our gazes meet. Passion burns within his eyes. He zeros back on my lips and takes possession of them. What begins as a loving, intimate kiss soon becomes lust-filled and frantic, leaving me lightheaded and breathless, impatient for more of his lips and mouth.

Tristian jerks his hips back, then thrusts forward. His pumping action increases, and his hips meet mine.

"Faster. Harder," I chant against his mouth. "Yes, just like that. More!"

He swivels his hips with each hard thrust. He repeats his extraordinarily talented actions, increasing his pace harder and faster with each thrust. Sending my body higher and higher.

And once again, my husband obeys his wife and does just what I demand for the rest of the evening.

Chapter Sixty-Six

IZZY

a contented smile plays on my lips as I savor the memory of last night's fiery passion and the tender joy of waking beside my husband. The sheets hold the scent of our lovemaking. If my married life continues like this, I will cherish every moment of being married to Tristian.

The alarm on my cell alerts me I have to get up. Damn. I have a 9 a.m. meeting this morning. My eyelids flutter open, and sunshine nearly blinds me. My eyes squint until they adjust to the light.

After Tristian's special wake-up call this morning, I must have fallen asleep again. I look over my shoulder, but all I see is the vacant bed. With a disappointed frown, I glance towards the clock on the nightstand. 7.34 a.m. Shit!

I have slept through two alarm alerts. Thrusting the bedding aside, I rush into the bathroom. Fifteen minutes later, I casually walk out of my bedroom door fully dressed and head to my son's room to check on him, but he was not there.

Huh?

I quickly take the elevator and head to the kitchen. Relief fills me seeing my boy in his porta highchair attached to the marble kitchen bench top and Tristian attempting to feed Rowan solids. By the look of things, I think our boy has more of the cereal paste on him and the bench top than he's probably eaten.

Once my boy spots me, he smiles and lifts his arms, and I smile back.

"No, buddy. You complain you were hungry. So, eat your breakfast," Tristian demands calmly.

Rowan turns his head towards his father, bangs his fists on the bench, and then smiles and laughs.

Dressed in my office attire, the last thing I require is baby food splattered on my clothing. I dodge my son's grubby hands and sit at the end of the island bench on the stool chair.

"Morning, Rowan. Are you enjoying your breakfast?"

Rowan nods and opens his mouth so that Tristian can slip the spoon into his mouth.

Cheeky little monkey.

"Morning, Izzy. Did you sleep well this morning?" Tristian asks with a knowing smile. Mel glances up from spooning another scoop of cereal into Trinity's mouth.

She glances from Tristian to me and back again before her eyes meet mine, and she gives me her knowing look with a smile.

With a roll of my eyes, I glance back at Tristian and reply, "Yes, I did, thanks. You should have woken me!" His lips twitch because we were both thinking of his wake-up call this morning, which had nothing to do with electronics.

"I thought I had!" He smiles and places another spoon of cereal into Rowan's mouth. "I might have to try something different tomorrow." His brow rises, and he gives me a knowing smirk.

"Morning, Izzy. I think my brother is annoying. Now I know why he was in such a good mood this morning," Mel says as she wipes Trinity's mouth.

"Morning, Mel." Avoiding what she said. "How are you both this morning?"

She smiles at her daughter before turning to me. "My little angel loves this cereal. She slept through the night last night."

"That's fantastic. But did you wake anyway?" I know when Rowan sleeps longer than usual, I still wake. Well, apart from this morning, that is.

She nods. "Yes. Thankfully, I rolled back over and went to sleep."

"At least that is something." The housekeeper, Mrs. Fraser, brings me over my morning tea. "Thank you, Mrs. Fraser," I murmur as I take a sip. Josie, whom I hired for my beach house, agreed to cook in the Astor manor and bring me my favorite fruit toast with melted butter. Yum! "Thank you, Josie. You both make my day," I say before taking a sizeable, delicious bite and making joyful noises as I savor the flavors while chewing.

"I think I'm jealous of toast," Tristian mumbles, and Mel laughs at her brother's words.

Chapter Sixty-Seven

IZZY

"*M*s. Delany, your 9 a.m. is here," my new secretary says.

"Thank you, Eliza. Send them in, please," I say. Thanks to Essy, she sent over another employee to replace Blade while he recuperates. Somehow, he survived his ordeal and is determined to come back and work for me. I'm thankful he lived after what happened in the conference room with CC. He was more than an outstanding employee.

As my office door opens, I stand to greet...

Tristian?

"Good morning, Ms. Delany. How are you today?"

My brow rises. "What's going on, Tristian?"

"Why, Ms. Delany? I am here for a business meeting."

Okay... I'll play along. I walk around my desk and reach out to shake my husband's hand in greeting. "Good morning, Mr. Astor. What is it you wish to speak to me about today?"

He smiles and firmly shakes my hand; the touch of his skin against mine sends a sensation straight up my arm. We release hands, and he sits in one of the office chairs.

"Ms. Delany, I have a proposal for you."

A proposal? What in the world is Tristian speaking about?

I lean on my desk. "What do you have in mind, Mr. Astor?"

He reaches inside his suit jacket, grabs what looks like a document, and places it on my desk. "This is for you," he says.

Now, what is going on? Keeping my mind clear, the last thing I want to do is have my mind race with different scenarios relating to what the document may contain.

I slide it towards myself, then lift the document, slowly opening it, and eye it and Tristian simultaneously. His face remains unchanged, not allowing his features to give anything away.

With the document open, my focus moves from Tristian to the paper in my hand.

Dear Izzibella,

Today, I am delivering this letter in person. Why? Because I will let nothing get between us again.

I will always cherish the recent time we spent together. Last night, you made me feel like a king and blew my mind, literally.

You gave me our son, Izzy, a child to cherish and love. I will always thank you for my son.

You gave me your body, and I didn't appreciate what I had until I let it slip away. For that, I will forever be sorry. I'm still not sure how to apologize for my stupidity. As I should have paid more attention to you — your past. I didn't consider your family history, schooling, or what you wanted.

I am forever sorry, Izzy.

You might have noticed I can be selfish. And for that, I apologize.

Please be by my side and help me navigate my future to become a better man.

I want to be a better father than my father was to his sons and daughter.

I want to be a husband you can rely on, one who loves and cherishes his wife and family.

So, if you are still reading, thank you.

I smile at his silliness and glance up. Huh? Where is he? Then I glance down. My husband is right in front of me, down on one knee.

"Um, Tristian. Should I complete reading your letter?"

He nods. I smile and continue reading from the last line.

So, if you are still reading, thank you.

I'm interrupting your business day...

Izzy. I love you and am asking for your hand in marriage.

Will you marry me, Izzy?

Yes, I know we are already married. However, because of the circumstances of our intimate home ceremony, I would love to have a wedding ceremony somewhere romantic, somewhere we can enjoy ourselves and then continue on a honeymoon.

Or, if you prefer, we can head to a romantic location and enjoy our honeymoon instead. We still have a lot to do.

I love you, Izzy.

I will love you for the rest of my days.

Forever, your sorry husband, who would prefer to make things right.

Tristian.

Okay, you can look back at me now.

My lips twitch before transforming into a huge smile as I glance back at Tristian.

"Seriously, Tristian?"

He nods. "Yes. You are the woman of my dreams. You're the breath for my lungs, the light to my soul. Today, I request you to remain in my life. Marry me,

Izzy, a second time. Let's have our honeymoon. Enjoy life on a getaway. Begin a new adventure and write our own story."

As hard as I can, I prevent myself from laughing. What Tristian was saying was not funny. He was serious. It is an unexpected moment. Unexpected question. Why would he want to get married again?

Without overthinking his words — I agree, though — we have not had our honeymoon.

The light bounces off Tristian's hand. A sparkle catches my eye. I glance down. In his hand, clutched between his thumb and forefinger, is a beautiful blue sapphire ring surrounded by small diamonds.

"Oh, Tristian. It's beautiful."

"Iz, what is your answer?"

My eyes meet his, and I reply, "We don't need a second ceremony, Tristian, to have a honeymoon. With everything that has happened, we deserve some time away."

"So, if you had the chance to marry me again, would you?"

This time, I laugh and nod at the silly man. "Yes, Tristian. I would marry you."

He smiles. He grabs my hand, slips the ring along my finger, and then stands and wraps his arms around me.

"I love you, Izzibella, my princess," he says before brushing his lips against mine, then deepens our kiss to a toe-curling passionate one, making our surroundings disappear.

I never thought I could love this man more than I do now. All we have to do now is work together as one and raise our son. If only my parents were here to see how much I have accomplished and how happy I am.

Chapter Sixty-Eight

IZZY

OVER TWENTY-ONE YEARS LATER.

"Mom, everyone is here," my nineteen-year-old son calls out.

"Thank you, Sebastian. I'll be there in a minute," I yell as I place the last of the forty-three candles on the cake.

"Iz, do you need a hand lighting the candles?" Mel asks as she steps into the kitchen.

My lips twitch. She bloody well knows I need help lighting all forty-two of the outside candles and the decorative twenty-first candle in the middle. It was her idea to have twenty-one candles each for Trinity and Rowan.

I nod. "There are two lighters on the shelf beside the large candles." We learned to keep matchsticks or a lighter beside the candles when the power goes out.

"Izzy, thank you for organizing and holding the birthday party here."

I nod. What else were we going to do? We canceled the kids' other party celebrations at the last minute.

Mel passes me a lighter, and we light all the birthday candles together.

I retrieve my cell from the bench and snap pictures of the cake before sliding my cell phone into my back pocket.

"That should do it. Come on, this thing is heavy," I say. We lift the cake, and I meet her eyes. "We're family, Mel. It is good to have all the kids under one roof." It is, especially after recent events.

"I know. With Nicholas passing away four weeks ago, a birthday party was the last thing I wanted to handle."

Yes. It's still a shock. Nicholas died on his speedboat. The police detectives speculated whether it was an accident or mechanical failure.

After all these years, Nick had straightened himself out and excelled in business.

We are confused about why his wife, Penny, left their five-year-old son behind at her parents' home three weeks ago and traveled to England. No one has seen or heard from her since.

Jackson, Mel's husband, and my original bodyguard is looking for Penny and following any leads he can find.

"How is Tristian holding up?" she asks.

Just before their brother's death, Nicholas had been busy with several business deals, leaving Mel and

Tristian arguing about which venture to continue and which to cancel. They've been squabbling ever since, and I am not getting involved. If she wants to know anything about her brother, she can ask him.

We go outside, keeping the cake balanced between us, and I reply, "You have to ask him." And leave it at that. The sound of her harrumph has my lips twitching.

As Mel and I maneuver the monstrosity cake to the back patio overlooking the ocean, I wonder why we didn't have the wait staff bring it out.

Too late now.

As Tristian walks our son toward the table, I see his face light up with laughter. It is good to see my husband smile again. This year has presented us with many challenges. Despite our vows, last year we did exactly what we said we wouldn't. Neglecting our personal lives, we allowed the pressures of work to dominate our relationship, taking each other for granted.

We've been working on our marriage for several months now, and thankfully, we are closer than ever. Tristian and I decided it was time for our kids to take on more responsibility in the family empires.

Our kids should learn now with them by our sides rather than being thrown in at the deep end if anything terrible should happen to us.

Rowan is with Heartson Industries, and Sebastian is with Astor International, with their cousin Trinity. Our only daughter, Lannah, loves learning everything about my mother's business, LaniD, with Aunt Hazel watching over her. Lannah will head to university in a week to continue her business and fashion design studies. We couldn't be more proud of our kids.

Alex's daughter, Amy, is learning all about Astor International. Her life has had its ups and downs. Thanks to Grandpa Joshua, he got her into some excellent schools and away from her mother's money-hungry family. Over a week ago, Tristian, Mel, Amy, and I gathered to honor her father's memory. We also lit a large candle, its flame flickering in remembrance.

As for MeBe Tech, Mel is still the boss. Her youngest son Jason is a wiz on the computer, apps, and coding. He will continue our IT business and expand it into gaming. Jason showed us a virtual game he had created two months ago. The prototype already has raving reviews.

My old business partner, Simon, is married and has two teenage children. He bought me out of Security Consults Today and expanded our old security business, doing exceptionally well for himself.

The guests begin singing Happy Birthday and stepping out of our way of the blazing candles as we head for the designated table.

I glance at Tristian standing beside our smiling son, Rowan, his eyes filled with pride. With Trinity bubbling with excitement, Jackson joins her in anticipation as they watch the cake's arrival.

My son is now a handsome, clever, and intelligent man. Rowan has displayed focus and determination in his studies and knows what he wants. In looks and talent, he resembles my father. My parents would be proud of my boy, just like Tristian and I are.

We place the cake on the decorated table just as the song ends, and everyone chants, "Hip, Hip, hooray! Hip, Hip, hooray. Hip, Hip, hooray."

As I step back, I reach for my cell phone from my back pocket and snap several photos of the kids blowing out their candles as several guests yell out for the pair to make a wish.

With most of the cousins under one roof, I had better make the most of it and capture as many pictures of everyone laughing and having a good time. We all need this time to be a happy memory after Nick's death.

Tristian steps beside me, smiling, and wraps his arm around my waist. Jackson steps beside and hugs Mel.

"We've done it. I am so proud of our son, Izzy," my husband states. I nod and meet Tristian's smiling eyes with my own.

"He has worked so hard to get to this point. Remember, we must keep him grounded," I remind him. I can still remember how Alex had turned out. I never want to see one of our children end up like their selfish uncle.

Tristian kisses my head and announces, "Come on, we better get the speeches over with so the younger ones can party."

With several photos taken, it is good to know I snapped a few of all the cousins together. Rowan and his siblings, Sebastian, and Lannah. Trinity and her two siblings, Travis, and Jason, and their cousin, Amy. Since they were little, they've had the nickname The Awesome Seven. With their busy lives, who knows when the kids will be together again to be in the one photo?

We reach for fresh drinks from one of the roaming waitstaff. You can't have a speech without a glass of bubbles. And glance over to see my Aunt Hazel resting in her chair, a glass in her hand and a raised brow.

My aunt is the head of our busy company, LaniD. The woman is determined nothing will stop her, even the recent hip operation which has left her chair-bound. Knowing my aunt, it will not be long until she gains enough strength and she will be on her feet once more.

I call everyone's attention, tapping my sapphire ring against my glass.

"Hello, everyone." The guests pause and turn towards me. "Thank you all for joining us today to celebrate Rowan and Trinity's twenty-first birthdays," I announce, looking at everyone. "Enjoy yourselves, and remember not to overdo the festivities." Several people laugh, and I face my son. "Rowan, I have a special gift from your grandfather, Philip Heartson." He frowns. His face shows that he's wondering what it could be. "I'll present it to you later." Even though we purchased a new car for him, we presented him with shares in Aster International and Heartson Industries. Each one of our children will receive equal shares on their twenty-first birthday.

His frown turns into his handsome smile. He nods and raises his glass in thanks.

I then turn to my niece. "Trinity, I hope you like our gift and will use it wisely." I had seen her open the present earlier. Tristian and I gave her a leather DIOR

Gallop briefcase with her initials in gold on the clasp. Inside it, we placed tickets and all-expense-paid vouchers for four people to travel to our holiday house in Australia on Hamilton Island.

We bought an old house on that island on the same street as Essy, Missy, and Laini's holiday houses and had it remodeled. The street name still cracks me up. Who would name it Plum Pudding Close? At least if we want to spend Christmas out of the cold, we can travel down to the small tropical island and have fun in the sun.

Lost in thought, I miss Tristian and Mel's speeches to the kids, followed by Jackson's.

Thank goodness that Jackson stepped into the role of Trinity's loving father. Corey never paid off his debts and was killed by the time Trinity turned one, leaving her without a biological father.

My son's voice grabs my attention. "I would like to thank my parents for holding the party at their beach house. And a special thank you to my gorgeous mother, who has given me the chance to learn the ropes by her side at Heartson Industries. Mom, I hope I make you proud."

I lift my glass, smile, and nod. "I love you, Rowan. Happy birthday," I mouth. Rowan winks back with his gorgeous smile and raises his glass back to me.

Tristian's arm tightens around me as his lips brush my ear, sending shivers through my body. "Can we leave early for our Christmas Pudding getaway?" he murmurs. See, I knew my husband would prefer to leave early to travel to Australia. A few days ago, Tristian and I scheduled quality time to travel to our

Australian holiday home. Thankfully, I have the jet on standby, our passports and summer clothes packed, and ready to fly out tonight.

"We can leave once the kids cut the cake if you like," I whisper and smile, turning my head and brushing my lips against his. Tristian increases our kiss, taking it over as his hands slide down my back to my butt.

Vaguely remembering we were surrounded, I lean back a little to create distance between us to take a well-needed breath.

Tristian smiles, and I notice that cheeky glint in his eyes. He whispers, "I knew I loved you for a reason, Izzy, my little princess. I love you more than all the stars in the galaxy. Never forget that."

Before I reply, he leans forward, tightens his arms around me, and seals our lips in a scorching, passionate kiss. Feeling his love and passion in every fiber of my body, Tristian's ability to turn my mind to mush and my body weak and eager for his touch spreads through me. Everything around us disappears, leaving me breathless and curling my toes as I swoon in his loving arms.

See, as a little girl. I meant it when I announced I would marry Tristian. I was a determined five-year-old with my sights set on her prince.

THANK YOU

Thank you for reading Secret Heiress, my fourth contemporary novella. I hope you enjoyed it as much as I loved writing about Izzy and Tristian.

After reading, consider leaving and writing a positive review, even if it is just a few words, such as 'I loved this book' or 'I enjoyed it! Or 'It kept me turning the page.'

It will assist other readers in selecting their next book.

By reading this book, you help keep me in work, so pass the word and tell your friends to grab a copy.

If you would like to learn more about what I am writing or competitions, sign up for my newsletter.

https://mltompsett.com/newsletter-signup/

If you're interested in reading one of my other books, check me out on my website www.mltompsett.com, Bookbub, or Goodreads, to name a few places.

THANK YOU
AND
HAPPY
READING

Secret Heiress

ACKNOWLEDGEMENTS

To my special people who have been there to encourage me to continue reading, thank you from the bottom of my heart. Your advice, ideas, and comments have been invaluable, big hugs guys. Without you, my book would not be finished.

As always, thank you to my boys — big hugs.
Your patience for your mother is a miracle. I bug you on our group chat with cover designs all the time. You must have known all those years ago when I taught you how to use a computer that there would come a time when you had to return the favor.

LOVE YOU GUYS 🤍

www.ingramcontent.com/pod-product-compliance
Lightning Source LLC
Chambersburg PA
CBHW020246120726
47904CB00001B/103